Conquering Passion

The Montbryce Legacy~Book One

Anna Markland

ANNA MARKLAND

ISBN:0987867318
ISBN-13: 978-0-9878673-1-5

The ruling passion, be it what it will,
The ruling passion conquers reason still.
~Alexander Pope

For Don, my Conqueror

CHAPTER ONE

Arques, Normandie,
January 2nd, 1066 A.D.

With a weary sigh, Lady Mabelle de Valtesse removed her grease-spattered apron, rolled it up, and gathered a meagre blanket around her shoulders. She sank down in exhaustion onto the stale rushes on the hard stone floor, tucking the apron under her drooping head. Her snoring father, the exiled lord of Alensonne, sprawled in the space allotted for them both in the Great Hall. As usual, she had to prod him to move over.

She'd been careful not to step on the slumbering forms—human and animal—in the communal sleeping area of the castle at Arques, a task rendered more difficult by the utter darkness of the early morning hour. A pall of blue smoke from the long dead fire in the hearth hung in the air, making her eyes water. Awakened by her attempts to find comfort, her father elbowed her and asked loudly, "Why are you so late to bed?"

Mabelle gritted her teeth, feeling her shoulders tense. Waking her unpredictable father was the last thing she'd wanted to do. "I wasn't allowed to leave the kitchens until all was tidy. The banquet for the New Year was larger than usual. I'm tired to the bone."

"It's intolerable," he replied, making no effort to whisper. "The only daughter of Guillaume de Valtesse, lord of Alensonne, working like a peasant in the kitchens."

1

"Papa, please, not now," she whispered. "The castle steward made it plain we must contribute if we want to avail ourselves of their hospitality."

It irritated her that her father never contributed anything.

"Hospitality!" he sneered. "Where is the chamber I should have, as befits my rank?"

"Hush there!" someone called. "It's the middle of the night."

Valtesse bristled and shouted back, "Don't tell me to hush. I am Guillaume de Valtesse, the *Seigneur* d'Alensonne."

"We don't care if you're the King of the English," came the reply. This sentiment was quickly supported by the complaints of others awakened after a day spent toiling for their master. Dogs yapped. Startled cats scurried away, screeching displeasure at having their nightly foraging disturbed.

Mabelle well knew the potential for the argument to escalate. In their wanderings, she'd seen her father thrown out of many a Hall because of his inability to control his tongue and his temper. This was the reason for their exile. It was during an argument over land, six years ago, that he had lashed out and blinded and mutilated the *Seigneur* de Giroux. In revenge, Giroux's family had captured the Valtesse castle at Alensonne and cast them out. Mabelle's half-brother, the bastard Arnulf, had aided the attackers.

"I will not sleep with ignorant serfs," her father began, reaching for the sword at his side.

"Papa, hush, please. I must sleep. You never cease complaining."

Her father sat up. "You are too impertinent, daughter. Young noblewomen don't speak to their fathers so rudely."

Mabelle rolled her eyes, itching to point out that her impertinence and resourcefulness had saved his miserable skin many times. She'd told him often enough she believed the only person with the power to end their banishment was their overlord, the *Comte* de Montbryce.

Muttering, Guillaume gathered his blanket over him, turned over and seemed about to fall back to sleep, but suddenly rasped, "Be ready at first light. We leave for Montbryce."

"*Oui*, Papa," she murmured, trying not to sound surprised. In the beginning of their exile, when she was three and ten, she'd followed her father without question. She'd learned quickly which servants to befriend. If she couldn't coax leftover food from a kitchen wench when a lord's hospitality was meagre, she filched it. She shared food with hungry stable boys and was rewarded with oats for their horses.

Aiding laundresses in their tasks provided her with clean clothing. She listened to gossip, and used what she learned to her advantage.

Living by her wits had been easier when she was a young girl. There was always something to trade. Now, six years later, it was more difficult. The ugly peasant garb she wore concealed the body of a woman, despite her efforts to hide it. Men now wanted something in return that she had no intention of trading. In a constant game of cat and mouse, Mabelle rarely felt like the cat any more.

For all his faults, her father had shown he was aware of the growing dangers and was quick to protect her, but his volatile temper often led to confrontations and a curtailing of some of her freedom. She appreciated his protection, but was afraid of his inability to control his temper. She'd tried repeatedly for the past year to set her father on the path to his liege lord, but he always made some excuse. She sometimes thought he was happier in his misery.

Now he'd agreed to go. What had made him change his mind? Perhaps the rumours concerning the imminent death of Edward, King of the English, had prompted him to take note of the winds of change blowing in Normandie. Every Norman knew their Duke William had been promised Edward's throne. The *Comte* de Montbryce might be willing to be the instrument to help regain her dowry, lands lost to Arnulf, and now of strategic importance to the Duke.

Her father's loud snores told her he wasn't lying awake worrying. She wrinkled her nose, pressing a finger and thumb over her nostrils, shutting out the odours of rotting food and sweat emanating from the rushes. Tucking her knees to her belly, she hoped sleep would come quickly and that on this night she would be too tired to dream of fine clothes, rich food and the comfortable bedchamber that had been hers at Alensonne—before Arnulf had usurped the castle.

Despite her exhaustion, sleep proved elusive as her restless mind thought of the journey to Montbryce. Would this be the means to at last regain the life of respected nobility to which she'd been born? She pushed away the insistent notion that if her dowry couldn't be won back, then marriage to a nobleman would be the only solution. How to accomplish such a thing? Did she truly want to exchange one overbearing noble for another? Perhaps the Year of Our Lord One Thousand and Sixty-Six would bring a change of fortunes for her as well as their Duke.

Mabelle curled into a tighter ball and covered her ears against the grunts of a peasant who'd taken advantage of his unexpected awakening to rut with his bedmate.

CHAPTER TWO

St. Germain de Montbryce, Normandie, March 1066

Rambaud de Montbryce stood in the stirrups and rubbed his hard saddle muscles. He complained to his brothers, riding alongside him, "After the years I've spent on horseback in command of our knights, my backside shouldn't ache as it does."

Antoine and Hugh had ridden out from their father's castle to welcome him back as he approached with a large contingent of Montbryce men-at-arms.

Ram smiled, always happy to see his brothers. "When did you two arrive home with your brigades? You must have been more anxious to get home than I am."

"Yesterday," Antoine replied. "But we didn't have as far to come. We were in Caen."

Ram wiped the dust from his lips with the back of his hand. "I hope you have a tall tankard of ale ready. It's been a long ride from Rouen."

Hugh smiled. "Father has it in hand."

Ram's heart lifted as the welcoming walls of his father's castle at Saint Germain de Montbryce came into view. Surrounded by fertile meadows which stretched as far as the eye could see, the imposing edifice sat atop a strategically important promontory at the junction of two river valleys. It watched over the *demesne,* which had its own extensive apple orchards. The serfs brewed for their lord a fine apple brandy, famous throughout the Calvados region, as was the golden honey and *fromage cremeux* they produced.

Ram's father, *Comte* Bernard de Montbryce, came out to the bailey to greet them as Ram eased his weary six foot frame from the saddle. "Ram, good to see you, my boy. It's been too long. You look fit. Campaigning for the Duke has toughened you up."

He punched his son in the shoulder, and Ram feigned injury. They clasped hands and embraced, his father pounding him on the back. "Your hair is long. Don't you shave it when you go into battle?"

Ram laughed, stretching his tired body, combing back his hair with his fingers. "Vaillon shaves it for me when we're going into combat. I encourage my men to do the same, though they don't need me to tell them it's more comfortable under a helmet. But my hair grows fast."

"I wish I could say the same for myself," his father lamented, running his hand over the few remaining grey wisps. He laughed and tousled Ram's hair. "No wonder they call you *Rambaud le Noir.*"

He pointed to the threatening skies. "Let's go inside."

Ram winced, throwing irritated glances at his grinning brothers, who had no doubt taken great pleasure at his father's teasing of him. "I believe the nickname *Rambaud the Black* has more to do with the discipline I expect of my men," he retorted with irritation.

His father seemed to sense his discomfort. "It's good to have the three of you home together. I'm proud of all of you. You're carrying on the noble military tradition of this family, in the service of our Duke. That you've stayed alive in these dangerous times is proof of your prowess. Many noble Norman families haven't been as fortunate."

Ram had been sixteen when he'd first fought at his father's side. He remembered fondly the pride in his sire's eyes as they faced the Angevins together. "We learned from you, Father. You were a great warrior."

Antoine and Hugh indicated they were of the same mind.

The *Comte* slapped Ram on the back. "Would I could still join you boys. With the dire news from England, I sense you will be going to war again?"

Ram concurred. "Duke William is incensed Harold Godwinson has claimed the Confessor's throne. You're right. It will mean war."

"Then your many abilities will be even more important to the Duke."

Ram dropped into a chair once they reached the solar and used his legs to drag over a footstool. "William is now our undisputed ruler. During my last visit to the ducal court, every major family had sent a representative. But military prowess won't be enough. If he becomes King of the English, the Duke will need capable administrators and I want him to see me as more than a warrior."

Two maidservants entered and served tankards of ale.

Their father waited until the women had left. "As my heir, whatever effort you put into the efficient running of our estates will benefit you. You'll continue our proud heritage as descendants of the original North Men."

Ram offered a toast. "To the honour of the Montbryce family."

"Montbryce! *Fide et Virtute*," the other men echoed.

The four sat for a while drinking deeply.

Ram licked his lips and belched, thumping his chest. "Good ale. Just what I needed after the long journey." He turned to his father. "I've asked the Duke if I can spend time assisting you with the administration of our estates. Before we go to war, I'll make sure all is in order."

Comte Bernard looked indignant. "You think I'm getting too old for the job, eh?"

Ram exchanged glances with his brothers, shook his head and smiled. "It will be good to leave the military life for a while, and the Duke recognizes you're an able tutor. He knows we've already learned much from you."

Relaxing in the comfort of the castle where he'd grown up, Ram had to admit his father had aged quickly after the death of his mother. His *maman* had been a quiet woman who always deferred to her husband. He hoped for such a wife, if ever he decided to marry.

His father had carried on talking while Ram had been daydreaming. "Well, there is a matter in which I must involve you."

Ram waited. His father walked over to the window, took another draught of his ale, then fidgeted with the lace on the cuffs of his tunic.

Finally, he cleared his throat and explained. "The exiled lord of Alensonne, Guillaume de Valtesse, has appealed to us with his complaints his bastard son, Arnulf, has usurped his lands. Valtesse and his daughter, Mabelle, were forced to flee. At first, it seemed a minor problem. You may not recall it? Guillaume de Valtesse was a competent lord, but unpredictable. Now those lands have become strategically more important, and Arnulf is tending more and more to make alliances with our enemies, his Angevin neighbours."

Antoine leaned forward. "I believe I've heard something of them in my travels. A *jongleur* in Caen performs a *ballade* that tells the tale of Valtesse blinding another nobleman. That can't be true?"

Their father corrected him. "Nigh on six years ago, there was an acrimonious dispute over, what else, land. Valtesse is an irascible fellow—he lost his temper and lashed out. As well as blinding Charles de Giroux, he cut off the unfortunate devil's ears. I've heard it drove Giroux to madness."

Hugh held out his empty tankard. "I've never heard this tale. What about Arnulf?"

Their father refilled their tankards. "If only it were a tale. Seeing an opportunity to advance his own wealth, Arnulf sided with Giroux. They challenged Valtesse to come out and fight, but without the support of his own son, his courage failed him. He surrendered and was exiled, taking his daughter with him, at Arnulf's insistence."

"He and the girl have wandered ever since?" Hugh asked.

"*Oui*, the only life his daughter has known is that of an outcast, regarded with scorn, and probably mistrust, as the landless daughter of a vicious murderer and mutilator."

"Murderer?"

"There are suspicions Guillaume de Valtesse killed his wife. She was strangled."

Ram scratched his head. Why had his father turned the conversation to the girl? "This woman—what's her name, Mabelle?—is either as evil as her father, or she has intelligence and has learned how to survive, despite his madness."

His father seemed intent on continuing the story. "There's no doubt she's lived a hard life. I believe coin has been a problem, and they've been forced to depend on the code of hospitality. Imagine a young woman, born into nobility but unable to take her rightful place. She's never had the opportunity to be who she was born to be. The only way to regain her position would be—marriage."

Ram didn't like the speculative look in his father's eyes. "Who would marry a landless refugee with no dowry, and what does this have to do with us?" he asked carefully, putting down his tankard.

His father shrugged his shoulders. "I may not like the horrid man, but he is my vassal, and he is the rightful lord of the lands in question. We can't have impertinent sons usurping their fathers' titles, can we?" He winked at Ram.

"*Non*, I suppose we can't," Ram said with a chuckle. Like him, his father was probably offering up a silent prayer of thanks for the unspoken bond of trust that would ensure nothing of the sort ever happened to the Montbryces. In such uncertain times, family treachery could put everything at risk.

His father's voice broke into his musing. "Besides, it's time for you to take a wife."

Ram felt his hackles rise. The ale suddenly had a bitter aftertaste. He rose, stiffened his shoulders and faced his father squarely, folding his arms. His brothers shifted nervously in their seats. This wasn't the first time his father had insinuated he should be getting married, but he'd never done it so blatantly.

"First of all," Ram said as calmly as he could, "I have plenty of time for such matters. In any case, our Duke will try to oust Harold and there will be war. This isn't the right time to be marrying. And what does this have to do with the Valtesse problem?"

His father took up an equally challenging stance. "You are five and twenty—past time to be married. You should be siring children while you're in your best years. Besides, I'm getting old and would like to see my grandchildren. Mabelle de Valtesse has grown to be a woman."

Ram was close to losing his temper, which he would rather avoid. He had managed thus far to deflect his father's attempts to get him to marry. He liked his bachelor life. "Why would I want to marry an urchin who has spent her life wandering, and who has no inheritance, titles or dowry? She wouldn't make a suitable *Comtesse*."

"One day she may have those things. Come, Valtesse expects us in his chamber."

"Now? But—"

"*Oui*, now."

Ram wanted to object. He'd just arrived home, but once his father made up his mind, it was useless to argue. Though he had no desire to meet this dubious nobleman, he didn't want to disobey his father.

"Let's get it over with then," he grumbled, rolling his eyes at the grinning Antoine.

"I won't attend, Father, if that's acceptable?" Hugh offered. "I haven't finished my ale."

"Fine. No need for you to be there, but Antoine, you should come."

Antoine's grin disappeared as they followed their father to the chamber allotted to Valtesse. Introductions were made. Valtesse's arrogant posture and angry face added mistrust to Ram's annoyance. And where was his daughter?

Bernard de Montbryce explained that his sons would undertake to travel to Alensonne to negotiate with Arnulf. Ram arched his brows and looked at Antoine, who seemed equally perplexed and confused. Wary of what he'd learned about the wandering nobleman, he approached the matter carefully. "Tell me, *milord*, your son—"

Guillaume glared at him. "Arnulf is a fat, lazy bastard. He stole my lands from me, and from Mabelle, my rightful heir. He took the part of the Giroux family to further his own ends and must be ousted. He has no right to the lands he occupies."

"Is Alensonne fortified?" Antoine asked.

Guillaume's eyes bulged and he paced. "All my castles are fortified. Arnulf forced us to wander as far away as Anjou. We had to flee from there because of Angevin animosity towards Normans—"

"But—"

"Because of Arnulf and the *Seigneur* de Giroux, we've been denied our rightful lands and have wandered from Caen to Fecamp, from Arques to Avranches. What kind of life is that for my daughter? At times, she's had to assist the cooks in the kitchens. My only daughter, a servant. It's intolerable."

"My father has suggested—"

Valtesse made no effort to listen to Ram and carried on, his mouth now twisted into an ugly sneer. "My daughter and I have been forced to sleep on pallets in musty unused chambers, if we were lucky enough."

He stopped, threw his hands in the air, arms outstretched, and raised his eyes, gazing at the ceiling beams. Ram opened his mouth to speak again, but Valtesse resumed his pacing and his rant. "Other times the stale rushes on dirt floors have been our resting place. The lord of Alensonne, Belisle and Domfort, sleeping with servants and serfs. God has abandoned us."

Good thing the Bishop, wasn't present to hear this heretical rant about God's mistreatment. He glanced at his father, who shrugged his shoulders. Antoine stifled a laugh. Ram felt sorry for the people of Alensonne if this raging fanatic did regain his lands. He felt a momentary pang of pity for the young girl who'd been forced to wander around Normandie with her irascible parent. But she was probably as angry and twisted as her father.

As they left the meeting, Antoine and their father started towards the Great Hall, but Ram went in a different direction.

"Aren't you supping in the Hall, Ram?" their father asked.

"*Non*, I have an appointment elsewhere."

His father shook his head and walked away.

Antoine wagged his finger at his brother. "Ah, the provocative Joleyne," he teased.

Ram put his forefinger to his lips and looked in the direction their father had gone. "Lower your voice."

Antoine snorted. "You think Father doesn't know? Besides, Mabelle de Valtesse will likely be in the Hall. Don't you want to see her?"

"Antoine, nothing will come of the idea of my marrying her. She's not suitable. Why should I forego the tryst I've looked forward to for days, to meet an uneducated urchin?"

Antoine frowned. "Joleyne isn't *suitable* either. She's a peasant, a woman to bear bastards, not heirs."

Ram's jaw clenched. "I'm aware of that, and I've no intention of fathering bastards with my mistress. I love you, brother, but I don't meddle in your *many* liaisons with women. I'll be dining privately with Joleyne. By the morrow, Father will have forgotten about Guillaume de Valtesse. I bid you goodnight."

***

Ram was proven wrong on the morrow when *Comte* Bernard remained insistent. Ram and Antoine were dispatched to Alensonne to force a solution to the problem of the contested lands.

The weather had deteriorated considerably. The brigade of Montbryce knights made slow progress along the road, harnesses jangling. Though he rode proudly at the head of the well-armed column, Ram peered through the rain with a sour gaze at the muddy track before them.

Why is my father adamant about this matter?

"I'll be relieved when we reach Alensonne on the morrow," Antoine complained. "Curse these March rains—they turn the earth to muck."

Ram grunted in agreement. Even his warhorse, Fortis, seemed weary of pulling his great hooves free with each step. Ram berated his father for sending them on this trivial mission. He'd been home only a day. But at least he'd had the chance to enjoy Joleyne's talents. He smiled at the memory of their tryst

CHAPTER THREE

A cloaked figure squeezed through the tiny postern gate of Alensonne, and paused to listen, his eyes darting from one darkened corner to another. The moonless night suited his plans. Heavy clouds threatened more rain, but the deluge had stopped for the moment.

He'd learned from recent gossip in the bailey that Rambaud de Montbryce, son of their overlord, would be arriving on the morrow. The guards would be more alert, and Montbryce would bring his own men. He had to act now to avenge his daughter's death. He'd waited long enough, since the thin sun had heralded the first day of this cursed Year of Our Lord One Thousand and Sixty-Six. That was the day a stillborn child had been drawn from Angeline's lifeless body, its soul at least preserved.

His daughter had been the one precious thing he had, a living reminder of his wife, dead in childbirth fifteen years before. His daily life, ploughing the few acres with his oxen team, planting and reaping, was a hard grind. His sole pleasure at the end of a gruelling day, the only thing that sustained him, had been the sight of his daughter's angelic face.

Then Arnulf had filled her with a bastard. Simon Hugo cursed. Why hadn't he paid heed to the whispers among his fellow peasants? Arnulf was known to prey on young maidens, yet Simon had sent his daughter to the castle to deliver turnips, grown on the meagre plot of land he tenanted. Arnulf was debauched and decadent, though he hadn't inherited the fiery temper of the father he'd ousted from the

13

castle, Guillaume de Valtesse. At least with the father, peasants had been able to prosper if they avoided angering him.

Simon's heart clenched when he remembered the night his daughter had returned to their hut, dishevelled and sobbing, and he'd known, known, what had happened, before she could tell him. He'd relived that night over and over, the words haunting him. Eventually he'd found his voice but couldn't look at her dirty, tear-streaked face. "We'll tell no one," he'd muttered.

For a long while the only sound had been Angeline's sobbing. Simon had clenched and unclenched his fists, his heart broken. "You'll never have to go to the castle again. Arnulf is a pig."

What words could he have uttered? How could he have comforted her? "It's not your fault, daughter."

Angeline had fallen silent. Her silence had worried him more than her wrenching sobs. "I've failed to protect you."

He'd wanted to rush to the castle and kill Arnulf, but he'd banged his fists on the crude table, knowing such vengeance would result in his being hanged, and Angeline left alone. He was a powerless cottar, a peasant. His lord owned the oxen and plough. He could do nothing.

Now, creeping through the darkened bailey, he was glad he'd waited and taken time to plan. It was close to midnight. Guards would still be on the turrets. He clenched the calloused fists with which he intended to restrain his victim. He'd nothing more to lose. If he hung for the murder he planned to commit, he didn't care. This lord had no honour, no morals.

It's a cruel man who wrests from young maidens the only thing of value they have.

Two sentries paused as their paths crossed on the battlements above. "*Mon vieux,* how are you this dark night?"

"I wish I was tucked up in a warm bed with my wife, old friend."

"I wish I was tucked up in a warm bed with your wife too!" One man slapped his comrade on the back.

Simon smirked and leaned his head back against the wall. His hood protected him from the cold roughness of the stone. He suspected the two men had exchanged this same jovial greeting many times over the years. Both snorted their laughter as they parted to continue their vigil. He was relieved their attention was on their jest and not their duty.

Simon moved stealthily through the darkened bailey, hugging the high stone walls, breathing a shallow sigh of relief when he saw there was no guard at the heavy door to the keep. Things were as lax as they usually were. The hinges of the oaken door creaked as he inched it open and paused, waiting, alert, his rough fingers gripping the smooth wood. No challenge came. His worn boots made no sound on the stone steps as he climbed to the chamber where all knew the master slept. He paused again to steady his breathing and his fingers closed on the vial concealed in his cloak. Reassured, he smiled grimly and edged the door open.

Loud snoring assailed his ears as he entered the chamber, and his disgust intensified. "*Cochon!*" he murmured. The *pig* was a man of thirty years, whereas Simon had weathered two score and ten, but the dissolute nobleman would be no match for Simon's strength, bred from years of toiling in the fields for this cruel wretch sprawled on his huge bed, and his father before him.

An echo of his daughter's last desperate wail for help in the throes of death, pressed in on his memory. Cowering outside their hut, his hands pressing his cloak to his ears, he'd been unable to shut out the sound of her screams.

He'd been helpless then, but he wasn't helpless now. Rage coursed through him as he grunted, "*Cochon!*"

Disoriented, Arnulf started and struggled to sit up in the large bed, confusion apparent in his half open eyes. Simon seized his victim and dragged him to the head of the bed, pinning him hard with his knee. Pressing Arnulf's head against the backboard, he used his big hands to force open the ugly mouth, silencing the scream that threatened to escape. Reaching into his cloak with one hand, his fingers closed on the vial. He flipped off the stopper with his thumb and slowly and deliberately poured the wolfsbane between Arnulf's protesting lips. He tried to move his head, his fat legs kicking frantically, but Simon increased his grip and brought his whole weight to bear on his lord's chest. A foul odour filled the air and Simon took grim satisfaction. Arnulf's bowels had failed him.

He will die in his own dung.

It took but a few minutes for the struggling to cease. Arnulf's eyes were wide with the knowledge he would soon be a dead man, and his paralyzed body could do nothing. Simon looked into the dying eyes and smiled grimly.

I have righted the wrong, Angeline! Vengeance is yours.

Then it was over. The lifeless body sagged as Simon withdrew his hands. In disgust, he wiped Arnulf's sweat on the frayed edges of the well-worn cloak that had concealed him. He moved the lolling head back to the pillow and covered the body with the linens. It would be hours before anyone became alarmed.

"Sleep well, pig. It was your destiny to die this night. It's too late to help my Angeline, but I pray other souls will benefit from your death."

***

"I'm getting curious about this Mabelle," Ram admitted to Antoine as Alensonne came into view. The prospect of his possible impending marriage to this unknown refugee filled him with misgivings. War was imminent. It wasn't a good time to be getting married. "How can a girl who has spent her youth wandering from place to place with a man like Guillaume de Valtesse make a suitable *Comtesse?*"

"If you'd supped in the Great Hall, you'd have seen her," Antoine replied with a grin. "Perhaps there'll be no treaty with Arnulf, and Mabelle will never inherit any part of her father's lands. You'll be free to marry someone more to your liking, someone more *suitable*, who'll bring you a rich dowry. Perhaps then I'll pursue Mabelle."

Ram cast a puzzled glance at his brother. "You already have too many women in your thrall, Antoine. How do you keep track?"

Antoine chuckled. "What can I say? I like women, and they like me. What's wrong with that?"

"Nothing, I suppose." How alike he, Antoine and Hugh were in many ways, and yet Antoine had women at his beck and call, whereas Ram doubted if the shy and gentle, happy-go-lucky Hugh had ever bedded a woman.

He shook his head, sending water droplets flying. "It's ironic I'm given the task of playing the diplomat on a mission I'd prefer not succeed. I'm sure there are prospective brides who've been more suitably brought up than this Mabelle."

Wiping the rain from his face, he thought again of Joleyne. She brought him relief from his physical needs, but it wasn't a satisfying relationship on any other level. He meant nothing to her beyond being a means to satisfy her considerable passion. He paid her well for her discretion. She came, whenever he summoned her, to a secluded chamber he kept for such trysts, not wishing to soil his own nest.

He smiled at the thought of his solar, furnished with military souvenirs and trophies. He loved to run his hands over the prized swords and shields mounted on the walls. It was his refuge. He was sure his father was aware of mistress, but it was a liaison he didn't flaunt. Few in the castle knew of it. Compared to Antoine he was a monk.

A thought suddenly occurred to him. He turned to his brother. "Imagine being a married man with a beautiful wife who is yours alone? A woman you loved and who loved you in return."

"Enough!" Antoine replied good-naturedly. "What are you thinking? Has the mud clouded your brain? You're the eldest son of the *Comte* de Montbryce. You'll have no say. None of our comrades in arranged marriages love their wives. It's a foolish notion to expect love from a marriage. You know that. We all know it. Though I'm the middle son, my bride will be chosen for me. That's one reason I'm enjoying myself now."

"You're right, Antoine. Look at our friend Pierre de Fleury."

"Exactly."

A cold shudder went through Ram as the possibility of a similar fate loomed. "Poor Pierre. How does he bear it? How can he lie with his shrew of a wife?"

He frowned, trying to recall what his father had said about Mabelle. He hadn't paid attention—perhaps he should have. It was his responsibility to ensure the succession of his family. He had to trust his father would ensure the woman who became his bride would bring them increased wealth and influence. Happiness wasn't an issue. Neither was passion. That could be found with the likes of the tantalizing Joleyne.

They rode at last into the Alensonne bailey, but no one came to tend their exhausted mounts. Blathering women ran hither and thither. Men shouted, with no apparent purpose. Indignant hens dodged the stampede. Dogs barked. The torrential rain added to the wretchedness.

What was the commotion about? Ram's body tensed and he gritted his teeth. He'd pushed men and horses through the deluge to get to shelter, yet they were being ignored.

"This Arnulf doesn't have his servants trained in the code of hospitality," he grumbled, feeling the cold damp seeping into his bones.

Antoine nodded his agreement, shrugging his shoulders.

"You there," Ram shouted to a terrified lad scurrying by. The boy stopped but avoided eye contact. "What's going on here? Is there no one to tend to our mounts?" he asked angrily, rainwater dripping from his helmet and chain mail.

"*Mi—milord*," the ragged urchin stammered, taking the reins, fear oozing out of him. "Our lord is dead. He's dead. No one knows what to do."

"Dead? Arnulf de Valtesse?"

"*Oui, milord.*"

Ram and Antoine exchanged glances. "How did he die?"

The lad glanced around furtively, as if looking for a means of escape. "No one knows, *milord*. His valet found his body in bed."

"He died in his bed?"

The urchin seemed confused by the question. "Our lord often slept late, but his servant became alarmed when the hour for the noon meal approached, and he hadn't risen."

The boy, his hair plastered to his head, was almost hysterical, apparently overwhelmed by the presence of two scowling knights and the hubbub around him.

"A lord who sleeps till noon," Ram remarked to his brother as he dismounted, knowing from experience the successful running of a castle required a leader who rose with the sun. Servants and serfs learned discipline from their masters.

Stable boys emerged to take the reins of their mounts.

"Make sure the horses are dried thoroughly," Antoine ordered.

"I am *Vicomte* Rambaud de Montbryce. Who's in charge here?" Ram asked the boy, who pointed timidly to a short, bearded man, standing with a group in the bailey, about twenty feet away. He scratched his head and looked at his feet, shoulders hunched, trying to coax shelter from a small overhang by the door. As Ram and Antoine sloshed angrily through the puddles towards him, he raised his head. He rushed towards them, his consternation evident.

Antoine smirked. "He's realized who we are, and that he's failed to provide an appropriate welcome."

The man bowed low. "*Mes seigneurs*, forgive me. I'm Michel Cormant, steward of Alensonne. As you see, we're in confusion here. Our master, Arnulf de Valtesse, is dead, the body recently discovered. We have therefore failed to give you the proper welcome, and we beg forgiveness."

"Rise, Cormant. I am Rambaud de Montbryce. I am accompanied by my brother, Lord Antoine de Montbryce. Your master was told of our visit. Have preparations been made for my men?"

"My son, Paul, will show them to their quarters, and I myself will take you to your chamber."

The Montbryce brothers followed the steward into the keep, where they ascended winding stone steps to the second floor of one of the three towers. They were shown into a well-appointed, circular room with two large beds, heavy draperies and exquisite tapestries. Ram nodded his approval to Cormant, then asked, "How did your master die?"

"We're not sure," the steward replied, shrugging his rounded shoulders and shaking his head. "Perhaps some kind of fit."

"We'll need to see the body."

Cormant hesitated a moment, then replied, "Of course, *milord*. It's still in his bed. Follow me, please."

Ram gave permission for two servants to enter, carrying trunks. "Leave us now, Cormant. We'll send our chain mail, swords and gambesons with these servants to be dried. Return shortly, and we'll go together."

Ram didn't want to hand over his sword. He felt naked without his *arme blanche*, a gift from his father, but it would rust if not dried. He'd dubbed it *Honneur* and pledged it to the honourable service of his Duke.

Cormant bowed and left.

"He hesitated when you asked to see the body," Antoine remarked, bouncing on the edge of the mattress.

"*Oui*, but he quickly dismissed his misgivings. He's no doubt relieved someone from the family of his liege lord has arrived at this time of crisis."

They stripped off their wet armour and clothing with the help of the servants, who hurried off with it. Ram found two luxurious drying cloths draped over a chair and tossed one to Antoine, who tucked the long cloth around his waist and rubbed his legs. Espying a bone comb on a table by the bed, he tugged it through his wet hair, and then handed it to his brother.

"*Dieu!* I grow to look more like you every day!" he lamented.

"What's wrong with that?" Ram retorted good-naturedly. "There's less than two years between us, and we both look like our father. Good thing your eyes are green."

19

Antoine shrugged. "Perhaps next time I shave my head, I'll keep it that way, so people don't keep mistaking me for you."

Ram smiled. "Strange, I've never been mistaken for you." The friction of the cloth warmed him. He worked hard to keep fit, ready for battle. His body was all muscle, yet lean. He rubbed dry the smattering of curly hair on his chest and worked his way down the faint line, to the thick nest of curls at his groin.

"*Dieu!* I'm soaked through," he said with a shiver. As he rubbed, Joleyne's erotic comments came to his memory. "You're so big, *milord*," she would croon. "I never saw such a weapon."

He was jerked from his self-absorbed reverie by the flick of a damp drying cloth against his buttocks, administered by his grinning brother. "Admiring yourself, Ram?"

Ram retaliated and they spent a few minutes indulging in their playful antics, chasing each other around the chamber, laughing, each with the glint of revenge in his eyes. Then they sobered as they remembered the unpleasant task they were to perform. "Better get on with it," Ram muttered.

"You're right."

They took fresh hose, linen shirts and woollen doublets from the iron trunks and dressed quickly, each assisting the other since they'd brought no valet. Ram had no choice but to lace on his still wet boots.

A soft tap at the heavy door heralded Cormant's return, and they followed the steward down the steps and across the hall to another tower, where they again mounted to the second floor. Cormant opened the door of this chamber after tapping.

"Why would he knock?" Antoine whispered.

"Habits of a lifetime," Ram murmured.

Cormant bowed. "After you, *mes seigneurs.*"

Their chamber was finely furnished, but the one they strode into now was opulent. An enormous, heavily-curtained bed dominated the room from a raised platform. The drapery was open, a shape visible. The bedspread had been thrown back. The pungent odour of human excrement cut the air like a sharp knife.

Ram approached the body resolutely, aware of Cormant still at the door. "No overabundance of mourning family members," he whispered sarcastically to Antoine, standing at the other side of the bed, his hand over his nose. Ram clasped his hands behind his back and looked at Arnulf's ugly body, reluctant to touch it. "He looks surprised. Death came unexpectedly. But was it by natural causes, or at someone's hand?"

Antoine kept his voice low. "No blood. No weapon in evidence."

When a lord died suddenly and mysteriously, all were suspect. Ram was thankful they'd arrived after this death and sympathised with Cormant's obvious nervousness. "Has a physician been summoned?"

"*Oui, milord.* He's not sure what happened. An attack, he thinks. An apoplexy. The lord had enjoyed a rather heavy meal last evening, and so—"

Looking at the fat jowls and bloated stomach of the dead man, Ram could believe this pig of a man might have died from his excesses. It confirmed his low opinion of the whole Valtesse family. "It's evident no one will miss this poor specimen of humanity," Ram whispered to his brother, who had moved to stand beside him as they conferred. "Or be sorry he's dead."

"His unexpected death might solve problems for the house of Montbryce."

"But what if someone murdered the wretch? In his own bed! Should an enquiry not be held?"

Antoine held his hand out towards the body. "You know as well as I the likelihood of finding the true killer, if one existed. It's far more likely some innocent scapegoat would be punished for this instead."

Ram turned to the steward, trying not to wrinkle his nose. "We must arrive at a decision as to our course of action and get this corpse cleaned up and buried."

"*Oui, milord.* It's that I don't have the authority, I mean, *milord,* you're the authority now. You are the highest ranking noble."

"I don't want to waste time conducting an enquiry into this death," Ram confided to Antoine. "I've more important things to do for Father, and our Duke."

He made a decision. "I declare his death to be of natural causes, in concurrence with what the physician has observed. We'll bury him on the morrow. Cormant, you'll see to the arrangements."

He glanced over to Antoine, whose eyes indicated agreement.

"*Oui, milord,*" Cormant replied, relief evident in his voice.

Ram regretted what had to be said next. "Antoine, we've just arrived, and it's a long journey, but I suggest you leave on the morrow, to take the news to Montbryce. I'll stay to assist Cormant for a few days."

Antoine agreed. "I'll leave after the interment."

***

At the funeral the next day, Ram wondered how a man of noble family could come to such a pass, that most of the people in attendance were the men of a baron's sons who hadn't come on a social call.

People from the castle were there—the steward Cormant, his wife and three sons, the cook, the chatelaine, the stable boys, servants, and village folk. All looked on with disinterest as Arnulf was interred with interminable solemnity by the incredibly obese Bishop of Alensonne. It took eight burly men-at-arms to lift the enormous lead coffin.

Antoine whispered to his brother, "I wonder where they managed to find that monstrosity?"

Ram shook his head. "I hope there are more to mourn my passing, when the time comes, and that they care about my death." His father was aging and it wasn't likely Ram would die first, unless he fell in the service of his Duke.

Who will weep for me?

He resolved to leave this castle as soon as possible. Shifting his weight, he looked up at the sky. "Praise be to the saints the rain held off. It's good to be dry for a while. A few days here will ensure the steward has everything in place for the successful running of the castle until Guillaume de Valtesse can return."

"Cormant seems a good man," Antoine agreed. "Even with Arnulf as his master, the steward appears to have kept things running well. But it's hard to tell whether he and the rest of the servants and serfs are looking forward to the probable return of their rightful lord or not.".

CHAPTER FOUR

Mabelle had never seen her red-faced father so excited, or for that matter, so happy. Antoine had brought the news of Arnulf's death a few hours ago and Guillaume had ranted gleefully ever since. Despite her relief, this wasn't the way to react publicly to news one's son had died. She determined to behave with more dignity than her father. She barely remembered Arnulf and wasn't saddened by his death, since it was he who'd cast her out. His convenient demise meant her dowry would be regained.

Her father calmed down sufficiently to have a conversation. "Didn't I tell you, daughter, your accursed brother would get his comeuppance? Didn't I tell you we would return to Alensonne in triumph and regain possession of our rightful lands? I can't wait to see what that miserable miscreant has been squandering my money on."

"Is it safe to go back? Is the castle ours again?" she asked, noticing he gave her no credit for pushing him to seek support from Montbryce. Would she always be a cipher as far as her father was concerned?

"Of course it's ours," her father roared. "The *Comte* de Montbryce has guaranteed it in writing. His sons signed the documents, confirming Arnulf's death was from natural causes. I am the *Seigneur* d'Alensonne, without question—and of Belisle and Domfort."

As if the mention of his name conjured him, the *Comte* de Montbryce appeared, and Guillaume bowed effusively. Mabelle curtsied, sinking to her knees.

Comte Bernard proffered his hand to her. "Rise, dear child."

Guillaume rushed to his side. "Ah, *Milord Comte*. I can't tell you how grateful I am for your succour and support over this difficult time, and now you've guaranteed the return of my lands."

"I've done nothing on your behalf, Valtesse. It's a coincidence your son died as my sons were embarking on their attempts to arrive at a diplomatic solution."

"But, *Milord Comte*, honour dictates I thank you for your help," Guillaume replied. Mabelle thought he was deliberately not listening. "I wish to repay you, by giving you my most treasured possession."

Comte Bernard's eyes went wide. "And what might that be?"

Mabelle held her breath. With her dowry regained, she could pick and choose her suitors. Perhaps she could find someone to love and honour her?

Her father didn't look at her. "Now that my beautiful daughter is the heiress to my lands and titles, she'll be a much sought after bride. But I offer her to you, in betrothal to your son, Rambaud."

Should she laugh or cry? Her father had never told her she was beautiful, yet now he was anxious to be rid of her.

"Papa—"

"*Silence*, child. I know what's best for you," he hissed. "So, *Milord Comte*, do you agree to my proposal that we join forces? Mabelle will bring to the marriage a formidable amount of land, power and influence in Normandie and Le Maine."

Comte Bernard hesitated only a few moments. He walked over to Mabelle. Placing his fingers under her chin, he tilted her face to his view. "You're a beautiful woman, Mabelle, and you'll make an exceptional wife for my son. You have strength, pride, intelligence, and perseverance. The future *Comte* de Montbryce will need such a woman at his side in the turbulent times I foresee for Normandie and its Duke. There's no doubt His Grace too will be pleased at the strategic lands that will come under our control. We must get some new gowns made for you."

Mabelle had never heard such words of praise from her own father. She wanted to throw her arms around the *Comte* and kiss him. He'd seen qualities in her that her sire had never considered. Perhaps strengths she hadn't seen in herself? She looked at her father and was suddenly afraid he might start strutting around the room crowing. He'd heard nothing of what *Comte* Bernard had said. She should have been happy but had a sinking feeling she'd quickly lost the long-desired control over her own life. Had she indeed exchanged one authoritarian for another?

***

Mabelle was thankful the next day for her mother's insistence she be taught to read and write, but determined not to let anyone see her trepidation when the documents for the marriage contract were brought in by the scrivener. Wearing a new linen chemise and dark green surcoat, tailored hastily by one of the castle seamstresses, she signed her name with care. To *Mabelle de Valtesse*, her father insisted she add *and of Alensonne, Belisle and Domfort*. The intended groom hadn't yet returned from Alensonne, and his father signed in his stead.

She'd lain awake, worrying she knew nothing of this man to whom she'd been given. Consequently, she'd arrived late for the ceremony, much to her father's chagrin. No one had asked her opinion. Hard as life was with her father, few paid her much attention most of the time. She was a person of no consequence. There'd been a chance, with her birthright regained, that she could return to her beloved Alensonne. Now another man, a stranger, would control her life. His brothers, Antoine and Hugh, had been warm and welcoming, but what was he like? She and her dead half-brother Arnulf were very different from each other.

At the celebratory banquet, she teased her father. "Now, Papa, the *jongleurs* will sing a different *ballade* about the Valtesse family."

"And now, daughter, we're seated *above* the salt."

The dark red wine and ale were plentiful, the courses many. They dined on roasted pheasants flavoured with tarragon from the herb gardens, pigeons sprigged with rosemary, and suckling pigs. The woman who reigned supreme in the kitchens, known simply by the name of her calling, *La Cuisinière*, had roasted the piglets on spits. Mabelle, used to wandering in and out of kitchens, had seen her shooing away, with a large wooden spoon, anyone who tried to steal the crisp crackling of the succulent meat. *La Cuisinière* used her secret recipe to produce a memorable dish with trout caught by the steward's men. There was yellow cheese in wedges, the famous *fromage cremeux* de Montbryce, and coarse black bread.

Guillaume's voice dominated, and Mabelle was content her father was happy, enjoying the honour he felt was his due. But she worried about her betrothed. Why had he failed to appear in the Great Hall the night he'd been home? *Comte* Bernard had apologised for his son's absence, obviously irritated. Antoine had muttered some excuse about an appointment. She had an idea of what that meant. Ram was evidently not in a hurry to meet her.

She should be relieved her father had given her to a wealthy family. Life would be much more comfortable. She would be the wife of a liege lord when her future husband inherited the title of *Comte*. Wasn't it everything she'd wanted for a long time?

***

"A messenger has arrived from Montbryce, *milord.*" Cormant handed the missive to Ram and turned to leave.

"A moment. I may need to send a reply." Ram unfurled the letter, scanned it, and swore.

"I trust it's not bad news from home, *milord?*"

Ram scratched his head. "I'm betrothed, Cormant. To a girl I've never met. I'd hoped it would come to nought, but my father has signed the betrothal documents."

Cormant, seemingly ill at ease with this moment of familiarity, offered, "It's often the way, *milord,* for the sons of great families."

Ram shrugged. "I wish I'd at least met her. You know her perhaps? The daughter of your lord."

Cormant looked at him with surprise. "Mabelle de Valtesse? I remember her as a child, before her father's ouster brought us Arnulf."

"So, you have no knowledge of her upbringing, her education? I'm not sure about her—suitability."

He felt uneasy. Perhaps he'd said too much to this servant already. He made an effort to explain. "I've met your lord—my future father-by-marriage, it seems."

Cormant remained silent. Ram looked him in the eye. "I don't envy you the task of dealing with Valtesse when he returns."

Cormant's face gave away nothing. "*Milord.*"

Ram read the missive again and rolled it up. Holding it in one hand, he tapped it absent-mindedly against his thigh. "Send the scrivener to me. I'll dictate a reply. I might remind my father this isn't the time to be marrying."

"Is there ever a right time to marry, *milord?*"

Ram smiled. The man had mistaken his meaning. "I'll be off to war with our Duke."

Cormant looked impressed. "You'll be accompanying his Grace in his quest for the English throne?"

Ram squared his shoulders, proud he could slap Cormant on the back and declare, *"Oui,* of that I'm sure." Then his thoughts went back to the news of his betrothal. "We must redouble our efforts to secure Alensonne now it's part of my betrothed's dowry. Seems I have no choice. My inevitable wedding is in a sennight."

***

Mabelle wanted to explore the castle Montbryce, where she would live when she and Ram were married and rule as the *Comtesse* in the future. "Perhaps if I can find my way around, it won't seem so overwhelming," she suggested to *Comte* Bernard.

He instructed the steward, Fernand Bonhomme, to conduct a tour. Mabelle was grateful for a knowledgeable guide to the immense place. They viewed halls, galleries and chambers. Mabelle had spent the last six years in one castle or another, but she'd not seen such beauty, nor felt such comfort and warmth, since she'd been a child in Alensonne.

"It's beautiful," she kept saying to Bonhomme. "Everything is beautiful." It was hard to believe it might one day be hers.

They arrived at a chamber with a stout oaken door. "And this, *milady*, is the chamber of your betrothed."

Mabelle entered nervously. It was a man's room. Red predominated in the hangings and furnishings. Weapons and shields adorned the walls, wolf skin rugs warmed the floor. A woven Flemish tapestry depicting a battle covered one wall. She ran her hand over the rich brocade of the bed coverings, snatching her hand away when she became aware of the tall steward's eyes on her.

The thought of sharing this bed with a man she'd never met was overwhelming, and her stomach turned over. She had little knowledge of men, despite the harsh life they'd lived. Her father was a difficult man, but he had protected her. Would Ram be patient? Would he treat her well? The room seemed so masculine, with no place for a woman. Would he expect her to keep to a chamber of her own?

"Shall we continue, *milady?*"

They toured the kitchens, the smithy, the chapel, the stores, the larder, the smokehouse, the herb garden, and even the chicken coop, though Bonhomme carefully avoided the manure pile. In the stables she found her mare.

"Sibell will love her own clean stable," she confided to the steward, who was also stroking the horse. "I used to bring her morsels from the tables. She'll be well taken care of here."

"*Oui, milady*. The Montbryces take good care of their horses."

He assisted her to ascend the stone steps to the ramparts, from where they looked down on the vast stretches of land surrounding the castle. "This is the Montbryce *demesne*," he declared, spreading out both his arms expansively. "As far as the eye can see."

Mabelle smiled. "You're proud of it."

"*Milady*, I've been the trusted steward of the Montbryce estate for many years, taking over from my father before me. One of my sons will succeed me when the time comes."

"Oh, look!" she exclaimed, pointing out to the west. "Over there—a patch of bluebells, at the edge of the forest." She closed her eyes, remembering the warm springs and summers of Alensonne, tucked away in the south west corner of Normandie, on the river Sarthe. She heard again her mother's tinkling laughter as they gathered armfuls of bluebells in the open fields surrounding the castle. Now the bluebells were a dim and distant memory, like her mother. "Is it safe to go there?"

"*Oui, milady*. Provided you don't go too far into the forest. There are wild boar."

"I'll be careful. Has there been any word from my betrothed?"

Bonhomme shook his head. "Not that I know of, *milady*. But don't worry, he's very punctual."

Punctual? I suppose that's a good thing. Unless he expects it of me!

Fernand took her hand and helped her descend the steps.

"*Merci,* Fernand. I appreciate your taking the time to show me everything. It's a big castle, and you run it well."

Now came his turn to blush. "*Merci, milady*. My pleasure," he gushed as his wife joined them. She bowed to Mabelle. "*Milady*, the seamstresses are waiting for you in your chamber."

Madame Bonhomme accompanied her to the fitting. The servant seemed friendly as she chattered on. "The dressmakers have never worked so hard. They've been plying their needles from morning till night, preparing shifts, nightgowns, wimples, hose, chemises and dresses for you. The *pièce de resistance* will be the gown for the ceremony itself."

Madame Bonhomme was seemingly unable to take small strides, and Mabelle had to run to keep up with her.

"I've never worn anything as fine. There have been so many fittings, pinnings, twirlings, and adjustments, I'm beginning to feel like a pincushion. Is there word from my betrothed?" It bothered her she seemed driven to ask about him.

"Not that I'm aware, but *milord* Rambaud is always—"

"I know—punctual. But what is he like?"

"Oh, he's a handsome devil. A great soldier, counsellor to Duke William, despite his youth."

Was he kind, thoughtful, or a tyrant? She couldn't voice these questions aloud to this loyal Montbryce servant.

When they reached the chamber, Mabelle submitted once more to the ministrations of the dressmakers, and the steward's wife took her leave. Mabelle looked down at the peasant woman adjusting her gown. Again, curiosity got the better of her. "Tell me, Bette, what is my betrothed like?"

Bette blushed and giggled. "Oh, *milady*, forgive me for saying, but *milord* Rambaud has eyes that could make women do foolish things."

"Ouch!"

"Sorry, *milady*, just a pin."

The pit in Mabelle's stomach widened further. She'd been chewing her nails—a new habit. She hastily curled her fingertips into her palms. Doing foolish things with a man was something beyond her comprehension. Such a man would want to dominate her. Would she grow to love him? She had to meet him first.

CHAPTER FIVE

The day before the wedding, a message had come from Ram with assurances to his father he was on his way home, and would arrive in time for the ceremony.

"He expresses frustration at being delayed in Alensonne. He wanted to ensure all was as it should be, now those lands and titles will be part of your dowry, Mabelle," *Comte* Bernard told her as they dined together in the Great Hall. "He received the message of the betrothal two days after we signed the document. He needed to investigate any lingering threat from the Giroux family but has heard no rumours of this. He sends you greetings."

"Greetings," she mumbled, struggling to control her disappointment that she wouldn't meet him until their wedding. These nagging doubts hadn't left her as the interminable night dragged on, and she woke from a fitful sleep before dawn on her wedding day, feeling tired and irritable, bemoaning the state of her fingernails.

She needed fresh air. Suddenly, she remembered the field of bluebells espied from the battlements. Bonhomme had assured her it was safe. Perhaps that was what she needed—an hour alone to recall happier days.

She leapt to her feet and dressed quickly, as she'd done for years, in a homespun chemise and sage green surcoat, with ample skirts down to her feet. She tied the braided woollen belt at her waist, pinned up her hair and stole out of the bailey, carrying a basket from the kitchens. Peasant garb had proven to be the surest way to pass unnoticed among servants already up and busy around a castle. They'd be looking for her soon enough to prepare for the ceremony.

She followed the path across the meadow. The fragrance of the apple blossom from the nearby orchard filled the air. Tension melted from her body as her bare feet touched the dew-laden grass. Turning to face the rising sun, she caught a glimpse of a lark high in the sky, filling the air with its tribute to the dawn, and shielded her eyes. Then, in a whirl of feathers, the bird had disappeared, snatched from the air by a sudden silent hawk. A chill swept over her, and her shoulders tensed. She blinked rapidly and hurried on.

She reached the carpet of blue and stooped to pluck the squeaky, hollow stems of the wildflowers, humming as the bunch grew in her basket. She tried in vain to think of something other than her impending marriage. Wandering in penury, she'd longed to be free to make her own decisions. Now that seemed unlikely, but at least she would no longer be sleeping on stone floors or working in kitchens.

Bees buzzed busily among the bluebells. She became flushed as the unseasonably warm April sun rose higher, and soon sought the shade of the white-barked birch trees at the edge of the forest, lured by the cooling sound of the warm gentle breeze rustling the leaves.

The basket became unwieldy. She set it down and bent to resume her gathering. She'd strayed far into the forest and was on the point of turning back when a glint of sunlight caught her eye. Venturing a few steps further, she smiled at the sight of a shimmering lake.

It was private and inviting, surrounded on three sides by sheer, moss-covered rocks. The clear water didn't appear to be deep. She was hot. Unable to see the castle, she felt secure no one could see her. It wouldn't be the first time she'd bathed in a lake or stream.

Glancing around nervously, she removed the belt and dress, setting them down on a small rock. The distant chirping and warbling of birds, newly hatched hungry nestlings, brought a smile to her face. She could hear no other sounds. The air here was still. The chemise quickly followed the dress, and she waded gingerly into the refreshing water, gasping as the chill assailed her body.

Not a strong swimmer, she waded, moving her arms to and fro, her breasts bobbing on the surface, nipples hardened from the initial shock of the cold water. A tingle snaked through her as she modestly cupped her breasts.

Before this day is out, I'll be married. Rambaud will expect his rights as a husband. Will he be gentle? Will he want me to call him Ram? Will

31

he like me? Everyone says he looks like his handsome brother, Antoine, who has been kind to me since I came here.

The long night and early rising caught up with her, and she yawned

I must make my way back. It will take a while for the sun to dry my skin.

She lay down in the grass, unpinning her hair to let it flow over her shoulders, easing her feeling of exposure. She spread the chemise over her body and gathered up a bunch of bluebells to clutch at her breast. The water had calmed her. With a smile on her face, she drifted off, dreaming of what it might be like to be kissed.

***

After riding at a steady pace for several hours, Ram was confident he would arrive home in plenty of time for the wedding, punctuality being one of the things he prided himself on. His muscles ached. He'd been riding with his body tense, preoccupied with the frustration of this unwanted marriage. The duty chafed. He had his immediate future planned, and this would interfere. He decided he'd take time to stop at his favourite lake to swim, not wanting his betrothed's first impression of him to be the unpleasant odour of horse and rider after a two day ride.

As the castle came in sight, he signalled his men to go ahead and veered off to take the familiar path into the forest, slowing his horse, then stopping and dismounting a little way away from the lake. He tied his stallion to a nearby birch tree and propped his helmet on the pommel of the saddle. "Fortis, old friend, you'll soon be back in your own stable, where you can have a rub down, some delicious hay and a well-deserved rest."

He walked briskly towards the inviting water, unsheathing his sword, eagerly stripping off his boots, padded chausses, surcoat, hose, undershirt and braies. He tossed them into a pile, placed his sword carefully on top, then slipped soundlessly into the water. It was bracing, but felt good against his skin. He swam lazily for several minutes, then floated on his back looking up at the clear blue sky, listening to the sounds of chirping birds, inhaling the fragrant apple blossom.

I love this place. Maman used to bring us there when we were boys.

The mysteries and frustrations of Alensonne melted away, and he looked forward to his marriage. He'd never bedded a virgin. Considering the life she'd led, was Mabelle untouched?

Reluctantly deciding he'd better make his way home, he strode from the water and perched on a flat rock, rubbing his hands through his hair, waiting for the sun to dry his body. After a few minutes, he wandered over to his clothing and pulled on his linen braies. Catching sight of a mound of blue in the grass nearby, he wondered idly what it might be. He sauntered over, fiddling with the ties of his braies. He discovered a basket of freshly picked bluebells.

He smiled and crouched down to touch them, but then his brow creased as his warrior instinct warned of a possible threat, angry he'd let his guard down.

Merde! My sword is with my clothing.

He stood, listening, but then the smile returned to his face as the notion struck him only girls picked flowers. His spine tingled at the recollection of floating on his back, naked. Had a woman watched him?

Surely I would have sensed?

He crept forward and his mouth fell open when he caught sight of a scantily clad maiden, asleep, half-hidden by the long grass. She'd covered her body with a chemise, but her arms and legs had escaped its folds. He licked his lips at the sight of her glorious golden hair and white shoulders. One long arm lay outstretched at her side. The other was bent, hand tucked into the side of her face. The steady rise and fall of the bluebells covering her chest drew his eye. Her bare feet were slender. He could see only part of her thigh, but her legs were long. They'd fallen open, the chemise bunched between them. Were the curls of the triangle at the top the same golden colour? Rosy cheeks and open lips, curved into the trace of a smile, gave her the face of an angel at rest. His body responded fiercely and he inhaled sharply.

Was she a vision? He squeezed his eyes shut, then looked again. He took in a ragged breath. Her long, brown eyelashes fluttered at the slight sound. She rubbed her nose and stretched, arching her back and bending her knees. The chemise came tantalizingly close to slipping off her breasts.

Icy heat rushed through Ram's body. He, the fearless *Rambaud le Noir*, felt something tighten in his chest. He'd never seen a more desirable woman. Crouched like a cat, he had an urge to spring up and pounce on her. Swallowing hard, he clenched his fists, struggling for the cool control that had made him a decorated cavalry commander. In the blink of an eye, a maelstrom of thoughts flew through his head.

He was to be married this afternoon. The clothing he now caught sight of indicated the woman was a servant. Having his way with her before going to the altar to meet his betrothed wouldn't be suitable behaviour for a Montbryce. He intended to try to be faithful to his new wife, and though his lust for the vision argued fidelity could come after the vows were spoken, he knew he wouldn't take advantage of this woman.

He wasn't married yet, didn't want to marry. This wasn't the right time to be marrying. However, he wasn't a ravisher of women. This stunning wench had aroused him, but he didn't intend to take her against her will. His legs were starting to cramp. He should move away before she—

Her eyelashes fluttered again. At first she didn't see him. Then she sat up, clutched the chemise to her body and exclaimed with a gasp, "Antoine! What are you doing here?"

The fruity huskiness of her voice startled him, and the taste and aroma of apple brandy suddenly filled his senses. He stood quickly, goosebumps marching up and down his spine, his mind whirling. She stared at him, eyes wide, mouth agape, obviously nervous, but not afraid.

She struggled to her feet, clasping her arms over her breasts, and glanced down, then back at him. He groaned inwardly when the long golden tresses fell forward across her shivering shoulders. The heat of embarrassment turn her body pink. He imagined her nipples hardening beneath the chemise she clutched against her. It made his already rigid arousal throb.

Striving to cover herself without revealing any more of her body, she looked vulnerable, in need of a champion. He wanted to be that man. No wonder his philandering brother was bedding this delectable woman—the devil. Thank goodness he'd donned his braies, but they weren't adequate to conceal his arousal, and the wench's gaze seemed fixated on his groin. His clothes were with his sword. He resisted the urge to move his hands to cover his erection and looking down would make matters worse.

He put his hand on his chest and shook his head. "I'm not Antoine. You're waiting for my brother?" he rasped.

"Your brother? You're—"

"I'm Rambaud de Montbryce. Who are you? I thought I knew all the servants. You must be new?"

"Ram?" she gasped.

He was on the point of remonstrating with a servant for using his given name, and the familiar form at that, but then she stammered, "I'm Mabelle."

A cold chill swept over him. He was speechless for a moment then exclaimed, "Mabelle de Valtesse? My betrothed? What in the name of all that's holy are you doing here, lying naked in the woods? Are you waiting for Antoine?"

Would my brother betray me thus?

The anger blazed in her eyes. "How dare you accuse me of such a thing? I wasn't naked. I came to pick flowers. I bathed," she cried. "I fell asleep, dreaming."

"Dreaming of Antoine, no doubt," he spat, not sure why anger had taken hold of him and why he wanted to hold on to such a preposterous idea.

"I dreamt of—"

"Clothe yourself, woman!" He turned his back to her. "You're supposed to be a future *Comtesse*. I've said repeatedly your behavior would be suspect.

She struggled breathlessly to hide her nudity, then her voice broke into his confused thoughts. "And what, pray, are you doing here, almost naked, watching a girl you don't know? You thought I was a whore. On your way to wed me, you intended to bed a whore."

He wanted to turn back to her, to explain how her beauty had bewitched him, but his anger and confusion held him in its thrall. His state of undress and obvious arousal left him feeling vulnerable. It wasn't a feeling *Rambaud le Noir* was used to. He was offended she thought so little of his honour. The word *whore* on her lovely lips sounded like an obscenity. It was a word a *Comtesse* would never utter. What's more, it was unacceptable for a woman to argue with him. "You must learn to be more obedient, and not answer me back," he spluttered.

"Obedient?"

She pushed him then with all her might as he crouched to conceal his arousal. Her strength took him off guard. He lost his balance, staggering into the water, falling full length with a great splash, cursing as he resurfaced.

Grabbing the rest of her clothes, she ran and stumbled over his sword. Her belongings fell to the ground as she picked up the long, heavy weapon with both hands, straining to hold it out in front of her as he advanced. He stopped a few yards away and raised his hand to calm her, unsure as to what she might have in mind for his beloved sword. His heart raced at the incredible sight of this desirable woman, the thin chemise clinging to the curves of her body, bluebells tangled in her hair.

He had to admire the way her heaving breasts thrust forward as she braced her feet, turned, and tightened her buttocks, gathering strength to heave the weapon. Through the thin fabric, he saw the outline of her bottom.

"Non! Arrête!" he yelled as she threw the blade as far as she could, into the water. She retrieved her clothing and fled. He watched her disappear into the forest, blonde hair flowing like a cloak behind her, wanting to pursue her but knowing he couldn't leave Honneur where she lay.

"She's stronger than she looks," he said to the trees.

Swearing a silent curse, he turned back to the water and began searching the muddy bottom for his weapon, shaking his head.

This isn't how I envisioned our first meeting.

***

Frantic, angry and breathless, Mabelle paused, listening. How far had she run in her panic? There were no sounds of pursuit. She gasped when she looked down at her chemise. She threw on the dress, hands fumbling with her belt, fervent prayers falling from her lips, mind racing. She wound the wimple round her head and tossed the ends over her shoulders.

She'd known as soon as she'd uttered Antoine's name she was mistaken. The strapping athlete before her was older and taller than Antoine. Antoine's eyes were green, not ice blue like the ones burning into her.

Dread and embarrassment had crept up her spine as she'd felt her face redden. She groaned as she remembered how she'd stared open-mouthed at the broad-shouldered, black-haired giant who'd leapt to his feet to stand before her, like a purebred stallion. He wasn't naked, but he might as well have been.

This was Ram. This ruggedly handsome knight was her future husband. The reality seemed to hold far more promise than she could have hoped for. She'd done nothing wrong. She could have explained, but he hadn't given her a chance.

His angry voice had rumbled over her like thunder, raising the hair on her nape. She'd never felt the least *frisson* when approached by men before, yet had quivered like a wanton in his presence. The storm of desire had swept over her, and for the first time in her life, she knew what it was to want a man. But then lightning had struck, and she'd known in a blinding moment of clarity that this proud, arrogant male she'd angered and embarrassed was her betrothed. She wanted to weep when she thought how furious he would be about his sword.

What an astounding sight he was, water dripping from his hair, running in rivulets down his broad chest, wet braies moulded to his very male body, his eyes burning with disbelief as she threw the weapon.

No wonder they call him Rambaud le Noir. But he thought I had a tryst with Antoine.

She cursed aloud and made the Sign of the Cross. "It's a spell I've brought on by picking the Fairies' Thimbles. God save me!"

She made for the wall, half running, half walking, biting her nails.

"*Milady*, we've been looking everywhere for you. Are you ill?" asked Madame Bonhomme, eyeing the peasant garb when she saw Mabelle stumble into the bailey.

"*Non,*" she gasped. "I'm well. All is well. I fell asleep in the meadow, and now I'm late. I'll go to dress—for the ceremony."

She felt the eyes of the steward's wife on her back as she walked away unsteadily.

CHAPTER SIX

Mabelle's head was full of thoughts of her betrothed when she came at last to her chamber, where the sound of an excited voice startled her.

"*Enfin*," cried her maid, Giselle. "Finally, you're here, *milady*."

Despite the frenzied preparations for the celebration, curious eyes had followed her from the bailey and she'd hoped to find a moment of quiet in the sanctuary of her chamber.

"It's not to be," she sighed, trying to calm her breathing.

The maid immediately got busy undressing Mabelle, who could see in Giselle's eyes a hint of disdain for the peasant clothing.

"I'm proud to have been chosen as your personal maid. I'm a widow, *milady*. My husband died many years ago in a skirmish, fighting for the Duke."

Mabelle nodded, only half listening, grateful the maid had said nothing about her attire or her tardy arrival. Once undressed, she leapt into the wooden tub, which had been filled earlier by the servants.

Giselle dipped her fingers in the water. "I was worried. Your bath water is cooling."

This diminutive woman, her red hair flecked with grey, was respected by the whole household. It would be wise not to alarm her.

"I've two grown sons, *milady*. People say I talk about them too much, but they are soldiers in the Duke's service, and I rarely see them. Let me help you. You've got weeds in your hair."

Soon the scented water and Giselle's soft chattering about her sons and their exploits calmed Mabelle and one certainty emerged from her jumbled thoughts. No one must ever find out what had happened by the lake. She would keep the truth hidden and was confidant Ram would too. Yet, her agitated heart was in turmoil. They might never have trust, or friendship, between them. Anger, something she'd lived with for too long, wasn't a good beginning. Ram wanted obedience. She craved love and acceptance.

Giselle helped her from the tub, grasped the drying cloth with her tiny hands, and dried her new mistress briskly and efficiently. The little maid was spry, despite her thickening waistline.

The seamstress arrived to help Mabelle into the wedding gown. The sleeves of the fitted white undertunic were made too long, so they could be pushed up, to give a wrinkled effect, which was prettily revealed by the shorter sleeves of the dress itself. The hem, the edges of the shorter sleeves and the neckline, were embroidered with ornamental bands of blue flowers. A blue embroidered silk girdle hugged her above the hips falling in a V to her mons. Fastened with a thin golden thread, the beautiful satin gown emphasised her curves.

"*Milord* Rambaud is a lucky man," Giselle whispered with a smile.

Once the gown was fitted, Giselle combed the tangles from Mabelle's long hair, and Bette pinned the finely wrought opaque veil on her mistress's head, drawing it over her face. The veil cascaded to the floor behind her. Satin slippers were placed upon her slender feet. She felt beautiful and giddy.

"What's *milord* Rambaud like?" she asked Giselle nervously, aware the woman had watched Ram grow up in the castle. She'd been a loyal servant to the Montbryce family for many years, having served Ram's mother until her death.

"Ah, *milady*, those blue eyes." Then she giggled. "Just like my own boys."

Mabelle took another big gulp from the goblet of dark red wine Giselle had brought to steady her nerves. She remembered the anger she'd seen in those blue eyes.

***

It had taken Ram several frustrating minutes of diving and resurfacing to find his treasured sword. Its weight and the distance his betrothed had managed to throw it had embedded it into the muddy bottom of the lake. He didn't want to step on the sharp blade. Cursing when he found it, he carried it to shore and dressed hurriedly, his hands fumbling with the points as he tried to reattach his hose to his wet braies. Running to his horse, he shoved his helmet back on his wet hair, mounted and rode at a gallop to the castle, his mind preoccupied with the vision of the angry beauty throwing the sword.

"*Milord*," shouted the stable boy, as Ram careened over the stone bridge and into the bailey. The boy reached for the reins, grabbing the sword as Ram thrust the hilt at him.

"Dry my sword at once. I don't want it to rust. Then lay on the oiled leather—not too much."

"*Oui, milord*," the boy replied. The boy's expression betrayed his curiosity as to how the magnificent sword had become wet and muddied.

Ram took the steps to his chamber two at a time. The vision he'd stumbled upon filled his head. He'd lost his temper, angered by her mention of Antoine's name and his own embarrassment. She wasn't what he'd expected. He'd envisioned a waif, a stray. His future wife was a woman of incredible beauty and perhaps deep passion. He had indeed been bewitched, more or less accusing her of being a whore. No wonder she'd been angry. But she would have to learn obedience. That was just the way of it. He didn't want a wife who would stare back at him defiantly, did he? A woman brave enough to shove him into the water? Perhaps this whole thing was a big mistake.

His valet had laid out his clothing. He arched his brows when Ram stripped off his wet braies and jumped into the bath Vaillon had prepared. He scrubbed his body quickly, then vaulted out and dried himself vigorously. He hoped the rubbing would help dry his hair. When he was ready to be dressed, Vaillon picked up the wet braies and looked at him curiously.

"*Milord?*"

"I went for a swim," he mumbled.

Soon, clad in pale hose with a long black doublet edged with gold worn over his cream linen shirt, he thought he looked presentable. Vaillon laced up his good black leather boots.

"Hmm—" Ram mused, running his hand over the crest embroidered on the doublet. His finger traced the Latin motto. "*Fide et Virtute*. It's a good motto. *Fidelity and Valour*. I hope I'll do nothing to dishonour it today."

Vaillon adjusted a short black cloak around Ram's shoulders, fastened it at his neck, and drew a wooden comb through his black hair. He brushed off Ram's shoulders and then stepped back. After his inspection, he announced his satisfaction with his Lord's appearance.

But Ram had made a decision. There were too many things bothering him about this arrangement. He would need to speak to his father.

The breathless stable boy came with his refurbished sword. Ram had just sheathed the weapon when a soft tap at the door heralded Hugh and his father.

"All is in readiness, my son. You should be at the door of the chapel before your betrothed arrives. I haven't had a chance to speak to you until now. I hope you'll be as happy as your mother and I were together. Mabelle has had a difficult life but I'm confident you can erase the memory of those years for her. Come."

They embraced. Ram marvelled his father would share anything intimate concerning his relationship with his dead mother, saddened by the knowledge of how much his father missed her. He'd never heard such words from his sire, and wondered how Mabelle had managed to reach his father's heart.

Hugh clasped his hand and smiled as he gave him a brief embrace. "This is it, brother. No turning back now."

"About that, *mon père*—a word please. Hugh, find Antoine."

"But he's waiting for you at the door of the chapel."

"Find Antoine and bring him here."

***

Mabelle's heart beat wildly. Her face was flushed. She felt lovely in her wedding finery. She hoped it would impress her betrothed and make up for—

Don't bite your nails.

Her father's unmistakable gruff, impatient voice echoed off the stone walls as he hurried his daughter and her attendants to their place by the chapel door.

There was no turning back now, though she'd been tempted to call the whole thing off, convinced discord was not a good beginning. She was to be married to an arrogant man she'd angered, a man who'd aroused feelings in her she'd never known before, a beautiful man.

Her breath caught in her dry throat as she rounded the corner. Her eyes fell on the unexpected sight of the *Comte* de Montbryce standing stony-faced, his hand on the hilt of his sword, his three sons behind him.

Perhaps they're upset because I'm tardy?

Antoine's face showed his anger as he chewed his bottom lip. Hugh was scratching his head, studying his feet.

Ram looked stunning in his black doublet and cape, but his expression was unreadable. His legs were braced, shoulders squared, ready for action, eyes fixed on Guillaume de Valtesse. She heard her father swear loudly as he reached for his sword.

She didn't hear exactly what *Comte* Bernard said, didn't need to. The only sounds that came to her ears were the thin metallic wail of swords drawn from scabbards, and her own anguished cry, "*Non,* Papa! Don't kill him, please don't kill him."

Then she fainted.

CHAPTER SEVEN

*C*omte Bernard de Montbryce felt older than his years. He was angered by his eldest son's unexpected behaviour. The usually decisive Ram seemed confused. He felt in his heart Mabelle was the right woman for Ram, and sensed that, despite his son's protestations about the marriage, he'd been drawn to Mabelle de Valtesse in the few moments of their first meeting outside the chapel. Ram had been adamant he be the one to carry the girl to her chamber. He'd rushed to catch her before her limp body crumpled to the hard tiled floor.

However, *Comte* Bernard had just left a confrontational meeting between himself, his son and a livid Guillaume de Valtesse.

"You've shamed my daughter, Rambaud de Montbryce," Valtesse screamed, so close to Ram his spittle sprayed across the younger man's face. "I've killed men for less. Jilted at the chapel door. I'll have to send her to a nunnery."

Ram wiped his face, obviously trying to keep his anger in check. "I haven't jilted her. I'm requesting a postponement, a time for us to prepare for this momentous step. I'll soon be going off to war and it isn't fair—"

Guillaume threw his hands in the air. "Rubbish! Many women will be sending their men off to fight for the Duke."

Ram ran his hand through his hair, the other still on the hilt of his sword. "But, Mabelle and I only met today."

Guillaume made a derisive sound. "Many noblemen meet their wives for the first time at the chapel door."

Ram took his hand off his sword and opened his hands in a gesture of conciliation. "I need more time. Will you not grant that?"

"*Non*, the betrothal will be cancelled and she must go to a nunnery." Guillaume strode off towards the door.

Ram's father felt he had to intervene if a solution was to be found. Ram tensed when the nunnery was mentioned. Bernard de Montbryce looked at his heir as he spoke. "My dear Valtesse, we all, including my son, are aware this marriage will benefit the Montbryces, the Valtesses and Normandie. Does it matter if it takes place now or in the future, as long as it takes place? We're on the brink of war. Ram is one of the Duke's closest counsellors. He's perhaps right that he shouldn't be distracted at this juncture by a new bride. It wouldn't be fair to Mabelle, or to our Duke. And if you send her to a nunnery, the Church will inherit your lands."

This last ploy seemed to resonate with Valtesse. After pacing for several minutes, he agreed to a postponement. "I'll take Mabelle with me to Alensonne."

"*Non*, she'll stay here."

Ram's vehement refusal took his father by surprise, and he was afraid Valtesse would lose his temper again, but his failure to continue the argument seemed to indicate the *Seigneur* didn't want to be burdened with his daughter.

Ram sensed the nobleman's capitulation. "We can't come to know each other if she's in Alensonne. She'll be chaperoned here. She won't be shamed. I'll oversee what she does and whom she sees."

Before Guillaume could object, Ram turned and strode out of the chamber, torn by a torrent of conflicting emotions. When Mabelle had come into view outside the chapel, he'd wanted to take back everything he'd told his father concerning the necessity of a postponement. He wasn't sure in his own mind why he'd asked for such a thing. He remembered how the expression of nervous anticipation on her beautiful face had turned to one of utter dismay. His gut clenched. He'd torn his gaze away from her face to concentrate on her volatile father.

When Guillaume had drawn his sword, Ram's brothers had responded, which was just as well because he'd rushed forward to catch Mabelle when she fainted. Gathering her up into his arms, he'd wanted to beg her forgiveness. Glaring at him as if he had two heads, Giselle had picked up the trailing veil and unfastened it from

Mabelle's hair. Her tresses had fallen free, prompting a desire to run his hands through the golden curls. His betrothed had felt light in his arms, her head nestled against his chest, yet his heart was heavy. What he'd done would turn her against him. He wanted her as he'd never wanted a woman, but he pushed the ache aside. Glory and honour beckoned.

***

Mabelle preferred to be in a stupor. Then there were no tears. When she was awake, they came unbidden and she couldn't cease sobbing, despite Giselle's best efforts to console her. For two days she couldn't speak of her humiliation. Then she could only stammer, "He—he—does—doesn't want me, Giselle."

Giselle sat on the edge of the bed and stroked her mistress's hair. "He's conflicted, *milady*, he's young. Young men don't like to rush into marriage."

Mabelle shook her head. "He—he doesn't—want me."

Giselle sighed. "*Milord* Rambaud isn't a cruel man. It's a postponement."

Mabelle blew her nose. "He—does—not—want—me."

"Soon there'll be war with Harold of England. *Milord* Rambaud must concentrate on his duty to his Duke."

"But—he doesn't want me. He doesn't like me." A fit of hiccups followed this outburst.

Giselle continued to stroke her lady's hair. "*Non*, that's not true *milady*. He's come several times a day to ask about you. He carried you here when you fainted. I've known *milord* since he was a boy. He cares for you."

Mabelle lay back against the bolster. "He abandoned me at the chapel door. I wish my father had killed him."

"Hush, *milady*. You know that's not true. You must eat something. That will improve your spirits."

Mabelle shook her head. "I can't eat. I'll be sick."

Giselle rose and went to fetch a goblet. "Drink then, a sip of ale."

After another day, Mabelle grudgingly accepted broth, but refused to leave her bed. In the years with her father she'd never known such humiliation. She'd allowed herself to hope, to have feelings, and Ram de Montbryce had ground her into the dirt. She'd disgusted him. He would never feel anything for her, and yet she still desired him, couldn't get the picture of him at the lake out of her head.

How can I marry him now? Twice he has betrayed me.

Eventually, Giselle coaxed her into a soothing bath. She felt better with her hair washed, but when the maid searched through her garments for a suitable dress, and Mabelle espied the wedding gown, she said loudly, "I never want to see it again."

Giselle took the garment with her and left the chamber, bumping into Ram. His arms were folded across his chest, a frown creased his brow. She bundled the dress more tightly to her body in an effort to conceal what she was carrying.

He fingered the material. "Don't worry, Giselle. I understand her hatred of the gown."

"You heard, *milord*?"

"*Oui*." He ran his hands through his hair. "I didn't think she'd be this upset."

Giselle snorted. "She's a woman, *milord*, a woman you rejected at the chapel door. How do you imagine she feels?"

Ram bristled. "She'll just have to get used to me. She's wilful."

Giselle pressed the dress more tightly to her body. "How do you know that? You only spent five minutes with her, and she was in a swoon for most of that time."

He knew he'd slipped, and looked away. "I mean, from what I understand—from what Antoine has told me."

She frowned. "Antoine? He barely knows her either."

Ram hoped that was true. He'd been reluctant to broach the topic with his brother and didn't like that this mistrust stood between them. Had she been waiting for Antoine in the meadow? He and his brother had always had a close bond, sharing everything. But he didn't want to share Mabelle.

Why does she rouse such strong feelings in me?

He'd reacted badly at the lake, but her beauty and state of undress had taken him unawares. When he'd carried her to her chamber, an intense feeling of longing had swept over him. He'd wanted to cradle her to his breast, to protect her. Now he stammered on, driven by a need to justify his actions to this little maid who knew him well, who he knew cared for him. "I'm told she rides her mare all over the estate, mounted astride. This isn't the behaviour of a future *Comtesse*. She must comport herself in a suitable manner, something she evidently hasn't been taught. She must learn to be a Montbryce."

"But her mare is one of her few pleasures, *milord*."

"Nevertheless, when she recovers, I'll speak with her. We'll come to an understanding of whose wishes and desires rule in a marriage. I must have obedience."

Giselle stared at him, open-mouthed.

"What? What's wrong? Giselle!" he shouted to her back as she stomped off.

I'll never understand women!

CHAPTER EIGHT

A sennight passed before Mabelle would agree to eat in the Great Hall with everyone else. Ram cringed when he saw her unhappy face. The spark had left her eyes, and she chewed her bottom lip nervously. She looked tired and ill-at-ease, but his manhood hardened at the sight of her.

This woman never fails to rouse me.

He took her hand and indicated the seat next to him. "Mabelle, sit here by me."

She didn't try to withdraw her hand, but her fingers were stiff. "That's not my place, *milord*," she replied coldly. "I'm not your wife. I have no right to sit at the head table."

He squeezed her hand, drawing her to the seat. "You're still my betrothed, Mabelle. Please obey me and sit here."

She raised her chin and looked him in the eye. A flash changed the warm brown, rich as the earth of his homeland, to an angry blaze, and he remembered her reaction at the lake to the mention of obedience.

Good, the fire is back in her eyes!

She took her hand from his, sat demurely, back rigid, hands folded in her lap. He suddenly missed the warmth of her skin, but resisted the urge to grab both her hands, press them to his face and kiss the palms.

Mabelle glanced over at Hugh and Antoine, seated further along the table, and smiled. Both returned the smile, but Antoine winked, sending pangs of jealousy searing through Ram. He wanted to leap up and pound his brother into the ground. Trying to control his temper, he turned to speak to Mabelle, ignoring Hugh's barely concealed snorts of laughter. "I'm glad to see you've recovered."

She shrugged her shoulders lightly and shook her head. "I'll never recover."

There was no anger in her voice, only resignation, and he regretted he was the cause. Putting his hands squarely on his knees, he leaned towards her slightly and offered, "Let me explain my actions. Perhaps then you'll not think so ill of me."

She looked up into the ceiling beams. "I'm all ears, *milord.*"

Ram fought the urge to tell her she shouldn't treat him with such sarcasm. "I requested a postponement, Mabelle. We will marry when I feel the time is right."

"And when might that be, *milord?*"

She's a feisty filly.

The idea brought new blood rushing to his manhood. He cleared his throat. "I'll be off to war to fight for the Duke in England. He is relying on me. Until then, you and I can come to know each other, perhaps repair some of the mistrusts, come to an understanding."

She turned to look at him. "An understanding of what?"

She's baiting me. She looks me right in the eye when she baits me.

He coughed again, rubbing his forefinger briefly over his top lip. "Well, of certain standards, codes of behaviour for a future *Comtesse.*"

She looked away. Even to his ears, his words sounded inane, but he couldn't seem to stop. He waited, knowing, *hoping* she would turn those disturbing eyes on him again. When she looked back at him, he held her gaze, wanting to make sure she knew he was determined. Their eyes locked. Could she tell a wave of heat had rolled over him? He could drown in those brown eyes.

"We must talk about your mare."

She lowered her long lashes and looked away and he felt her tense beside him. Still he pressed on. "I can't allow you to go riding alone all over the *demesne.*"

She looked back at him, her eyes boring into his. "Why not?"

Again she questions me! Keep calm.

He took a deep breath. "You ride astride. It's not seemly. And it's not safe."

She stood. "Excuse me, *milord.* As you've said, I'm not a *seemly* woman. You wish to deprive me of my only pleasure. I can no longer sit here."

He shoved his chair back abruptly, and it toppled and crashed to the floor. "Mabelle—"

But she'd flounced off, head high, back rigid, and he didn't intend to embarrass himself further in front of his grinning brothers.

Her only pleasure.

The challenge in those blazing eyes held the promise of passion, and he wanted desperately to be the one to introduce her to many other pleasures.

***

"*Milady*, you seem upset," Giselle observed a sennight later, as Mabelle stormed into her chamber yet again, slamming the door with both hands.

Mabelle whirled around, shoulders heaving. "Giselle, you love my betrothed like a son, but he's the most infuriating—"

"He's a man, *milady*."

Mabelle walked towards her bed, her fingertips pressed to her forehead. "But he wants to control everything I do. First he forbids me, *forbids* me to ride my mare. That's not considered *Comtesse*-like behaviour. Then it was how I dress. Next he forbade me to express my opinion of the conflict with Anjou. When I dared to tell him what I overheard people saying about the Duke in the castle at Arques—what will be next?"

She sank down to sit on the bed.

Giselle sat down beside her, put her arm around her lady's shoulders and took hold of her hand. "Rambaud wants to live up to what he sees as his father's expectations. He believes his parents' marriage was dominated by his father, and to the outside world it was. But I can tell you differently. The *Comte* loved his wife and never made a major decision without her. Rambaud's view is women are for—well—obedience. And bedding—and the begetting of heirs, but he'll change, as did his father."

Mabelle leaned her head on Giselle's shoulder and blushed. "I don't think the bedding will be a problem—I have to admit we seem drawn to each other that way. When he looks at me with those startling blue eyes, I want to surrender, to be obedient, to agree with everything he says. And he knows the power of those eyes to make a woman do foolish things. His voice is like the beat of a tabor drum rolling through me."

She blushed and paused, fiddling with the sleeve of her gown. Had she betrayed too much of her intense feelings? She rose from the bed and went to sit in a chair. "I long to bear a child I can love. But what Ram wants is dominance."

Giselle came to massage her lady's shoulders. "He's a soldier, *milady*. Above all else he's a warrior. But he's ambitious and such men believe they have to control everyone. His life has revolved around discipline."

Mabelle leaned her head on her hand. "But I can't sit all day doing nothing. If I'm to be a *Comtesse,* I need to learn things about the castle, the estates, the world. Ram will let me do none of that."

Giselle came to kneel in front of her mistress. "Rambaud is a good man, *milady*. Sometimes, men rebel when they think they've been forced into a marriage, though their hearts tell them it's what they want. They feel they have to assert their authority. Rambaud has never been cruel, or unreasonable. He'll come to see you're not a threat, but you must make him see you can help him achieve his ambitions."

Mabelle moved her head from side to side as Giselle stood again and kneaded her tense neck muscles. "How did things get so complicated, Giselle? I want a husband who can love me for myself, let me be myself."

"Don't give up hope, *milady*. Someday Rambaud de Montbryce will be that man. Help him grow."

Mabelle placed her hand atop the maid's. "Thank goodness I have you, Giselle, I would feel alone here without your guidance."

***

"You seem upset, *mon fils*—again," *Comte* Bernard remarked to Ram, who'd stormed into the solar, slamming the door, the second loud bang to reverberate through the castle that evening.

Ram whirled around, his eyes wild. "This woman you want me to marry is insufferable. She's wilful."

His father smiled. "*I* want you to marry? Sit down, Ram. What has she done now?"

Ram sat, but on the edge of the seat. "You think highly of her, *mon père*, but she needs to learn to be more obedient."

Bernard rolled his eyes. "Don't you find her pleasing, Ram?"

She pleases me so much I can't control my arousal whenever I'm near her.

He stood again and paced. "*Oui*—er—she's pleasing—I agree—but—"

Comte Bernard stretched out his legs and crossed his feet at the ankles. "Don't you think she's intelligent?"

"*Oui*—very—but—"

"Would you prefer an empty-headed wife?"

"Well—*non*—"

"Is she not beautiful?"

Ram sank back down into the chair. "She's breathtakingly beautiful, but—for example—it's my right to decide what should be done with Alensonne when her father dies, isn't it?"

Comte Bernard stood, walked to the hearth and stared into the flames. "Alensonne is her birthright, Ram. True, it's part of her dowry, but she grew up there. She lost that childhood home when she was a girl." He turned to face his son. "Why do you want to deprive her of a say in what happens to it?"

Silence reigned. Ram got to his feet again, and resumed his pacing, his arms folded across his chest. His father waited.

"I didn't think of it that way."

Bernard put a hand on his son's shoulder. "Mabelle isn't a threat to you, Ram, unless you turn her into one. She's survived worse tyrants than you, and is wily. If you want her on your side, you'll need to be more subtle, more appreciative of her talents and opinions. If you're not, she'll find a way to achieve what she wants, despite you."

Ram looked up at his father and their eyes met.

"She'll make a much better ally than enemy. She's listened to gossip in castles the length and breadth of Normandie and may have a better idea of people's sentiments than even our Duke. Mabelle is an exquisite rose and roses have thorns, but we tolerate the slight pain they may cause so their intoxicating beauty can enrich our lives."

Who is this man I thought was my father?

"I suppose I could indulge her a little more."

***

That evening, in the gallery, Giselle curtseyed when she arrived for her appointment with *Comte* Bernard, whose family she'd worked for most of her life.

"Please be seated, Giselle. How fares your lady?"

Giselle made herself comfortable in the upholstered chair. Her feet swung free of the floor. "Just as she has for the last fortnight. She's frustrated with *milord* Rambaud's insistence on obedience."

Comte Bernard shook his head. "And my son is still complaining about her wilfulness."

"*Milady* has agreed to be less confrontational, to try to get him to understand she can be a support to him and not a threat."

Bernard chuckled. "And Ram has agreed to be more *indulgent*."

There was a silence between them, and *Comte* Bernard sensed Giselle's hesitation, but he knew this diminutive woman well. Sooner or later she would say what had to be said.

"I hope my advice to her is correct. I'm only a maidservant but I love *milord* Rambaud like my own sons and don't want to see him destroy his prospects of marriage to this intelligent young woman."

Bernard nodded. "I'm glad she has you as a confidante, Giselle. My dear wife relied on your good sense, as do I. You're much more than a maidservant."

Giselle inclined her head. "*Merci, milord*."

Comte Bernard stood, and offered his hand to Giselle to help her out of the chair. "I hope my son will soon understand that love and respect will bind Mabelle to him, not *indulgence*. She's the kind of woman whose love and support Ram will need in the turbulent times ahead. You and I won't always be here to guide them."

Giselle indicated her agreement. "Perhaps they'll one day see how fortunate they are to have each other."

He chuckled. "We can but hope, Giselle, we can but hope—and perhaps continue our discreet meddling?"

The maidservant was about to take her leave, but turned back to face him. "Do you ever get a sense there's something else between them?"

Comte Bernard frowned. "Such as?"

"I'm not sure. I have the feeling something happened on the day they were to wed. Perhaps I'm imagining it."

CHAPTER NINE

On the morrow, as the golden streaks of dawn lit the sky, Mabelle stole down to the stables, saddled her mare quickly, a skill born of necessity and learned early in life, and rode out into the fields.

"Sibell!" she exclaimed gleefully as the mare tossed her head. Urging the horse to a canter across the meadow, she headed for the apple orchards. The wind caught her hair and ballooned in her cloak. Exhilaration swept over her. She too tossed her head and laughed with joy. "I've missed you, Sibell. Let's gallop until we get to the trees. We can't allow an overbearing nobleman to come between us and our fun, no matter how preoccupied we are with him."

Once in the orchards, she dismounted and led the horse by the reins, inhaling the scents of late spring, remembering ruefully the last time she'd been in the woods beyond the orchards. "I'm confused, Sibell. I can't get my thoughts off Ram de Montbryce but I'm afraid to trust him with my feelings. I'm nervous whenever I'm with him, I can't think properly."

Sibell whinnied and pricked up her ears. Mabelle looked around nervously. Had the horse sensed someone? Seeing no-one she became calm again. "It's good to be out of the castle for a while. I feel Ram's presence everywhere there. He's a complicated man. Will I ever understand him? Will he ever understand me?"

***

Ram had spent most of the night tossing and turning, the restful sleep he usually enjoyed in his own chamber eluding him yet again. Thoughts of Mabelle's luscious breasts and beautiful hair kept intruding on his thoughts. If he'd gone ahead with the marriage, he would now be suckling her nipples, wrapping golden tresses around his body, held tight in the grip of those impossibly long legs, as he plunged deep—

Abandoning any hope of sleep, he rose in the predawn darkness, donned a linen shirt, tied his hair back with a leather thong, and pulled on breeches and boots. He climbed to the battlements as the sun rose, hoping the fresh air would clear his head. Looking out over his family's *demesne* gave him a sense of peace. But he tensed as an unknown rider trotted out of the bailey, waving to the guard.

It can't be!

He watched in disbelief as the mare cantered and then broke into a full gallop, heading for the orchards. Mabelle's cloak ballooned behind her and the wind whipped her wheaten hair like a blazing banner, liberating her long legs from her skirts. He remembered the last time he'd seen her hair streaming behind her, down to her *derrière* as she fled him at the lake. She looked back over her shoulder for a moment and he saw the naughty grin on her sunlit face. Then she turned back and bent low, one with the horse.

She looks magnificent.

In less than five minutes he was mounted bareback on Fortis, pursuing her. Once in the orchards, he proceeded more slowly, following her trail. It led him into the woods and he suspected she'd gone to the lake. He dismounted and edged forward stealthily.

She was perched on an outcropping, close to where he'd first found her, feeding something to the horse, crooning soft words. He froze. She looked peaceful and happy, her tangled tresses covering her cloaked shoulders. He longed to bury his face in her hair, inhale the intoxicating scent that was peculiarly Mabelle.

She tucked a stray lock behind her ear and he imagined running his fingertips along the edge of that dainty ear, taking her head in his hands and drawing her lips to his. He stilled, afraid her horse would sense him. She pulled the cloak tighter around her shoulders and glanced around, peering into the trees. Had she felt his presence? Did she know his scent as he knew hers?

What is she thinking? How to be free of me?

Why was he intent on denying her this simple pleasure? Why did he feel such need for control?

She sat for a good while, laughing as the horse nudged her, begging another morsel. Ram wished he could make her laugh. He became rapt in his gazing and when she stood abruptly, it took him off guard. She saw him. He hated the flicker of fear that flashed across her face as she stopped, looking to escape him.

"Don't be afraid, Mabelle," he said softly as he stood, holding out his hands to her. "I'll never hurt you."

"*Milord.*" She bowed her head briefly and then looked directly at him. "You have a habit of watching me in the woods." Her eyes raked over his linen shirt and tight breeches and her mouth fell open. He was being devoured and it excited him. Slowly, he rolled the loose sleeves of his shirt to his elbows, braced his legs, pulled the thong from his hair, and put his hands on his hips.

"I asked you not to ride, Mabelle."

She looked at the ground. "You did."

"Yet here you are, wilfully disobeying me."

She shrugged then looked right at him. "I *am* wilful, as you've often said. I'm not suited to be a *comtesse*. You should free me from our betrothal so I can seek another husband who will think my dowry *is* suitable."

My father was right. She's wily and knows her worth.

He strode towards her. She still looked nervous but obviously determined not to let it show. She raised her hand and tucked the errant strand behind her ear again, never averting her eyes from his. Her courage excited him. He wanted to touch her, to gather her up in his arms but that might alarm her. He put his hands on her shoulders and felt her shudder. Her lashes fluttered and she closed her eyes but didn't pull away as he'd feared.

"Mabelle, you infuriate me, yet I find myself longing for your company, for the touch of your hand in mine. I want to know how your lips will feel as they open to me." Her face reddened and the heat rolled through his own body. He could feel her trembling.

"Please don't make fun of me, *milord.*"

"My name is Ram," he breathed, pulling her body to his. Her spine went rigid. Her sensuous mouth enticed him. Would her lips be warm or cold? How would she taste?

"You rouse me, Mabelle. You are my betrothed, yet we've never kissed."

He brushed his lips over hers. The moist warmth made his skin tingle. She moved her mouth away from his lips, but he held her against him, his arms now around her shoulders.

"Please don't tease me—Ram."

She seemed more afraid now than when she thought he was angry. He held her away from his body and rasped, "Are you wishing it was Antoine and not me kissing you?"

"*Non*," she murmured, shaking her head, tears welling. "Why do you torment me with this?"

He kissed her again, more deeply, his tongue coaxing her to open to him. He sucked her lower lip, bit it gently, then darted his tongue once more over her lips, whispering, "Open your sweet mouth for me."

The fight seemed to go out of her. She opened her mouth and twirled her tongue around his. A deep groan escaped her that reverberated through his body. His hand went to the back of her head and he raked his fingers along her scalp. She groaned again and then sucked his tongue into her mouth.

"Mabelle!" he rasped when he could breathe again, "You certainly know how to kiss a man." As soon as the words were spoken he regretted them.

She stiffened. "Of course I do. Have you forgotten? I'm a whore."

His grip on her shoulders tightened. "Don't utter that word. You're not a whore. I didn't mean—aagh!—by the saints, Mabelle, why is it that when I'm with you—?"

He shook his head, and moved away from her. He paced, running his hand through his hair, unsuccessfully willing his arousal to abate. "I'm a decorated cavalry commander, a counselor to the Duke. One day I'll be the *Comte* de Montbryce. I've faced many dangers, and yet I can't say or do the right thing when I'm with you."

She swayed and leaned against Sibell, her eyes closed. "It's the same for me. I've survived all manner of trials and tribulations but you—make me—quiver. I've—never—I've never kissed a man before."

His mind struggled to reconcile the idea he was the first to kiss her with what he suspected to be true—that she was no longer a maid. But, the taste of her had excited him. She looked vulnerable, leaning dejectedly against her horse. What had happened to the spirited woman he'd seen ride out from the castle? He liked the idea of the feisty Mabelle better. He wanted to reignite that flame.

He strode towards her, captured her mouth again and kissed her deeply, his hand at her throat, his thumb caressing her neck. He swirled his tongue around the inside of her mouth, feeling the warmth, the textures. Then she drew his tongue into her mouth, welcoming him. He felt her breasts rise and fall as her breathing became more rapid. His hand moved down slowly until he cupped her breast, lifting it, feeling the weight of it.

"I've wanted to hold your lovely breasts from the moment I first saw you," he whispered. "You fill my hand."

"Ram—" she breathed, as his thumb and forefinger fondled her nipple through the fabric and he felt it harden. Were her nipples pale or dark, their haloes large or small? He shook his head and gently pushed her body away from his. He would soon lose control of his arousal.

"Mabelle, I want to possess you, but not here, not like this. I'm an honourable man. When our bodies join, it will be in our marriage bed. The wait will be purgatory, but it'll be worth it."

It's a purgatory I've brought on myself. We could have been married by now.

"If Harold of England hadn't stolen our Duke's throne, things would have been much simpler. Duke William will be here within a sennight to discuss the coming invasion of England. I must stop touching you, or my proud words will be for nothing, and I'll take you right here. I'm close to the point of no return. You inflame me."

She gasped and swayed slightly, her mouth, swollen with his kisses, still open. She looked dazed.

Sibell ambled over and nudged Ram.

"She likes you," Mabelle whispered.

"I like her too," he smiled, "and I know you love her."

It would be a simple thing to grant her this happiness.

"I'll *allow* you to ride her—provided you never ride alone."

At first she seemed upset, but then murmured, "Astride?"

He hesitated. "If you wish."

She kissed his palm, held it to her face and smiled at him. "*Merci*, Ram. That means so much to me."

Waves of heat radiated up and down his spine. "Perhaps sometimes you and I can ride together."

Have I ever ridden with a woman?

"I would enjoy that, Ram. Sibell will love it. She likes Fortis."

For the first time since he'd met her, Mabelle's face blossomed into a smile. She was beautiful. He wanted that smile bestowed on him every day of his life. Something tightened in his chest and he coughed to conceal the tumult that had coursed from his heart, down through his belly and into his groin. "This talk of riding is—stimulating, Mabelle. We should go back."

They rode back in silence as far as the meadow, where Ram reined in his horse. "I lost my temper concerning Alensonne. I wasn't thinking about how important it is to you, to your childhood. This castle, my home, means everything to me. I should have understood."

"*Merci*, Ram. I'm sometimes impatient. I didn't mean to question your decisions."

"I want us to be friends, Mabelle." He reached over and tucked the curl, his finger lightly touching the edge of her ear. It sent another jolt of desire through him.

"We can be friends—if there's trust," she replied, then urged Sibell to a gallop. He sat atop Fortis, watching her disappear into the bailey, shaking his head, wishing it was him she rode.

Mabelle trembled from head to foot when she arrived in the bailey. She could barely dismount and had to lean her head against Sibell while she regained her balance. The feelings Ram's touch had aroused in her were so intense she was afraid she might swoon.

If he hadn't been honourable, if he'd wanted to make love to her in the woods, would she have given herself to him? She was inexplicably drawn to him, but what made her giddy was the notion he wanted her.

As she'd grown to womanhood, she'd seen men lust for her. She knew the signals and had learned to be wary of them. Ram's every gesture had spoken of desire and when his thick, glossy hair sprang free from the thong and fell to his shoulders, she was lost.

The heat of his hands on her had travelled down to her toes. She'd never been kissed, and the intimacy of Ram's tongue shocked her. But she'd suddenly understood what kissing was all about as the ache grew between her legs, and her own tongue became a thing beyond control. She wanted to suck him right into her mouth, to join their bodies in some way. He tasted of apple brandy, the unique scent of his maleness on the stubble of his morning beard, excitingly rough against her face.

What came over me?

When he'd withdrawn and forced her body away from his, she'd felt bereft, cold. It wasn't lost on her that this proud man had been willing to concede to her wishes concerning her horse and her childhood home. But William was to arrive soon, and above all, Ram was a warrior, sworn to his Duke.

She looked up and watched him ride in. Sweat beaded along her upper lip and she breathed heavily as chills chased down her spine. He'd looked at her as if he wanted to eat her. The touch of his hand cupping her breast, the playful squeeze of her nipple—*when our bodies join*—dizziness overwhelmed her again at the persistent memory, still tugging deep in her belly.

He desires me. Me, the unsuitable comtesse!

CHAPTER TEN

"Everyone in this castle is in a state of nervous apprehension," Ram exclaimed to his brothers with exasperation, watching the flurry of activity in the Great Hall. "Just because Duke William is coming to pay an official visit. He's been here before."

"But never on an official visit and never at such a turbulent time in Normandie's history," Hugh retorted.

Antoine put a hand on his brother's shoulder. "Worry not, Ram. *La Cuisinière* is in full command, bellowing orders to the scullery maids and serving wenches, making sure everything is in preparation for the finest meals ever concocted in her kitchen.

Madame Bonhomme has an army of maids and houseboys cleaning every last nook and cranny. Chambers are being swept, rugs and tapestries beaten, draperies and bedding aired, cobblestones scoured.

Fernand is making sure the stables are spotless, the horses immaculately groomed, the men-at-arms properly uniformed and equipped, new *enseignes* run up the flagpoles and overseeing everything else about the preparations. He even has boys up in the oak beams of this great hall, sweeping out the cobwebs." He took a deep breath, pointing to the urchins perched precariously above them.

Antoine was right and Ram had been pleasantly surprised at the way Mabelle assisted in any way she could. She seemed to enjoy the work and was friendly to everyone, though she still maintained aloofness towards him.

He dragged his thoughts back to the business at hand. "William is coming to speak to us specifically about the future. He'll no doubt be commanding us to accompany him to England for the invasion to oust Harold. Father has pledged all of us to his service."

"I'm sure you're right, Ram," Hugh replied, helping himself to a tankard of ale from the servery. "But I expect it's you he wants as his right hand man during the invasion. Your rewards could be rich."

"Whatever honour and rewards we earn are for the advancement and glory of the Montbryce name," Ram replied, aware Hugh's observations were probably correct.

I must get Mabelle off my mind and concentrate on what's important.

The sun was high in the sky when William, proud descendant of the Viking Rollo, first ruler of the Normans, rode to within sight of the castle Montbryce at the head of an impressive force of one thousand well-armed men. Sixth Duke of the Normans, he had held that title since the age of seven. In the stiff breeze, the deafening noise of the green and gold *gonfanons,* emblazoned with the Papal cross, was music to his ears. His square face, furrowed brow and determined jaw bespoke a man on a mission.

The steeds of the mounted knights behind William snorted and pranced. The spears and shields of the infantry clattered. The archers moved as one, longbows over their shoulders, newly fletched arrows rattling in their quivers. He knew it was an awesome sight and the leonine features of his face showed it.

He left the bulk of his troops to pitch camp in the freshly scythed meadows, knights under canvas, men-at-arms out in the open. Riding majestically into the bailey with a handful of knights and servants, he was greeted by all the men of the Montbryce family down on one knee, and the women of the castle in deep curtseys, their wimpled heads bowed.

"Not bad for the bastard son of a Duke and a tanner's daughter," he chuckled as he dismounted. "And Ram's betrothed. What a beauty! Why hasn't he married her yet?"

He'd been gladdened by the news of their betrothal. It would bring a great deal of strategic land in both Normandie and Le Maine under Montbryce control.

"*Non,* rise, *Comte* Bernard de Montbryce. Your family has served me, and Normandie, well. You need not bend the knee to me. Let's enter and enjoy your hospitality and discuss how we'll teach Harold a lesson he won't soon forget."

"Please, your Grace, enter," replied *Comte* Bernard, rising stiffly with Hugh's help. "You do us great honour. Ram will show you to the chambers we've prepared for you. I trust they'll meet with your approval."

Later, when the Duke's trunks had been taken to his chambers and his servants had bathed and dressed him, he descended the stone steps in the company of his senior knights to the Great Hall. A feast was served that he suspected was more sumptuous than any other meal eaten there before.

The immaculately groomed servers were resplendent in their green tabards with the Montbryce crest. The mutton meatballs were excellent and the roast chicken glazed with eggs delectable. So many multicoloured boars' heads made an appearance, the iron pans in which they reposed held aloft by brawny lads, William wondered if there could be any boar left in the Montbryce forests. *La Cuisinière's* signature dish of rainbow trout was the *pièce de resistance,* and everyone sighed as the succulent juices of the golden baked apple flesh of the *pommes d'orées* dripped from their mouths.

The famous Montbryce apple brandy was a favourite of William's and he savoured it as he watched Ram and Mabelle. Leaning over to his trusted commander, he jested, "Ram, *mon ami,* I'm heartily pleased for you that your upcoming nuptials have been welcomed, a far cry from the torment my own marriage to my tiny wife Matilda caused."

"*Merci,* your Grace," Ram responded.

The Duke had regaled Ram many times with the story but appreciated his friend would humour him as he retold it.

"I wanted the union because, with a princess of Flanders as my wife, I would have the Flemish as my allies. She at first refused me, saying she would rather become a nun than marry a bastard? Hah!"

He took a sip of apple brandy before continuing. "However, once I went swiftly to her side, I rapidly convinced her to change her mind." He winked knowingly. "But—Pope Leo was enraged by the marriage and excommunicated us both, as well as the whole of Normandie, when I refused to annul it."

Ram interjected, "I recall it took the persuasive powers of our staunch friend and ally Lanfranc, the prior of Bec, to convince a new Pope that returning Matilda to her father, *Comte* Baduin of Flandres, would be seen as a gross insult, and Nicolas relented."

William chuckled. "*Oui*, but it cost me a pretty penny because the Pope insisted I build a monastery and a nunnery in return, which I built in Caen, not to mention the hospitals I had to construct. That reminds me, I'll have to repay Lanfranc in some way once I get rid of the scheming King Harold in England. Perhaps Archbishop of Canterbury might suit our friend?"

William enjoyed the feasting and suspected he would eat no such fare in England. He so relished the food, he sent his compliments to the kitchen, particularly regarding the trout dish.

Watching Ram and Mabelle, he saw the fire in their eyes when they looked at each other. Did they recognize they were in love? He regretted the coming war would mean separation for them but was gladdened his friend Ram had found his perfect mate, even if he didn't know it yet.

"Why haven't you married her yet, Ram? I thought the nuptials were—"

His question was interrupted by the voice of *Comte* Bernard. "Your Grace, on behalf of our family, my eldest son will propose the toast."

Ram stood, goblet in hand. "Your Grace," he began, "You have done us a great honour by visiting our humble castle. You are the pride of Normandie and we salute you. We wish God's blessings on your voyage to fight the Saxons in England, where you will take your rightful place as the King. Every Montbryce knight will do what he can to further your cause."

He turned to the assembly and raised his goblet. "Fellow knights of Montbryce, rise and join me in a toast to our beloved *Duc de Normandie*, soon to be William the Conqueror."

"Duke William the Conqueror." The toast echoed around the huge room, followed by a resounding cheer and loud banging of tankards and goblets on tables.

The Duke stood to reply. "Thank you, Ram. It's only because of families such as yours that Normandie is a great power. With your family's help, though we're his vassals, we drove out Henry the King of France when he dared to invade our borders."

With a wave of his hand William indicated *Comte* Bernard. "Your father distinguished himself at the great victory which decimated our enemies at Mortemer, and though you were a mere lad at the battle of Varaville, you both helped us soundly defeat the Angevin dogs. We will similarly punish these puny sons of Danes, who have usurped the throne promised to me by my cousin. Our legacy wherever we conquer will last forever. You have pledged many knights and your brothers to our campaign and they will cover themselves with honour and glory."

Applause and cheering broke out.

"However—" William raised his hand, and the cheering stopped, as he'd known it would, and he paused to make sure his words had the desired effect. "However, there is one Montbryce for whom I have a special honour and responsibility."

A hush fell over the large hall. William loved theatrics and knew how desperately Ram wanted to accompany him on his campaign. He was aware of the pride his courageous and capable friend took in being his counsellor.

"It will take many months to complete our fleet to invade England. I've left Normandie ungoverned while overseeing the preparations. Too many have taken advantage. I can't be worried about trouble at home while I'm preparing to fight the accursed Harold the Oath-Breaker."

A hint of murmured agreement stole round the room.

"I must have a capable commander in charge of finishing my fleet, someone I can trust implicitly."

He turned to Ram, seated beside him. "Rambaud de Montbryce, you are that man. You'll oversee the completion of our great fleet and the gathering of men, weapons, horses and provisions. Your decisions will be my decisions. You and your family have never failed me. You've supported me against the rebellious barons who would take Normandie for themselves, including my own uncles."

"You served brilliantly in our successful campaign to extend our influence into Le Maine, a few short years ago. Your skills as a negotiator helped bring Harold Godwinson into our grasp when he was shipwrecked on the lands of Guy of Ponthieu—*without* our paying a ransom for him."

He slapped Ram on the back and the laughter and cheering echoed in the room. "Too bad we let him go then—we wouldn't be in this predicament now."

More cheers, laughter and agreement.

Ram rose and bowed deeply, his hand over his heart. He cleared his throat. "Your Grace, I will build a fleet of ships so mighty and gather an army so great, it will strike terror into the hearts of all Englishmen. The honour you do me, my betrothed and my family is humbly accepted." He turned to Mabelle and held out his hand. She rose and bowed to the Duke.

"You're fortunate, Rambaud de Montbryce, to have such a beautiful and capable woman to support you in your formidable task. *Mes seigneurs et mesdames*, a toast to Mabelle de Valtesse."

The toast echoed around the room. "Mabelle de Valtesse."

Custom dictated she reply. "*Majesté*," she began, swallowing hard. William was pleased and flattered by the exalted name she used to address him.

"Your majesty, I thank you from the bottom of my heart for the honour you have bestowed on my betrothed. I know he will serve you, our beloved Duchess Matilda, and Normandie well."

She raised her goblet, took a sip, licked her lips and looked into the Duke's deep blue eyes, and then, nervously, at Ram.

The Duke of the Normans inclined his head in acknowledgement, relieved his ducal robe concealed his arousal.

***

For most of the next five months Ram was away, supervising the building of the ships. Whenever he could, he rode home to Montbryce and kept his family apprised of their progress and his challenges and frustrations. He came to the surprising realization it was a desire to see Mabelle and share these matters with her that drew him home. She was often present when the Montbryce men discussed the preparations, and he came to see, as his father had indicated, that she was intelligent and pragmatic. Her insights were often impossible to ignore.

"We're felling the trees from the forests around the coastal town of Dives-sur-Mer. Shipwrights shape the wood into vessels, armour and weapons. The building will be more or less completed at the mouth of the Dives and then the fleet will move to Saint-Valery-sur-Somme."

"I suppose that will shorten the crossing?" Mabelle remarked.

When the move to Saint-Valery was undertaken, it was hampered by foul weather and several men drowned. Ram was angry and upset, worried the same might happen when the day came for the invasion. It was Mabelle who reassured him. "You won't be forced to launch the invasion during bad weather," she soothed.

During one of his visits, they were discussing the comet which appeared and remained visible for fifteen days. "William has taken it as a good omen. His astrologers declared this portends the transfer of a kingdom. I'm to start gathering horses."

"You're taking horses?" Mabelle asked with surprise.

"*Oui*. William and I have discussed it with the commanders and we believe it's essential we take them."

"You're right. How can you win without your horses? Normandie's strength is in her elite mounted troops."

Ram's heart swelled with pride that she recognised the importance of his life's calling.

On another occasion, *Comte* Bernard, Ram and his brothers were seated around the table in the Map Room, discussing the landing in England. Ram explained, "We're concerned about our arrival on the coast. We'll need a fortification of some sort, but that will mean time lost gathering materials, building and the like."

They pondered the problem for a while. Mabelle sat off to one side, saying nothing until she suddenly suggested, "Why not make a fortification here in Normandie and take it with you in pieces?"

Comte Bernard glanced at Ram, who was nodding, scratching his chin.

"What an intriguing idea, Mabelle," Hugh exclaimed with a smile.

By early September, Ram came close to the breaking point. He paced back and forth in the Map Room. "I have seven thousand men and six hundred and ninety-six ships ready to move, yet we've had to sit and wait for an interminable five and thirty days for the wind to shift from north to south, to fill our square sails. The wait is driving me out of my wits."

He strode over to Mabelle's chair and went down on one knee before her, taking her hands in his. "Thanks be to the saints I have you to listen to my interminable ramblings, Mabelle. William is becoming maniacal about his *crusade* and maintaining morale is difficult."

Mabelle raised her hand and stroked his hair. He wanted to rest his head in her lap. He felt better sharing his frustrations with her. It was an odd feeling. He'd never confided in a woman before. "Horses and men have to be fed, and I've forbidden pillaging. William doesn't want the ordinary people of Normandie trembling at the sight of his soldiers. It might have been easier if they were all Normans."

She stopped stroking his hair, and he instantly missed the soothing gesture. "You have men who aren't Normans?"

He took her hand, kissed her fingertips and put it to his forehead. "My head aches."

She massaged his temples with her fingertips. He let out a sigh and slumped to sit at her feet. "That feels good. *Oui.* Many of them are mercenaries, allies and volunteers from Bretagne and Flandres. A few have come from other parts of France and some from as far away as the Norman colonies in Italy. I've maintained strict discipline but it's not an easy task when old hatreds and feuds reassert their ugly heads."

I could sit here all day, letting her massage my head.

Mabelle's next words brought him back to reality. "Does King Harold know you're coming?"

He didn't want to tell her spies had informed them Harold had assembled a large force on the south coast of England to repel any attack.

CHAPTER ELEVEN

Harold Godwinson, King of the English, sat in stunned disbelief in his headquarters on the south coast of England, where he had gathered his forces to await William's arrival. He re-read the message that had sent chills down his spine. The Viking king, Harald Hardråda, his Norwegian rival, had landed unexpectedly on the north east coast of England near York with a huge force of more than fifteen thousand men, intent on claiming the English throne.

"What's worse, Gyrth," he told his brother, "Our wretched half-brother, Tostig, has apparently joined with Hardråda, incensed I drove him out of his earldom of Northumbria, after he rebelled against me. What did he expect?"

Harold crushed the parchment in his hands. "What's your advice? Do we stay here and wait for William, or make haste to York?"

"We must oppose Hardråda," his brother decided without hesitation. "The threat from him is real. William is still waiting in Normandie for the wind to change."

Harold had been of the same mind. "You're right. We have no choice."

The forced march north was gruelling. The strategic northern town of York had surrendered to Harald Hardråda on the twenty-fourth day of September. In an effort to avoid battle, Harold arranged a meeting with Tostig and reluctantly offered him a third of his kingdom.

Tostig thought on the offer for a while and then asked, "What will you offer the King of Norway?"

Harold had no intention of giving the Norwegian anything. "Six feet of ground, or as much more as he needs. He's taller than most men," he retorted sarcastically.

No agreement was reached and the battle was joined the next day at dawn at Stamford Bridge. The opposing forces fought hard until noonday. The Norwegians were forced to retreat under the weight of superior English numbers. It was an unusually hot day and many of the Norsemen had taken off their heavy byrnies. They were driven across the river Ouse, where they made a fresh stand. A lone Norwegian giant took up a post on the bridge over the river and hewed down more than two score Saxons with a battle-axe. This stayed the advance of the English army for many hours.

Watching the massacre from his command post, Harold asked his commanders with exasperation, "Who is that formidable warrior?"

"No one knows, Sire," replied one of them, with equal irritation. "But we cannot advance with him there. I have a plan to send a boat beneath the bridge, and skewer him with a spear from below."

Harold looked at him sceptically, then shrugged, "Sometimes the simple plan is the best."

To the king's surprise, this ploy was successful, and the Norwegians were overrun. Harald Hardråda was killed by an arrow through the throat.

After the battle, Harold went to examine the Norwegian king's body. He poked at it with his foot. "Hardråda has spent his life fighting in such faraway places as Asia and Africa, yet he falls on the banks of the River Ouse here in Yorkshire," he commented wryly. "He's a tall man and goodly to look upon, but his luck has left him."

Gyrth gloated. "We've thrashed the Norwegians. Of their three hundred ships, only four and twenty are returning with their wounded, and Tostig, the traitor, is dead."

Harold scratched his head and adjusted his gold circlet. "We've defeated one rival, Gyrth, but now we're hundreds of miles from the south coast where William might arrive any time. Our army is tired, bloodied and aching to return home."

***

A few days later, the winds of change blew across the Narrow Sea between Normandie and England. William and his army of seven thousand, the Montbryce brothers among them, boarded their longboats, after loading the horses, armour, weapons, provisions and wine.

"An army can't be victorious if it runs out of food," Ram had told Mabelle, "And we'll be a long way from the fertile fields of Normandie."

The deafening sounds of drums, trumpets and pipes filled the air as they set sail.

"If Harold is waiting on the coast, he'll surely know we're coming now," Ram jested to his Duke.

William smiled. "According to reports delivered to me yesterday, he's in the North. The Norwegian, Hardråda, has attacked unexpectedly. My plan is to sail through the night and land on the morrow, as day breaks. Ram, you and I will be aboard the Mora. Is the muster roll complete? Do you have it?"

"*Oui*, Your Grace, it's complete and in the good hands of the clerks who assisted me to compile it. Every man fighting for you is listed."

When all was in readiness, William ordered the signal to be given by use of a lantern on the mast. "Matilda gave me this ship, Ram. See the figurehead? It's a young boy with a bow and arrow pointing towards England."

As the sun set, Ram held his breath, his heart beating erratically as he watched the hundreds of ships he had helped build set sail on this momentous undertaking. All seemed to be going well, but as darkness fell, the flagship became separated from the main fleet. Ram could tell his friend didn't want to appear perturbed as he calmly issued commands. "Cast out the anchor. We'll break our fast while we wait for them to catch up. Bring some spiced wine also."

Servants scurried to do his bidding, and soon Ram and his Duke were savouring the wine. "You know, Ram, when I visited Edward the Confessor in England all those years ago, he promised me the throne as a lawful gift. I sometimes wonder why he sent Harold to us as an Ambassador. Did the wily old Confessor think it humorous to have two rivals size each other up?"

He cupped his goblet in both hands and inhaled the aroma. "I regret I'll have to kill Harold. I like the fellow. He's tall and handsome, has remarkable physical strength, courage and eloquence. He's known for his ready jests and acts of valour. But what's the use of those gifts without honour? It infuriates me he swore an oath of loyalty to me at Bonneville, two years ago, over the relic of a saint's bones. Harold claims he wasn't aware the bones were there, and in any case had crossed his fingers when he took the oath. You were there, *mon ami.*"

The wine was beginning to ward off the chill of the sea air creeping into Ram's blood. "I was indeed, your Grace." He knew what came next.

"When he came to Normandie, I greeted him with splendid hospitality after his difficult journey. He was shipwrecked, as you know, and we rescued him from Guy de Ponthieu. He assisted us with our campaign against the Bretons, saving two of our commanders who'd fallen into quicksand. I knighted him for that."

William took a long draught of the wine and bit into a pastry. "He swore an oath, of his own free will, that he would represent me at Edward's court and would do everything in his power to ensure the throne came to me, after Edward's death. He promised to garrison my troops in the castle at Dover, and anywhere else I might choose—at his expense, I might add."

"I can testify to that, as a truthful and honourable man who was present." Ram had heard the story many, many times over the course of the past six sennights, and his attention was more on the play of the moonlight on the rippling water. Did Mabelle watch the same moon?

William suddenly threw his empty goblet down angrily, and it rolled back and forth with the swell. "Then comes the unwelcome report, that this insensate Englishman has not waited for public choice, has broken his oath, and has seized the throne of the best of kings on the very day of his funeral. But, unfortunately for Harold," William laughed, "The Pope doesn't approve of oath-breakers and has given my crusade his blessing."

Watching the rolling goblet made Ram's stomach clench and he felt the familiar bile of *mal de mer* rise in his throat. He wondered if William would be as free and easy with his confidences and friendship if he did become King. Only six years separated them in age but William had been the Duke since he was a boy.

"I'm not naive, Ram. I recognize the real reason most of the Normans have supported my *crusade*—the promise of titles and lands in England, for anyone who would help me get my throne."

He jumped to his feet and braced his legs against the movement of the ship. "I'm offering them the investment opportunity of a lifetime. If we can take England away from Harold, we'll divide up the kingdom. The Pope has legitimized our violence as necessary, in a just cause, to depose an oath-breaking upstart."

He raised his hand and pointed. "He's even given me this fine consecrated Papal banner."

Both men became lost in their thoughts as the longboat bobbed in the waves. Ram wasn't a good sailor and, if he had to be in a boat, would prefer it wasn't anchored. He didn't wish to retch in front of William. The Duke was probably envisaging thrones and crowns and coronations. Ram thought of Mabelle, and his father's magnificent castle, his home. He wondered if and when he would ever see them again.

As dawn broke, they heard the cry from the prow, "We've sighted the fleet."

"Signal to regroup, and continue on to the coast." William sat, legs wide, hands on his knees, his back rigid, as the longship resumed its journey.

At Pevensey they heaved the longboats up on the shore, but when William stepped off his boat, he slipped and fell into the mud. Trying to avoid the accident being perceived as a bad omen, Ram quipped, "His Grace already has the earth of England in his hands."

William smiled his thanks at his quick-thinking friend, and raised his fist full of the muck. Everyone cheered, obviously relieved this awkward moment had passed.

"This is a good omen, Ram. We've had a safe crossing, and Harold has no one here to oppose us. Our spies were correct. He didn't expect us to come so late in the year."

Knights and nervous horses poured out of the boats.

"They are relieved to be back on dry land," William commented.

"As am I," Ram agreed.

When all were ashore, William summoned his commanders to his tent. "Eude," he indicated his half brother. "Eude will send out men immediately to raid the surrounding countryside for supplies. We'll move a few miles inland to the east, to Hastings, and erect the temporary wooden stockade we brought with us in pieces. An excellent idea of yours, Montbryce."

Ram swelled with pride, squaring his shoulders and jutting out his chin as he inclined his head in acknowledgement.

Merci, Mabelle.

William paced as he went over his plans for what Ram felt must have been the hundredth time. "Then we await Harold's inevitable arrival. We could advance on London, but it would be better to lure Harold to the coast. We have a sheltered harbour here. It's a good defensive position, and Sussex is Harold's territory. He'll ride to defend his people from our harassment. We must continue to forage from his lands, though we brought enough provisions with us. The English fleet will regroup to cut off our escape by sea. We must attack people and property in the vicinity, incensing Harold and drawing him here quickly."

***

"This castle feels empty without my boys," *Comte* Bernard said sadly, as he and Mabelle supped. "They've gone off to fight before. I should be used to this by now."

Mabelle understood his concern for their safety. His life revolved around his sons—they were the hope of his family's future. He seemed to have aged considerably in the few days since the departure of the fleet.

"We'll pray daily for their safe return, *milord*." She kept her voice calm, but her heart thudded in her ears, her head ached and she was filled with a sense of dread.

Pray God he returns to me.

They'd received no word of the crossing. Had the ships arrived? How had Ram weathered the sea journey? Was he safe? She couldn't get him out of her head, couldn't forget the taste of his lips, the feel of his hands. It had been challenging and stimulating to sit discussing the preparations for the invasion, but now it was a reality and the potential loss to the Montbryce family, and to herself, overwhelmed her. An atmosphere of nervous expectancy, tinged with fear, pervaded the castle.

CHAPTER TWELVE

Harold's forces began arriving back on the south coast in groups throughout the day on the thirteenth of October, in the year of Our Lord One Thousand and Sixty-Six. These men had won a hard-fought battle eighteen days before, two hundred and sixty miles to the north and were now expected to fight another.

Harold, his brother, Leofric, and several other knights were poring over charts in Harold's tent.

"Despite the hardship, morale is high," Leofric told Harold. "Soundly defeating Hardråda has boosted confidence."

Harold bit his bottom lip. "But not our numbers. However, we've recruited many more to our cause on the trip south, and collected fresh troops in London. I assume a battle is inevitable since no form of parley has been offered. I've made the decision to fight William, before he can consolidate any further."

Leofric put his hand on his brother's shoulder. "You're the King the people of England want, your Majesty. They didn't want Hardråda, and they certainly don't want William. Edgar the Aetheling is much too young. You're the dead Confessor's brother-by-marriage. He wanted you to have the throne."

Harold believed the decision of the powerful Witan to support him, instead of Edgar, had nothing to do with the Aetheling's age. Stigand and Ealdred, the Archbishops of Canterbury and York, and the other powerful members of the Witan, recognized him as the more capable monarch. Harold knew in his heart they were right.

In the few months he'd been king, and despite the conflicts he'd been embroiled in, he'd struck down several iniquitous laws, and established just ones. He'd ordered thieves and wrongdoers arrested, and had improved England's land and sea defences, placing infantry garrisons at key points along the coast.

Now he needed to clear his head after the long ride from the north, and concentrate on the coming battle. Some, including his own mother, advised him to wait before joining William in battle, but he was adamant. He hoped the confidence in his voice would resonate with his commanders as faced them squarely, one hand on the hilt of his sword, his back rigid, his crowned head held high. "We can't afford to give the Norman time to make friends and allies in England. My decision to surprise the Norwegians is what brought about their defeat."

One knight raised his hand, as if to speak, but Harold's glare silenced him.

"We will fight William *now*. We need to choose the location of the battle with care."

He looked around for any further signs of opposition but saw none. "I've opted for Caldbec Hill for a number of reasons. It gives a natural advantage because of its all round visibility. It's protected on each flank by marshy ground, and there's a forest behind it. It's easy to reach from London and is close to William's position."

Many indicated their understanding and agreement.

"The Old Hoare Apple Tree is a well known landmark and will make an excellent rallying point. By nightfall, I estimate at least seventy-five hundred of our men should have arrived. Preparations must be laid to challenge William as soon as possible. He's in Hastings. Tomorrow is Saturday. I was born on a Saturday, and my mother has always said it's my lucky day."

At first light, the English set off towards the enemy. The common soldiers wore conical leather helmets, the wealthier helmets of iron and as much clothing as possible under their hauberks, to serve as padding. The rich knights had hauberks with hoods worn under the helmets. All were on foot, armed with battle-axes, swords, shields and spears.

Gyrth came to the King. He went down on one knee before his brother. "Harold, there will be great danger in the coming battle. Let me take your place to lead the army against the Normans. You're too important, as our monarch, to expose yourself, especially tired as you are after Stamford Bridge. England can't risk losing her King."

Harold took Gyrth's hand and pulled him from his knees. "No, Gyrth. I thank you for your love and concern. William is deliberately victimizing my people in Sussex. It's personal now. I'll lead our victory against him."

***

Prayers were offered in the Norman camp throughout the night prior to the battle, and the men confessed their sins. Ram sought out his brothers and they received the Sacrament of Penance together. He wanted to clear the air, once and for all, between Antoine and himself. He'd never truly believed his brother had a relationship with his future wife, but the unfounded jealousy was there, in the back of his thoughts. Mabelle had uttered Antoine's name at the lake. He and his brother could both die during the coming battle. Antoine had sensed his coolness, he was sure. The crackling campfire held their gazes.

"Antoine, brother, there's no easy way to ask you this, but I must."

"I know something's on your mind, Ram, something that's bothered you for months."

"It's Mabelle."

Antoine shook his head. "I've never understood why you didn't marry her that day. I was ashamed of you, I have to admit, the way you treated her. You're lucky she still speaks to you."

Ram hesitated. "You're part of the reason I didn't."

Antoine looked startled. "Me?"

"I chanced upon Mabelle in the woods, on my way home that day. She seemed to be waiting for someone."

Hugh and Antoine looked up suddenly. "And you thought it was I? Why?"

"She spoke your name."

"My name? What do you mean?"

"When she first saw me, she thought I was you."

Antoine had straightened his back. He stared intently at Ram. "I'm confused. You saw her in the woods, and she thought you were me?"

Ram shifted uncomfortably on his camp stool. Now he would have to tell the whole story. "She was asleep."

"In the woods?"

"She'd been bathing—at the lake—and fell asleep."

Antoine looked at Hugh and the two burst out laughing, drawing the curious stares of other knights nearby. Hugh almost fell off his stool.

When Antoine could speak again, he stammered, "What you're trying to tell us, older brother, is that you stumbled across Mabelle lying naked in the woods and—but, wait a moment—did you know who she was?"

"*Non.* And she wasn't naked. Not quite, anyway."

"So, let me see if I have this right." Antoine held up his thumb. "One, on the way to your wedding, you stopped to watch an unknown, *almost naked* maiden?"

He held up his forefinger. "Two, you became angry with me?"

His middle finger popped up. "Three, you were so furious with her, because she thought you were me, that you called off the wedding."

Another fit of laughter from Hugh caused Antoine to pause.

"I *knew* something had happened that day. I could tell there was tension between you," his younger brother said.

"Four," Antoine continued, "You're an idiot, and five, you should fall to your knees and ask the woman's forgiveness." He thrust his five outstretched digits in front of Ram's reddened face.

His brothers continued to mock him, and soon he was laughing and shaking his head at his own folly. He stood and dragged Antoine off his stool and into his embrace, choking back tears. "I'm sorry, Antoine. Forgive me. When I'm near Mabelle, I lose my senses."

"That's called love, brother," Antoine replied.

Ram's spine stiffened. "I have no time for love."

"You're a fool if you drive her away," Antoine said gently.

They talked for an hour about their father, their family, their castle, their orchards. Each swore to bring honour to the Montbryce name. Despite their earlier laughter, Hugh's wide eyes, tense lips and crossed arms told Ram his brother was terrified.

"Hugh, there's no shame in feeling fear. I'm afraid, as is Antoine. My gut is tied in knots. Any man who tells you he's not afraid this night is a liar. The important thing is not to let the fear control you. Bravery is born of fear. Engrave our family motto on your heart, as it is on your shield, *Fidelity and Valour.*"

"I know. I can't stop shaking but I'm not a coward."

***

78

William ordered a Mass to be said, during which he placed around his neck the relics on which Harold had sworn his oath. He assembled his army, and informed them what was expected. Astride his destrier, William proclaimed, "It's all or nothing. There's no going back without a victory. We will win because we are the righteous side."

He intoned a *laisse* of the Song of Roland to inspire his soldiers with that warlike example.

His castles all in ruin have you hurled,
With catapults his ramparts have you burst,
Vanquished his men, and all his cities burned.

The Normans set off from the coast in a long column, because of the forested terrain, their wagons loaded with sharpened weapons, armour and provisions. Startled birds took flight as the horde marched through the trees. No words were exchanged. Did each man ponder his future, or his past, hypnotised by the muffled sounds of horses' hooves and leather booted feet, as they made their way to the inevitable horror ahead. Did each rider focus on the swaying tail of the horse ahead, as he did, sphincter muscles clenched?

They completed the nine mile march behind the Papal banner. William set up his command post behind the cavalry. Ram joined him astride Fortis.

"It's as well the situation is coming to a conclusion. Morale is beginning to wane amongst the foot soldiers." William confided. "They're less concerned about moral crusades, and promises of wealth to the nobility, than staying alive."

Ram quickly checked his equipment, the hooded hauberk and iron helmet, spear, shield and trusty sword in its scabbard. He smiled at a brief memory of Mabelle heaving *Honneur* into a muddy pond but quickly banished the thought. He couldn't afford to be distracted from the dire business at hand. His hauberk, with three layers of metal circles, looped and soldered together, would give him good protection, especially with the extra rectangular breastplate of chain mail secured to protect his chest. The bottom of his hauberk tunic, split at front and back, covered his thighs like a skirt, and made riding more comfortable. He wished it covered the lower part of his long legs but would have to make sure the pointed end of his tapering wooden shield did that. He was proud of his leather covered shield, one of the few with a coat of arms. *Fide et Virtute.*

Vaillon had shaved the back of Ram's head, Norman style. He would be doing a lot of sweating this day, and couldn't afford to have his vision obscured. The nosepiece of his helmet, protecting his nose, and to some extent his eyes, was enough of a distraction.

William positioned his army looking towards Caldbec Hill. Ram's gaze ranged slowly over the front ranks of archers, then to the six rows of infantry behind them, and then to the cavalry, the fearsome Bretons on the left, the Flemish contingent on the right, the Normans in the centre. As he surveyed the daunting sight, Rambaud de Montbryce knew with dire certainty this would be a different fight from any he'd been in before. It would be a mighty battle to the death that would change the course of history. His own, his country's and his Duke's.

Immense pride and sheer terror coursed through his veins.

CHAPTER THIRTEEN

"We will meet his challenge," Harold shouted decisively, seeing the Normans take up their position. "Move the men down from Caldbec Hill to within five hundred yards of the enemy. The Normans won't deploy a shield wall."

His *housecarls* were in the front rank and were responsible for forming the shield wall, developed by Alfred the Great and used ever since. This tactic was particularly effective against the initial onslaught in any battle. Behind the *housecarls* were the *fyrd,* or militia, ten deep, led by the thanes who carried swords and javelins. Many of the ordinary soldiers were armed with iron-studded clubs, slings, reaping hooks, scythes and haying forks. Harold set up his command post behind them, centrally positioned to give him an elevated view of proceedings. Confidence coursed through him, heating his warrior blood.

It was still early in the morning. He ordered the signal to be given. His standard bearer raised the Wessex Wyvern dragon and waved it proudly. Suddenly on the air came the Saxon battle cries, "*Godemite*", "*Oli Crosse*".

The Normans responded with a plea for God's help, "*Que Dieu nous aide.*"

Trumpets sounded. The pivotal battle began.

"What's that fool doing?" screamed William, as one of his men broke ranks to rush forward *alone*, juggling swords, to attack the Saxons. He was quickly cut down, after managing to slay a standard bearer of the astonished Saxons.

"Loose the arrows," William commanded. The Norman archers let fly their arrows in a concentrated barrage. This had limited success against the shield wall. A serious problem soon became apparent to

Ram. "Your Grace," he shouted breathlessly, when he arrived back at the command post. "I'm not sure why, but the English are not using archers, and we require an exchange of arrows to keep the ammunition levels up. We'll soon run out."

William cursed. "If that happens, our archers are not trained for hand to hand fighting. Bring forward the crossbows."

Ram shook his head. "But, your Grace, the Pope has forbidden the use of crossbows. We're fighting Christians."

William clenched his fist. "We must win. We must defeat Harold. That's our only concern, and crossbow bolts are more effective against shields."

"*Oui*, your Grace."

With prearranged hand signals, William ordered his foot soldiers forward. The English responded. The quiet of the countryside soon filled with the clang of swords, the sickening thud of clubs on helmets and bone, the battle cries of the living, and the groans of the dying. Iron helmets and weapons clashed. The English on the high ground had the advantage. The Saxon line remained virtually untouched, the arrows having done little damage to the impenetrable armoured monster. The barrage of traditional weapons as well as anything that could be collected in the vicinity, including rocks from homemade slingshots, caused serious problems to William's men.

"We'll need the cavalry earlier than I would have wished," William shouted. "Too many heavy casualties." He turned, looking for someone. "Montbryce," he yelled, as Ram galloped into view.

"Your Grace?"

"Order the cavalry to charge on the shield wall, before it advances much further."

Ram rode at full speed into the bloody mayhem, to deliver the order to the cavalry. Both his beloved brothers were among the mounted Norman ranks. He encouraged his horse, knowing the weight, speed and impact of Fortis might prove to be his best weapon against the unmounted Saxons. Secure in the large saddle, raised front and back to give him a solid seat, he used his spurs sparingly on the beloved horse. "I'm thankful it's you beneath me, Fortis. Many questioned the wisdom and necessity of bringing horses on the ships, but I would wager they see the right of it now. You could be the difference between victory and defeat."

Why is the English army not using its horses? Perhaps neither the horses nor the men are trained to fight as cavalry.

As a youth he'd learned to fight from horseback as a noble pursuit. The idea of a mounted elite was a heroic notion in Normandie and Bretagne, as Mabelle had rightly observed. But now, hard as the Normans tried, they couldn't break down the shield wall. The Saxons brought down riders and horses with a single blow of their lethal Danish battle axes. The slope, quickly becoming a muddy slide, made a speedy ascent difficult for the horses. Fortis struggled as Ram swung and hacked with his sword, severing limbs and heads.

He noticed suddenly that the much feared Bretons, on the left, were having a particularly difficult time. They retreated back down the hill, and Ram watched in horror, left with no alternative but to go back to the command post. The corded muscles of his sword arm were on fire, his face spattered with blood and muck. His heart raced. He turned back to look at the scene of chaotic terror. He caught sight of another Montbryce shield, the knight carrying it still mounted, and breathed a sigh of relief.

Hugh or Antoine?

"The retreat of the Bretons leaves us vulnerable to a pincer attack," William bellowed. "Our men are panicking." He cursed and Ram sensed he could see his dreams of taking the English throne in serious jeopardy. Ram thought he might never see Mabelle again.

Why do my thoughts go to her?

Rumour started to spread along the ranks that William had been killed. Panic was widespread amongst the Normans. The Bretons were in full retreat back down the hill but were slowed down on the lower slopes by the stream and marshy ground below, giving the Saxons more opportunity to inflict casualties on them.

The rumour of his death reached William and infuriated him. "I am not dead yet," he shouted in loud disgust, pushing his helmet to the back of his head. He rode along the ranks that still stood to dispel the rumour. "Look at me! There is no way back. You are fighting for your lives."

"You're Grace," Ram panted, swallowing hard. "Look. Eude is rallying the cavalry." Two of William's commanders, his half brother, Bishop Eude, and Eustace of Boulogne, had indeed seen the action on the left flank, and were rallying their confused cavalry. They rode to the area the Saxons had advanced to. Seeing the horses approaching, the Saxon infantry broke off battle and tried to return to their lines. The uphill trek proved to be too far, and they were cut down by the Norman cavalry. Ram suddenly saw his gentle brother

Hugh viciously strike down an enemy soldier, but then lost sight of him.

"Harold has seen the advance on the Saxon right," William cried. "I wager he didn't order it. It was undisciplined, and against all military strategy. He's hesitating to take up the challenge of a full frontal assault. We have a chance to regroup, re-arm and take food and drink. Montbryce, order Pierre de Fleury to take a party of men to remove our wounded from the field. Harold's men are taking advantage of the break in the hostilities to do the same. Tell de Fleury they must put the wounded horses out of their misery."

What of the men's misery?

"The cursed Saxons will win if they hang on until dark. We can't stay here all night. We would have to retreat, and retreat means defeat." William seemed to be at his lowest ebb, trying to plan a new tactic to break down the Saxon defences. "The terrain makes it difficult," he shared with his commanders gathered around him. "We can't try a flanking movement, because of the trees and marshes on either side. Harold chose this place well. We can't break the shield wall. Perhaps we can feign a retreat and draw the Saxons forward?"

Most of his commanders were doubtful it would work, but Ram, wiping the spatters of blood and brains from his face, urged, "It's our only chance. We need to draw the Saxons forward by giving the impression it's a genuine retreat, and not a tactic. Normans have used it successfully before, at Saint-Aubin against Walter Giffard. Ask him yourself, he's on our side now, and is fighting with us today."

William thought for a while, shifting impatiently in his saddle. "Feigning a retreat worked for us in Sicily, not long ago. We'll resume the battle. Montbryce, order the infantry to advance, and then lead the cavalry, at speed, up the hill behind the infantry. Engage the Saxons, and then turn around and make it appear we're running. You'll have to choose the moment carefully, so as not to arouse their suspicion it's a trick."

Ram rode back into hell, his blood pumping so fast his heartbeat echoed in his ears, in time with his steed's hoof beats. The sound had an oddly comforting cadence to it, "Ma-Belle, Ma-Belle, Ma-Belle."

Thanks be to God, Fortis still lived. The Duke had already lost three horses in the melee. He clutched the leather straps of his shield tightly, couched his spear like a lance, and leaned into his horse.

The infantry advanced with limited success. Ram regretted he couldn't inform them of William's plan. Most of them would be killed, sacrificed for the greater good. Shouting the battle cry *Fide et Virtute*, he led the cavalry at a gallop up the hill and engaged the Saxons, narrowly avoiding being decapitated by a gigantic Saxon, wielding a battle axe. He felt the cold draft of the huge weapon as it swung close to his ear, heard the *whoosh*. For a moment, he couldn't understand why he wasn't looking at his own bloodied head on the ground, instead of into the startled, disembodied gaze of the Flemish knight who'd ridden at his side. He thrust his spear into the Saxon's throat, then had to pull hard to retrieve it. He looked back over his shoulder. Judging the moment to be right, he shouted the order to turn, giving the impression they were retreating. He shifted his shield to cover his back.

"Unbelievable—it seems to be working," William chortled, as he watched the Saxon army break ranks and follow Montbryce's cavalry down the slope, only to be cut down by them as they turned again.

Ram became vaguely aware of arrows flying overhead. He surmised William must have sent his archers forward, to retrieve the arrows loosed earlier. Firing over the heads of their own men, so that the arrows would land on the rear English lines, had caused a number of casualties. Wheeling round, he saw King Harold raise his hands to clutch an arrow that had struck him in the face. The monarch fell to the ground.

"Your Grace, Harold has fallen! He has fallen!" Ram's throat was so dry he hoped his strangled cry had reached the Duke's ears.

Reining in his horse and swivelling in the saddle to look at where Ram pointed, William yelled, "This news will cause widespread confusion. We must launch a full frontal attack now."

It didn't take long for the news of Harold's demise to spread like wildfire through the Saxon ranks. They became dispirited, and fled up the hill and into the forest on the other side, taking any horses that had previously been withdrawn for safety. The exhausted, and often wounded, English warriors were pursued relentlessly, and cut down in the woods or trampled beneath thundering hooves.

The dead and injured of both sides, and Norman horses littered the battlefield. Severed body parts lay everywhere on the bloodied earth, now churned to mud. The Saxon line had broken. The mangled bodies that had been the flower of English nobility and youth, covered the ground as far as the eye could see. Only the King's *housecarls* were prepared to continue the fight. They valiantly surrounded their dead king. With battle-axes and swords, they fought to the last man.

The Normans at last broke through to where King Harold had fallen. William had won against the odds, but, as darkness fell, showed his dismay at the sight of so many promising young men, both English and Norman, lying dead and broken on the field of battle. An eerie silence hung over all.

As they picked their way through the carnage, William confided to Ram, "If Harold had waited only one more day for his full force to arrive, the outcome of this battle may have been very different. If he'd decided to outwait us, the more difficult it would have been for us to maintain our position here, far from home. I can't understand why he had no archers. He always was too impetuous. It's ironic that after all the tactics of the battle, my decision to send the bowmen back in to retrieve and reuse their own arrows turned the tide."

He gazed distractedly at the Wessex Wyvern dragon banner, still fluttering sadly in the breeze, and Harold's personal standard of the Fighting Man, captured near his body. It was sumptuously embroidered with gold and precious stones. William pointed to it. "I want that standard borne to the Pope."

He turned and Ram could see the exhaustion etched into his friend's face.

"By the way," William said. "Speaking of impetuous, who was the fool that charged the Saxons alone, at the outset of the battle?"

"According to the rumours, a *jongleur* named Taillefer," Ram replied.

"Hmm. The man must have had a death wish. I suppose *jongleurs* will be singing about him soon. He'll be more famous than I."

Ram de Montbryce and his future king looked at each other and laughed.

***

While Ram was fighting for his country and his life in England with his Conqueror, a vile pestilence swept through the villages of the Calvados. It attacked the elderly and the young, and the village healer could do nothing in the face of its horror.

Madame Bonhomme succumbed, and then Mabelle faced the swift illness and death of her beloved future father-by-marriage. As he lay dying, *Comte* Bernard took her hand. "You're the only one now, Mabelle. Ram needs you."

A fit of coughing seized him and there was blood on his spittle.

"I sense you're my son's destiny. Take good care of my boy. I always believed I would die with honour, on the battlefield. But it's not to be." He smiled at her as his life ebbed away.

In her anguish, she keened Ram's name over and over, in sorrow for his loss and her own. *Comte* Bernard had been her champion. There was no news from England. Was her betrothed alive or dead? It was her darkest hour. Why did she ache for a man she should loathe?

There's no happiness for me at Montbryce. The only person here who truly loved me is dead. Ram will never love me. I need to go home. How many years have I longed to return to Alensonne.

The lead coffin was laid to rest in its tomb in the crypt, beneath the chapel. Bonhomme and his sons were lost in their own grief. Giselle and *La Cuisinière* embraced each other tearfully as they watched their future *Comtesse* climb wearily to her lonely bedchamber.

CHAPTER FOURTEEN

As soon as William gave leave, Ram searched frantically for his brothers. To his great relief, they'd both survived the slaughter. The three stood together for long silent minutes, their arms around each other's shoulders. Hugh's left arm hung by his side. He had suffered a sword slash to his upper arm, which had been tended by one of the camp physicians.

They spent time calming and reassuring their horses, knowing the important role the stallions had played in keeping them alive. It significant all three Montbryce horses—his own Fortis, Hugh's Velox, and Antoine's steed, Regis—had survived. Few Normans could claim that, and it was a testament to the care with which they were chosen, and the attention lavished on them.

Antoine lamented, "My body stinks. It disgusts me. Let's go bathe in the river."

They stripped off their armour with the help of their squires and joined many of their countrymen who were trying to wash away the stench of blood, sweat and their own waste.

"I feel I'll never be clean again," Ram complained as they dried off. Vaillon handed him his clean tunic.

None of them slept, and as dawn broke the following morning, all were summoned for the solemn reading of the muster roll. Ram was saddened to discover his handsome friend, Pierre de Fleury, had lost his life.

"He'll no longer have to lie with his ugly wife," Ram said bitterly to Antoine. "Perhaps he'd rather be alive and lying with her, than stone cold dead on this bloody field."

The Montbryce brothers left the marshalling area after the ceremony and huddled under the canvas hastily erected by their squires. They looked out over the distant battlefield, sickened by the sight of scavengers still combing over what remained of the bodies. "We should be grateful our rank saved us from the duty of searching for reusable weapons and armour," Hugh murmured.

"My squire has scrubbed my armour with vinegar and sand, but I can still smell the stench of blood. It clings as do fleas to a dog," Antoine scowled.

"It's the piteous moans of the wounded I find the hardest," Hugh murmured. "We were lucky to escape as we did."

His brothers grunted their agreement. They sat in strained silence. Eventually Hugh spoke, his voice full of anger. "The Duke has arranged for the proper burial of the Normans who fell, and Bishop Eude is to say a Mass. A few Saxons took their dead away, but most of the English corpses have been buried in a mass grave."

Antoine looked hard at Ram. "There are rumours His Grace wanted to verify the identity of the body they thought was Harold's. It was so mutilated his face couldn't be recognized. William ordered Harold's mistress, Edith Swanneck, to attend and verify identifying marks which only an intimate would know."

"That's true. I can vouch for it. The body was a gruesome sight," Ram admitted, shaking his head. "The woman was distraught."

"What about the other rumour, that Harold's mother sent messages offering the weight of her son's body in gold, if she could be allowed to bury him, but William perversely refused?" Hugh asked.

"That's also true, I regret to say. He ordered Harold be buried in an unmarked grave, near the sea shore he'd fought so hard to protect. Even I don't know the location."

The three men were silent for a long while, holding their hands to the warmth of the campfire. Ram spoke first. "I'd hoped to return home to Normandie," he told them, "But William is sending me to Ellesmere, in the west. There has been trouble for many years between the Welsh and the English. News has arrived, from Normans who settled there years ago, that there have been more recent raids on the Welsh borders. A rebel by the name of Rhodri ap Owain has been attacking the towns and villages near Ellesmere. William has promised me an earldom there."

Antoine and Hugh were delighted for their brother and shook his hand. Ram accepted their congratulations, knowing they were genuine, then continued, "William wants us to assert our authority now over this rabble. I'm to reconnoitre the area and inspect my castle at Ellesmere at the same time. I'll request you be assigned to accompany me. Your wound shouldn't prevent you from travelling Hugh?"

His brother's hand still trembled

"*Non, mon frère.* I'll be fit to travel. Thank you for your words of courage before the battle."

Ram nodded. "Hastings has taken a heavy toll on all of us. We will never forget this battle as long as we live. I wouldn't admit this to anyone else, but you're my brothers. I miss Mabelle. I want to share the victory with her—perhaps confide something of the terror and disgust I felt, and tell her the news of the promised Earldom. I want to lie with her, bury my head in her breasts, fill her with my seed and feel whole again. You're right, Antoine. I was a fool many times over not to marry her."

His words had resonated with Hugh, who rasped, "Why is it the thing a man feels compelled to do after courting death is lie with a woman? Most of the survivors in my brigade are hobbling round trying to hide tree trunks at their groins. Look at me." His trembling hand went to his manhood. "I can't help myself."

Antoine shifted uncomfortably. Both of them believed Hugh had never lain with a woman. Ram thought his young brother might be close to his breaking point. "Much as I would like to hasten home to wed Mabelle, I'll have to do the Duke's bidding, if I want to keep the title he's promised. At least we'll have each other's company as we travel to Ellesmere, and I'll know you're safe. I'll dispatch a messenger to Montbryce."

***

William was incensed. "Since Hastings I've waited for the Witan to formally surrender the English throne to me, and now we have news they've proclaimed Edgar the Aetheling king. They have the gall to support the Confessor's grand-nephew. I give my oath, Ram, he'll never be crowned, as long as I draw breath. We'll evidently have to take London by force."

Ram's heart fell. This would mean another delay before he could return to Normandie. He struggled not to let his agitation show. William was upset enough. "It seems ironic Stigand and the others now want to support Edgar, when they were previously willing to favour Harold as king over him," he offered.

"You're right. It makes one question their resolve. First we march to Dover. It's strategically important and we must secure it."

In Dover an epidemic of the flux broke out among the troops after they ate tainted meat and drank the water. Many died, and still more had to be left behind in Dover to recover as the invading force advanced to the religious centre of England, Canterbury.

After taking Canterbury, they marched on London, where the core of resistance was centred on Edgar. Meeting fierce opposition at London Bridge they circled to the west of the city, setting fires and leaving a trail of devastation.

"We'll cross the Thames at Wallingford," William ordered. "Wigod, the Lord of Wallingford, is a Norman sympathiser."

At Wallingford, Stigand abandoned Edgar. The Aetheling's forces were dwindling rapidly. He met William at Berkhamsted, with a group of English nobles, and offered him their fealty, bringing to an end the Anglo-Saxon kingdom that had lasted for hundreds of years.

CHAPTER FIFTEEN

Ram wasn't present at the historic surrender, having left the main army after the Wallingford crossing. The three Montbryce men had escaped the ravages of the flux but were sickened again by the excessive brutality of the victory at Wallingford. They set out, with two hundred of the best surviving knights and men-at-arms from Montbryce, to make the journey from the River Thames to the Welsh border region. He felt it a sufficient number to deter any attack from disgruntled locals.

Ram told Hugh, "We should cover the seven score miles to Ellesmere in four days, if we're lucky and the November conditions don't make the track difficult. Pray for cloudless skies."

Their route took them through Oxford, a fortified burgh, founded two centuries before by Alfred the Great. Antoine and Hugh rode at Ram's side. The inhabitants fled upon catching sight of them.

"William has talked about the possibility of building a castle here, and I'll report it's a good idea, given the town's location and burgeoning reputation as a place of learning. I'm impressed with the way the streets are laid out in an orderly pattern, and the town looks to have about a thousand houses, which probably means there are close to five thousand inhabitants."

Antoine replied, "I suppose, since the Danes burned the town fifty years ago, much of what we see has been built since then. There's a market, and the town seems prosperous. It's ironic, don't you think, that a council was held here earlier in the century to choose a King of the English? No wonder William wants to build a castle here. No doubt he appreciates the irony too."

They shared the humour of it as they left Oxford, following the Cherwell River bound for Warwick, another walled town William had his eye on for a castle. The three of them agreed a piece of land on a sandstone bluff overlooking the River Avon, site of four houses belonging to the Abbot of Coventry, would be an ideal location for such a project.

"I'll bring back that piece of important information. This inconvenient journey might turn to my advantage, and augment my importance in William's eyes."

Ram was glad of the company of his brothers. He could keep an eye on Antoine and Hugh, and the presence of family made him feel better. They'd proven themselves as warriors in the hell of Hastings, but Hugh had withdrawn into uncharacteristic moodiness. The seemingly uncontrollable tremor in his younger brother's hand worried him.

Passing through Bridgnorth on the River Severn, Ram resolved to ask William for this town as part of his holdings. Though somewhat far removed from Ellesmere, it was a good location, and William hadn't mentioned it for a royal castle.

They decided to stop at Shrewsbury before going on to Ellesmere, to ascertain the latest news of Welsh incursions. He learned, from Norman sympathisers, that Rhodri ap Owain, the rebel chieftain, had been creating havoc around the town of Oswestry.

"This is surprising," he remarked to his brothers as they left the meeting. "I understood winter normally keeps the Welsh in their mountain hideaways. Perhaps they're changing their strategy? I propose you both take most of the men and ride to Oswestry. I'll rejoin you once I've inspected Ellesmere."

He watched the small army ride off towards the west, then ordered his remaining men to set their mounts in motion. After only a few miles they suddenly caught sight, as they neared Ruyton, of a group of riders galloping west.

"Gervais," he shouted excitedly to his second-in-command, "I would wager those are Welsh rebels, fleeing Ruyton."

"*Oui*, you're probably right. We could give chase. Our mounts are still fresh. They have some way to go to the border, and won't be expecting pursuit."

"Give the command to pursue."

The veteran Norman soldiers eagerly spurred their horses, and had closed the gap on the Welsh band significantly before the rebels became aware they were being chased. The lead rider, a mountain of a man, turned and saw them. He alerted the others, and they increased their speed and split up. The moorland terrain was rugged. One false move could result in a horse's hoof plunging into a pothole in the rolling landscape.

Suddenly, the leader's horse lost its footing, and animal and rider went down. With incredible agility, as if it were an everyday occurrence, the huge warrior quickly found his feet, and had his dagger out immediately. One Norman soldier fell from his horse with a bone-chilling scream as the barbarian slashed the dagger across his belly, almost severing the lad in two with the power of his thrust.

Ram's warrior blood rushed to his head. "Gervais, continue the pursuit. I'll deal with this ruffian," he yelled, reining in his snorting horse, dropping from the saddle and unsheathing his sword in one fluid movement. The men continued on after the fleeing rebels.

Ram yanked off his helmet, threw it to the ground, and faced the barbarian, noting with surprise the man didn't look afraid. Ram felt he had the advantage. His opponent had no sword, but he'd seen what the man had done with his dagger and would have to be wary.

Perhaps sending the other men on wasn't a good idea.

The two warriors squared off—the tall Norman noble trying to make the thrust with his sword that would disarm the rebel, the powerful Welsh barbarian attempting to plunge his dagger into a momentarily unguarded part of the other man's body. It occurred to Ram he rarely came face to face with an enemy who matched him in height.

"I am Rambaud de Montbryce, Earl of Ellesmere. On the authority of King William, I command your surrender," Ram declared with calm assurance.

Is that a smile on the barbarian's face?

"I am Rhodri ap Owain, Prince of Powwydd. Ellesmere has an Earl, you say? The Norman bastard isn't my king, not anyone's king yet, therefore I cannot and will not surrender to you."

Ram thrust again and Rhodri made to deflect the blow. Sword and dagger became braced together as the two powerful men struggled, their intense gazes locked on each other. Ram suddenly used a well practiced maneuver and pulled away from the deadlock, taking Rhodri unawares, and his sword flicked the dagger out of the

Welshman's hand. Ram advanced on the unarmed man, again offering him the chance to surrender.

"You don't understand, Norman invader. Welshmen don't surrender," Rhodri sneered. Suddenly he lunged at Ram, knocking the wind out of his body, and *Honneur* out of his hand. As he fell, Ram felt a painful blow to the back of his head.

I survived Hastings to fall here?

His knees buckled and he reeled into oblivion.

CHAPTER SIXTEEN

R am didn't recognise the unsmiling face of the woman bending over him, but it showed concern. Weren't the angels supposed to be smiling when he reached paradise? He sank back into the murky haze.

"If I'm in heaven, why does my head feel like it's broken?" he murmured groggily when he awoke some time later.

"That's because you're not dead, *milord*."

"Gervais?" he muttered, half opening one eye. His Second stood at the foot of the bed on which he lay.

"*Oui, milord*. I'm relieved you're awake. *Non*, don't try to get up. *Milady* says you must rest. You had a blow to the head."

"*Milady*? Who is *milady*?"

"She's the mistress of this manor, *milord*. We brought you here because it was close and we were afraid you wouldn't make it to Ellesmere. This is Shelfhoc Manor, near Ruyton, and *milady* is Lady Ascha Woolgar."

"I don't understand what happened," Ram said with great exasperation.

"*Milord*, it's not good to get agitated. When the barbarian lunged and knocked you off balance, you hit your head on a sharp rock. The wound bled a great deal. You have a large gash on the back of your head. We were on the way back and I could see what had happened, but couldn't get there in time to aid you. The rebel's horse wasn't hurt, and he was able to remount and flee. I had to make a decision to either follow them, or help you. We'd killed two of their men, but three of ours had fallen. I didn't think it wise to pursue them into Wales."

Ram felt like an incompetent fool. So much for the prowess of the great warrior *Rambaud le Noir*. The scourge of the border, the threat to peace had been at his mercy. He wondered why the Prince of Powwydd hadn't just finished him off.

"You did the right thing, Gervais. He must have laughed his way back to Wales. Who is this Woolgar woman?" he demanded, his head throbbing. He remembered Mabelle's soothing touch on his aching temples.

"She's a Saxon noblewoman, *milord*."

He dozed off again and awoke later, sensing a presence. He didn't know how much time had passed.

"Gervais?"

"I'm Lady Ascha Woolgar. This is my home," a soft voice replied.

Ram opened his bleary eyes and saw the woman he'd previously thought was a vision. She stood beside the bed, and looked to be about the same age as he. What he could see of her hair, at the edges of the wimple, was brown and curly. She was slender and her long thin fingers held a bowl and spoon. She had a look of defeat.

"I've brought you some nourishing vegetable broth," she said, without emotion. "You should eat only broth for a few days, until you feel more recovered."

She was polite but didn't smile, and he sensed she didn't welcome his intrusion into her life.

"My Lady Woolgar, I thank you for allowing my men to bring me here." There was no warmth in his voice.

"They didn't give me much choice, my Lord Montbryce."

"I regret—"

She raised her hand. "Don't worry. It's a reality I must accept. I'm a Saxon, a widow. You're a Norman. You're the conqueror, I'm the conquered."

He had to keep his wits about him. He struggled sit up but dizziness overwhelmed him and his stomach roiled. "My Lady, we're Normans, not savages like the murderous Danes. Our King, your King, wishes peace and prosperity for his people, Saxon and Norman."

As he mouthed the words, he was certain there would be much bloodshed ahead as William embarked on his plan for the total subjugation of these lands. He wondered why he should bother to justify all this to a woman, especially a Saxon.

She bowed her head slightly. "I'll let you finish your broth yourself. A manservant will see to your needs."

An elderly man entered a few minutes later, assisted Ram to stand so he could relieve himself, and then removed the chamber pot. He too was polite, but the undercurrent of Saxon resentment was palpable. The effort exhausted Ram, making him more dizzy, and he slept again, relieved he had managed not to retch.

Later a warm hand on his forehead woke him. It felt good.

"Mabelle," he croaked, still half asleep. He raised his hand and lay it atop the one on his forehead.

"It's Lady Ascha."

Ram's eyes shot open, sending pain shooting through his head. He quickly removed his hand from hers, bothered he'd found the warmth of it comforting. Ascha seemed to pay no attention to the abrupt movement.

"There is no fever. You're fortunate, Lord Montbryce."

Ram's head throbbed and his throat was dry. "Please, Lady Ascha, my name is Rambaud," he said wearily.

"As you wish, Lord Rambaud. Who is Mabelle?"

"She's my betrothed—in Normandie. When I felt your touch, I was half asleep and I thought it was she."

Surely I'm not blushing?

"Were you dreaming of her?"

"Perhaps I was," he admitted, thinking it a strange question.

"You're not a married man?"

"*Non*, not yet," he said with regret.

For a few minutes she gazed down at him, not with animosity but with a strange sort of longing. He felt uncomfortable, and wished he wasn't lying in a bed.

"I don't dream of my husband," she whispered, and her eyes glazed with unhappiness.

"You told me you're a widow."

"Yes. My husband was a warrior, a thane of the king. He's dead."

A feeling of dread crept over Ram. Many Saxon nobles had died on the field at Hastings that terrible day.

"You don't want to ask me, Lord Montbryce, so I'll tell you, since there's no shame in it. My husband, Sir Caedmon Woolgar, was a *housecarl* to King Harold. He died at Hastings. At least, we assume he did, since he hasn't returned home."

Ram thought of the mass grave where Harold's *housecarls* lay buried. They'd been determined to fight to the last man. Could the Saxon giant who'd come close to removing his head have been Sir Caedmon Woolgar? He saw no point in avoiding the truth.

"I fought at Hastings," he said forthrightly.

"Yes," she replied quietly, smiling an enigmatic smile.

Convinced though he was of the righteousness of William's conquest, this woman's plight brought home to him the often terrible consequences of war for those left behind. Men might fight and die and glorify what they did, but there was no doubt women were left to bear the burden of sorrow, and the weight of castles and manors with no man to defend them or provide.

None of this would have happened if Harold hadn't broken his oath.

By the next day, the dizziness had abated, and he left his bed. The manservant came to help him dress, and informed him Lady Woolgar would receive him in her solar, to which the man directed him. Ascha was seated on a wooden bench by the window, the oiled covering drawn back, despite the chilly air. The embroidery on her lap lay untouched as she gazed out at the surrounding lands. A maidservant sat by her side, sewing.

"Leave us, Enid," she said softly when she saw Ram enter.

"Lady Ascha, I trust you're well today?" he ventured.

She didn't look up at him. "As well as can be expected."

"I would offer my condolences, but we both know it would sound hollow. I was your husband's enemy. I strove to kill him and his comrades. I don't regret it. I could have been the one to deal his death blow."

Had her expression softened slightly?

She looked him in the eye. "I don't lay blame at your door. My husband was a fierce warrior. He gloried in war. He died doing what he was born for. In a conflict there must be winners and losers. Sir Caedmon wasn't on the winning side this time."

He waited a few minutes. Those sad grey eyes had momentarily distracted him. "What of this manor, Lady Ascha? I don't wish to add to your burdens, but it's our King's wish that we strengthen this border region against the Welsh. You're not in a position of strength here, through no fault of your own. Many would covet this manor. Rhodri ap Owain was close by, as you know. Gervais tells me you hold more than five hides of land, and that there's a parish church, a kitchen and a fortress gate. While you do have a rampart and ditch, it wouldn't hold off a large attack."

She fidgeted nervously. "I don't know what will happen, Lord Rambaud, the grief and uncertainty is too new. I'm a woman alone."

She sobbed, so quietly he wasn't immediately aware she was crying. The embroidery fell to the floor. He strode across to sit by her side, hesitant to take her hand, not knowing how to bring comfort. Why did he want to?

He retrieved the embroidery, but as he returned it to her lap, their fingers touched. She seized his hand and gripped it with both hers. Trembling, she leaned into him and he nervously put his arm around her shoulders, trying to bring comfort.

As the sobs wracked her slender body, the wimple slipped from her hair, and brown curls tumbled to her hips.

She's younger than I thought. And beautiful.

His body responded. He ran his fingers through her hair. She appeared embarrassed by the crack that had appeared in her armour, but he continued to comfort her, and soon her weeping subsided. She was aware of his obvious physical reaction to her. He cleared his throat, extricated his hand, withdrew his arm, and stood.

"Lady Ascha, I'll place you and your manor under my protection. I don't intend to take your manor for myself, but others will no doubt try. I'll station a contingent of my men-at-arms to protect you, and provide a steward to help you manage your estate."

He suspected fellow Normans might be more of a threat than the Welsh, but said nothing of this.

She stared at him, open mouthed. "I thank you for your unexpected compassion but I can't accept. I've nothing to give you in return, Lord Montbryce."

"I want nothing in return, Lady Ascha. If my future wife was in a similar position, I'd like to think some champion would protect her."

His conversation with Ascha started Ram thinking about Mabelle. How would she feel if he fell in battle? If he'd fallen at Hastings? She would likely never be in the same perilous position as Ascha because he had brothers to protect her, but how would she *feel*? Would she mourn him? He'd not seen her since September, and then only briefly. He needed to get home. Had the message he'd survived got through? He resolved to leave the next day to inspect Ellesmere, and then make his way home to Normandie.

He took his leave and returned to his chamber.

***

Ascha liked the sound of the word *champion* but not Ram's reference to his future wife. She'd been drawn to this attractive Norman warrior deposited into her care. He had a sensitivity her brutish husband had lacked. She'd held on to his hands like a rock in her sea of fear and uncertainty, and the unexpected intimacy of his arm around her shoulder had sent a warm shiver through her body.

And he's not married yet.

***

"I wish you weren't leaving. Head wounds can be dangerous and the effects can linger. You should rest here longer, Lord Rambaud," Ascha cajoled the next morning, when he told her of his decision to leave forthwith. Now she wasn't cool and detached. Her hand lay on his arm as she spoke, and she looked into his eyes.

Ram looked back, surprised at the intimacy of the gesture, and the use of his given name. Desire flickered in the grey depths.

She's lonely. She desires me.

The thought aroused and dismayed him. She was an attractive woman who'd been without a man for a considerable time. What would it matter if he gave them both a few pleasures? It wouldn't obligate either of them to the other. Her eyes told him that.

Perhaps a kiss? What harm could a kiss do?

He'd been without a woman for months. Since meeting Mabelle, he'd lost interest in Joleyne. In these dangerous new lands he could be killed before he ever made it home to Normandie. Since Hastings he seemed to be constantly hard, constantly needy. Hugh was right.

"Lady Ascha," he murmured as he bent his head to kiss her.

His lips brushed hers as she breathed, "Lord Rambaud."

They kissed. The blood rushed to his groin. His tongue coaxed her lips and she allowed him entry. The kiss was sweet and gentle, and she responded to him as he pressed his arousal to her body. "I didn't love my husband," she whispered. "War was his life. He didn't understand the needs of a woman."

Intense emotions, pent up since Hastings, swept over him—the terror of the battle, the horror and stench of the bloodshed and broken bodies, the sickening brutality, the constant homesickness, the exhaustion of travel, the heavy responsibilities put upon him by his Duke, the unbearable aching for his infuriating Mabelle, the frustration of Rhodri's escape, the concern for Hugh—all conspired to render him senseless, his only instinct a need to possess and be possessed. He held a woman in his arms who'd admitted never knowing the pleasures of passion. It was more than he could resist. He wanted to tear the clothes from her body and take her on the floor, to liberate her from the sexual frustration she'd endured.

He ran his hands over her body, along the swell of her breast, the curve of her hip, the flesh of her thigh. He gathered her up, intending to carry her to the chamber where she'd tended him. He felt a momentary dizziness as he rose, but braced his legs and steadied himself. She curled her arms around his neck and rested her head against his chest. Once in the chamber, he laid her on his bed. She undressed, her eyes fixed on his face. He helped her, then tore off his own clothes. She gasped and licked her lips when she saw his rigid manhood, and her eyes burned with wanting.

He didn't have to spend long preparing her. As a spasm of release tore through her body, he raised himself above her, positioned his shaft at her opening and groaned as he slid inside. They quickly found each other's rhythm and she smiled, her hands reaching up to his chest, thumbs brushing his male nipples. In a moment of clarity he rasped, "Have no fear Ascha, I'll spill myself outside your body."

She dug her nails into his shoulders. "No, Rambaud."

"But—"

Her hands went to his hips and she gripped him fiercely, pulling his body to hers. "No! Fill me! I can't keep you. I want every bit of you I can now. These moments are all I have."

The intensity of her words inflamed him. He shuddered and revelled verbally in his euphoria as his seed entered her body.

Later, as his wits slowly returned, an image of Mabelle lying by the lake, barely covered by her chemise, rose up in his mind. It was so vivid that he abruptly rolled away from Ascha.

"Ascha—I shouldn't have," he said hoarsely. "My obligation to my betrothed—I shouldn't have. You're a widow. It was wrong to take advantage of you."

But it had nothing to do with obligation. How could he have sacrificed what he wanted to give to Mabelle with another woman, no matter how great her need, or his? Mabelle was his destiny, brought to him through some miracle he didn't understand, which he'd tried to deny. He'd betrayed her with this woman. What he'd experienced with Ascha was simply physical release.

Yet again I have betrayed Mabelle.

"You didn't take advantage of me, Rambaud," Ascha whispered languidly. "I took advantage of you. I know you're a man in love. My husband didn't love me, didn't understand the importance of touch for a woman. I envy your betrothed. She's a lucky woman. I thank you for the gift you've given me today. The memory of it will help see me through many difficult days. I don't regret what we've shared. I don't expect you to love me."

Confusion whirled through Ram's head. "Ascha—I must leave now. I'll be your champion but I can't be your lover."

He dressed quickly, and prepared to leave.

She became agitated and knelt up in the bed, wrapping the linens around her body. "Rambaud," she stammered. "I lied. I need you—please. Stay a few days."

He shook his head, desperate to be gone from this manor. "I can't."

He strode out of the chamber. She would be safe under his protection, but he prayed she would find a good husband some day. She was a woman with a deeply hidden passion Caedmon Woolgar had been unable to ignite, and he silently thanked God for Mabelle and the erotic joys her touch and her kisses promised. A chill went up his spine when he thought of Mabelle finding out about his liaison. Had she been faithful to him? He wanted to believe she was still a virgin but, given the life she'd led, the odds were—

If there's no love, if it's only about passion, why not? What's the harm?

His fury grew at the idea of Mabelle sharing another man's bed, and he was dismayed he'd bedded this woman, and was now hurrying away. This wasn't behaviour worthy of a Montbryce.

He left soldiers to guard Shelfhoc but the contingent that rode away with him was still a force to be regarded with respect. As he made for Ellesmere, he deliberately pushed away the tantalizing vision insinuating itself into his head of a maiden with golden hair, lying on a grassy bank. He'd denied his passion for Mabelle, but Ascha's words echoed over and over—*I know you are a man in love.*

Through the window, Lady Ascha Woolgar watched until the Normans were completely out of sight, her fingers absent-mindedly rubbing the oiled window covering she held. From the moment she'd set eyes on the magnificent Norman Lord when he'd been brought to her home, feelings had stirred within her she'd never known with her husband. She'd tried to deny them but couldn't. She sank to her knees sobbing, swathed in bed linens, feeling more fulfilled, yet more bereft than she'd ever felt. She would never see Rambaud de Montbryce again, but she would remember the feel of his touch, the fulfilment of his manhood inside her, forever.

CHAPTER SEVENTEEN

The tragic news of his father's death caught up with Ram as he stood surveying the crumbling Anglo-Saxon timber fortification that was Ellesmere Castle. It guarded the only dry approach to the town, which seemed to exist in a sea of mud. Anguish brought him to his knees as he grieved his loss.

His brothers were devastated. They had rejoined him at Ellesmere after hearing of his injury. All Ram could think of was returning to Normandie and his Mabelle.

How did she cope with this alone? Will she turn to someone else for solace, as I did?

Ram swore to someday build a magnificent castle for Mabelle at Ellesmere that would be warm and welcoming, instead of this abomination, and to return to her side as soon as he could. What more did he want in a wife? He set himself, his horse and his men a punishing pace to the south coast where they took ship for Normandie. A sennight after receiving the tragic news, he, Antoine and Hugh were galloping into the bailey of the castle Montbryce, long after sunset.

He'd expected Mabelle to come out and meet them, and was disappointed when she didn't. He was anxious to tell her he was sorry, that they would marry as soon as possible. He longed to tell her about Hastings, about his promised Earldom.

Fernand Bonhomme appeared and grooms came to take their mounts.

"Fernand." Ram embraced his trusted steward, who looked haggard. "We are all desolate at the news of your wife's death."

"*Merci, milord.* Vangeline was a good wife and helpmate. We'll miss her sorely. And your father—It was a desperate time, but he succumbed quickly and didn't suffer. Your betrothed nursed him night and day. He found comfort in her. And now you're the *Comte, milord.*"

"*Oui,* Fernand, but I would prefer our dear father was still with us. The hour is late. I suppose my betrothed has retired to her chamber?"

"*Non, milord.* She's gone."

They'd walked as they talked, and were standing in the Great Hall. He noticed Giselle coming towards him, her face grim.

Dread tore at his gut. "Gone? Gone where?"

Not dead, please God, not dead.

"*Milord,*" Giselle cried, "I tried to stop her, but she wouldn't listen. She was unhappy here."

"But where would she go? She has no-one, only her father—*Non!* She's gone to Alensonne?"

"*Oui, milord.*"

"Ram!" Antoine shouted, as his brother's fist smashed into the wall. "Ram, be calm. You can go after her, convince her to return."

Ram leaned his forehead against the stone. "There won't be time. I have to go back to England for the Coronation. She's left me, and no wonder. But I'm not a man to go crawling on my hands and knees."

Hugh put his trembling hand on Ram's shoulder. "Let's go down to the crypt. I'm tired, and I want to pray by our father's tomb."

As Ram stood in the cold, candlelit crypt, flanked by his grieving brothers, his arm across Hugh's shaking shoulders, a tear slid down his cheek. They felt their loss keenly, but his heart ached too for Mabelle, the beautiful refugee he'd done his utmost to alienate.

The three returned to the Hall, where they reminisced together until after midnight, then Ram decided to clear his head out on the battlements before retiring. If he slept at all, it would be from sheer exhaustion.

He came at last to his chamber feeling calmer, but as he slumped onto the bed, he noticed a parchment tucked under the bedcover.

A letter.

His hands shook as he removed the seal.

To Comte Ram de Montbryce
If you and your brothers yet live, you will have been devastated by the news of your father's death. I found it difficult to bear. He was the only loving father I've ever had.

Montbryce is a place I have known only humiliation, unhappiness and now death. Will any of you ever return?

I must turn my attention to my beloved Alensonne, where by all accounts my father is making life difficult.

Now you're the Comte de Montbryce, you must marry a bride more suited to you. I release you from your obligation. You will not now receive Alensonne, Belisle and Domfort in dower, and I don't yet know how to resolve that problem, as I'm sure they are lands you covet.

Perhaps my diplomatic father will have a solution!
Mabelle de Valtesse (and d'Alensonne)

"Mabelle!" His fist pounded the bolster over and over in frustration, until he collapsed onto it. "I don't want to be released. I don't covet your lands, I covet *you*. I want you as my wife, the mother of my children."

He must have fallen asleep, but felt exhausted when he went to break his fast.

Antoine and Hugh greeted him, their eyes wide with excitement.

"What scheme have you two plotted now?"

"If you leave immediately, you can reach Alensonne in two days. Two days to get there, one day to persuade Mabelle to return with you, two days back, a day to wed her and bed her, three days to get to Westminster. *Voilà,* you'll arrive a day early for the Coronation on Christmas Day."

"Antoine, if I'm not at William's Coronation, I can bid *adieu* to my Earldom. We could miss the right tides, encounter the wrong winds."

"The choice is yours. The Earldom or Mabelle de Valtesse. Hugh and I are willing to ride with you. You may need some protection from Valtesse. Or perhaps from Mabelle."

Ram hesitated. What if he went to Alensonne and she rejected him? But he had to try. If he didn't go now he could be mired in England, possibly for years. "Tell Bonhomme to get provisions ready for the journey. I'll get the horses saddled and the men-at-arms organized."

***

"Normandie is abuzz with the news of the upcoming coronation of our Duke as the King of the English," Guillaume de Valtesse announced to his daughter as they broke their fast. "It's to take place on Christmas Day. His victory over the Saxons has earned him the name of *Conqueror*."

His words sent Mabelle's mind reeling back to the banquet at Montbryce, when she'd returned the Duke's toast. "Ram foretold he would be known as the Conqueror," she whispered.

"I'll never understand why you broke the betrothal. You're obviously smitten with the man, and we'll be in great difficulty here if he comes to claim his dower rights."

Her father shuffled out of the Hall, mumbling. They had argued long and hard when she'd come home to Alensonne. She'd thought to find peace here but all she could think of was Ram de Montbryce—the feel of his lips on hers, his strong arms around her, his hands fondling her hair, her breast—she couldn't erase the memory of him at the lake, standing almost naked, his arousal obvious. She longed to run her hands over his thighs, his chest, his shoulders. She ached in places she'd never ached before. Her body tingled when she thought of him, and she longed to see him *sans* braies.

However, she'd made her decision. There was no going back now. He wouldn't want her, never had wanted her. How angry he must have been when he read her letter.

The sound of raised voices disturbed her reverie. Her breathless father reappeared, steward Cormant with him. "I told you he would come for his due. Your betrothed is at the gates, demanding entry."

He has come?

Her heart lurched when she heard her father giving orders for the men-at-arms to ride out against Ram.

"*Non*, Papa, I don't want to see blood spilled. We'll allow him entry, and perhaps negotiate some settlement for the lands. Leave this to me. You're too apt to lose your temper. Cormant, pass the word the *Comte* de Montbryce is to be allowed entry. Show him to the Great Hall."

She went to stand on the dais, hoping she looked like the *Milady* of the castle, in control. She wiped her sweaty palms on her dress.

Don't bite your nails.

"He's bigger even than I remember," she murmured when Ram, Antoine and Hugh entered the Great Hall five minutes later. She could tell they'd ridden hard and fast.

What has he done to his hair?

She balled her fists, trying to still the wild beating of her heart. The sound filled her ears, and she was sure everyone else could hear it. She held out her arms to the three men. "*Mon seigneur, Comte* de Montbryce, my Lords Antoine and Hugh, welcome to my home. Welcome to Alensonne. I grieve with you on the loss of your father—I loved—" She could barely speak the words.

Antoine and Hugh moved quickly to her side and embraced her. "Mabelle," Antoine whispered in her ear, "Be patient with him."

She smiled and whispered back, "He looks like his blood is boiling because I'm whispering in your ear."

Hugh laughed out loud.

Ram clenched his jaw. "Mabelle, I've come about our betrothal."

"You wish to discuss the dowry?"

"*Non!*" he exclaimed. "I haven't come to discuss the dowry."

"What he means is he's here to beg you to come back—" Antoine began.

"I haven't come to beg," Ram interrupted.

"He has come to *ask* you to return to Montbryce."

"I'm capable of speaking for myself. Why not go to tend to our horses, dear brothers?"

"I'm sure the steward—"

"Go! Leave us."

Antoine and Hugh shrugged their shoulders and left, scarcely able to contain their mirth.

Mabelle took a deep breath. "You seem comfortable giving orders here, but Alensonne isn't yours yet."

She fought to control the excitement flooding through her as Ram quickly crossed the space between them. Would he touch her? Take her in his arms? Cradle her to his chest?

He took her hands. "I don't care about Alensonne. I want you to return to Montbryce with me so we can be married."

She swayed as she struggled to control her voice and the threatening tears.

"*You've* decided this is the right time?"

"My father pledged me to you. It would dishonour his memory if I reneged."

Her heart sank. She pulled her hands away from his grasp. "I told you, I've released you from that pledge. I have no desire to dishonour your father. I loved him. But I don't want to be wed to a man who is marrying me for the sake of duty."

She sensed his agitation at her words. He paced nervously for several minutes, running his hand over his short hair. She had to resist the impulse to rush over and tell him of her relief he was alive, that she would be his wife under any circumstances, that she couldn't bear the thought of losing him.

He turned to face her. "Mabelle, you're the woman I want, the woman I need. I am sure of it now, after Hastings. You were my talisman. After the battle, I wanted to join my body to yours, to lose myself in you. I can be overbearing but I'll try to—why are you crying?"

He brushed a tear from her cheek with his thumb.

"Ram," she whispered.

He kissed her fiercely, and her body cried out for him. His hands were on her waist, pulling her to him. She felt his hard male length against her, and the pent up longing burst over her.

"Ram," she whispered again, her breath catching in her throat as she reached up nervously to run her fingers lightly over his shaven head. "You're alive—but what have you done to your beautiful hair?"

He laughed and put his arms on her shoulders. "Vaillon shaved it, for Hastings. It will grow back, but it feels strange."

She leaned on him, her arms around his waist. They clung together for long minutes. She could hear his breathing, feel the beating of his heart. She'd never felt so safe.

"Return to Montbryce with me, Mabelle. Come be my wife, my *Comtesse*."

She swallowed hard. She'd run away, denied her attraction to this man, but he was her destiny. "I'll return with you. I invite you to rest here a few days. You've had a long journey and the grief of your father's death. Enjoy Yuletide at Alensonne with me for a while."

"It would give me great pleasure to see you enjoy your childhood home for a while longer, but I've been summoned to the Duke's coronation in Westminster on Christmas Day. I want to take you there as my bride."

"But that's only a few days away!"

"William has promised me an Earldom in England, but if I'm not at the ceremony—"

"You risked it to come here—to get me?"

"You're the woman I want to marry."

He'd spoken no words of love but he wanted her enough to risk what was important to him—lands and titles. He would make sure she was safe. Alchemy drew them to each other. They would at least have passion.

"Then we must summon Cormant to prepare for our departure on the morrow. I'm used to travelling fast and light."

CHAPTER EIGHTEEN

Hugh and Ram walked together to the door of the chapel, and Ram took his place with the Bishop, and Antoine. The two brothers grasped each other's hand as their forearms crossed in a familiar gesture. Antoine slapped him on the back and smiled. Ram kissed the bishop's ring as he bowed to the cleric.

He wished with all his heart his father still lived and regretted deeply he'd deprived him of the pleasure of seeing him wed. The trio waited a few minutes in nervous silence, then heard a rustling of gowns along with feminine whispers.

Ram's breath caught in his dry throat when Mabelle came into view on the jaunty arm of her scowling father, who'd insisted on riding to Montbryce with them. He licked his lips. She seemed to be carefully examining the elaborately tiled floor.

Guillaume passed her warm hand into his, and Mabelle stole a glance at him as a jolt passed between them. As the long ceremony progressed, Ram became aware that the tall woman holding his hand tightly with her long slim fingers, was swaying. Was she going to faint? His head filled with images of running his hands over her breasts and hips—they promised fertility and many healthy children.

"Do you, Rambaud de Montbryce, wish to take this woman, Mabelle de Valtesse, de Belisle, d'Alensonne and de Domfort, to be your wedded wife?"

The bishop's voice brought Ram back to reality. Immersed in his daydream, he'd lost track of where they were in the ceremony.

"I do so wish."

Mabelle let out her breath.

She thought I might betray her again.

"Do you, Mabelle de Valtesse, de Belisle, d'Alensonne and de Domfort, wish to take this man, Rambaud de Montbryce, to be your wedded husband?"

This may be the moment she's chosen for her revenge.

"I do so wish," she whispered, her head bowed.

He'd been holding his breath and exhaled slowly.

"I now declare, to all present, they are husband and wife. *Comte* Rambaud de Montbryce, you may kiss your bride."

They both stood perfectly still for a moment before turning to face each other. His heart racing, he lifted the veil and smiled, scarcely able to believe the erotic passion she provoked in him. Then the unhappy thought came again that he'd come cross his bride lying barely clothed in a meadow. *Had* she been expecting someone? It wasn't Antoine, but perhaps another man? His smile turned to a frown. Why was she so cool? He bent his head to kiss her. At first she didn't respond, but as he darted his tongue into her mouth, she opened to him.

Oh yes. She definitely feels the passion.

"Mabelle," he whispered. "You're beautiful."

"*Milord* Ram," she faltered. "*Milord*, you are—oh what a beautiful weapon!" she giggled, pointing to his sword, a naughty grin on her face. "Is it a family heirloom?"

The Bishop looked at her curiously. Ram suppressed a chuckle at the look of confused perplexity on the cleric's face. *L'évêque* wasn't a man who usually showed any emotion. Ram doubted the Bishop had ever known a new bride openly admire her husband's weapon. He bent to whisper in her ear. "*Oui*, Mabelle, my weapon is a family treasure," he replied with a smile. "It's always ready to be of service."

She reddened and averted her eyes.

None of the guests had heard the exchange. Ram and Mabelle signed the book of records and walked out of the chapel to the Great Hall. Ram gripped her hand, momentarily nervous she might loudly denounce him. Or perhaps he should accuse her, cast her off? But that would mean never experiencing the fulfillment of the passion she aroused in him. No, the die was cast. These were the confused ravings of a newly married man.

Hugh embraced him and took Mabelle's hand in his, bowing slightly to her as he bestowed a kiss upon it. "Welcome to our family, Mabelle. I'm confident you'll make Ram very happy."

"Patience, dear sister. You will need lots of patience," Antoine teased.

His remark warmed Mabelle's heart. She'd never had a brother who cared.

Her father shook Ram's hand vigorously, and then gave his daughter a perfunctory kiss on the cheek.

"I depart for Alensonne on the morrow," he informed her.

Soon the invited guests were pressing around, congratulating the newlywed couple. Ram and Mabelle became separated.

She lost track of him, until she saw him a while later, beckoning to her from the dais, a hint of uncertainty in his blue eyes. She had to admit grudgingly she was happy to find him again, having felt strangely bereft without him at her side. A jolt had passed through her when their fingers had touched at the beginning of the ceremony. Determined not to look up, she'd stolen a glance at him and felt her throat go dry. During the long nuptial ritual she'd lapsed into a daydream. A tall, dark, naked man rose from the shimmering depths of a pool to possess her, his manhood erect—

"*Arrête!*" she chided herself then, opening her eyes, trying to get back a sense of what was next in the sacred ceremony, not sure of how long she'd been distracted.

She breathed a sigh of relief when Ram spoke his vows. She wouldn't need the dagger concealed in the sleeve of her gown, ready to thrust into him if he betrayed her again.

She'd felt *his* hand twitch and close tightly around hers when she spoke. By the time the rest of the ceremony was over, the vows completed and the ring blessed and placed by Ram's large, firm hand on her trembling finger, she was worried that when he lifted her veil, she would be withered by his look of mistrust.

Was that indeed what she saw as his smile turned to a frown? When he kissed her, she tried not to respond, but the wanton, aching feelings returned. She couldn't help herself when he darted his tongue into her mouth. Then the courage which had helped her survive for many years came to her rescue, bolstered by the wine she'd drunk rather rapidly a short time before, and she made the remark about his weapon, shocking the bishop.

This man had accused her of inappropriate behaviour, and yet, on his way to his own wedding, he'd hidden in the woods, watching a scantily clad maiden. That she'd felt aroused by him was immaterial. It was a betrayal. Then he'd abandoned her at the chapel door. He'd called her his *talisman*—but could he be trusted? She steeled her emotions as he approached her.

"The servants are ready to serve the feast, *milady*. Please come and take your place by my side." She allowed him to lead her to the head table, saying nothing. The touch of his hand made her incapable of speech. This would never do. She would need to be wary.

CHAPTER NINETEEN

The festivities began. The servants brought out massive plates of food from the kitchens. Two liveried serving lads appeared, carrying on their shoulders a large iron pan with the traditional boar's head. There was crusty fresh bread. *La Cuisinière* had spared no effort to provide a sumptuous spread for the wedding of their *Comte*.

A large serving dish of roasted chicken was placed between the newly-weds on the head table, a symbolic shared first meal. Ram broke off a piece and offered it to her. She accepted with a nod, eyelashes fluttering, and bit into it, the succulent juices dripping on to her trencher. She licked her lips and fingers, savouring it.

"I've eaten nothing all day," she whispered.

Ram was aroused and pressed his thigh against hers. He wished it was his fingers she licked. She seemed to sense his arousal as she stole a blushing glance at the tight bulge in his hose. He wondered how he would get through the next few hours of food, wine, ale, ribaldry, *jongleurs,* toasts and speeches without ripping the clothes from her body and making love to her on the tables.

It was a heady thought he'd married a passionate woman. He could stir her with his kisses, his touches. But she harboured resentments, and it sobered him. He had some grovelling to do, but she too had things to explain.

There was a sudden flurry of activity. Antoine and Hugh were up on their feet, indicating to the diners in the hall something was about to happen. People were being ushered into lines.

"What is it, Ram?" Mabelle asked nervously.

"We're going to have a ceremony," he replied, rising from his seat.

She frowned. "Ceremony? We just—"

"Allegiance. Everyone will swear their allegiance to me, as their new *Comte*. And to you."

"To me?"

Ram turned to her. "Mabelle, you're now the *Comtesse* de Montbryce. I would expect my people to honour and respect and serve you. They're your people now."

It's the first time he has acknowledged I can be a good Comtesse.

She quickly wiped her greasy hands and lips with a napkin. Vaillon came forward to refasten the short cloak Ram had shed during the meal. Her husband took her hand and led her to stand at the front of the dais. He drew his sword, braced his legs, pushed the cloak further back on his shoulders and took up a stance with his sword pointing down, his left hand on the hilt.

He looked at his wife. "Place your right hand on top of mine."

She obeyed, her knees turning to water. He put his right hand on top of hers. His hands were warm, and soon those hands—

Ram gestured to Antoine. "Begin."

Antoine came first, followed by Hugh. Each brother bent the knee, placed his hand atop Ram's, and pledged, "In the name of our Lord, and in the presence of all gathered here, I acknowledge that you, Rambaud de Montbryce, are my *Comte*, and my liege lord, and I am your loyal man, and I acknowledge that you, Mabelle de Montbryce, are my *Comtesse*, and I am your loyal man."

The knights and men-at-arms followed suit. When all had pledged themselves, Ram turned to Mabelle and declared in a loud and authoritative voice, "I'll accept your pledge now, *Comtesse*."

Something inside her rebelled at the notion. Ram wanted to use the occasion to demonstrate his dominance. But what choice did she have? Kneeling before him, she placed both hands on his, looked into his eyes, and made her pledge, hoping her voice didn't betray her nervousness. "In the name of the Lord, and in the presence of all here gathered, I acknowledge that you, Rambaud de Montbryce, are my *Comte* and my liege lord, and I am your loyal woman."

I am your woman!

The words echoed in her head, and her mouth went dry. She was this man's woman. This baron she barely knew was her future, her forever. Ram bowed to her slightly, and she saw a smile tug at the edges of his mouth. He took her hand and helped her to rise, and she silently thanked God for the strength she felt in his grip. She assumed he would lead her back to her place, having established his superior position.

Instead, he handed her the sword, placed her hands on the hilt, covered them with his own, and knelt on one knee before her. Staring at her intently, he gave his oath. "I, *Comte* Rambaud de Montbryce, in the name of the Lord, and in the presence of all here gathered, acknowledge that you, Mabelle de Montbryce, and de Valtesse, and d'Alensonne, and de Domfort and de Belisle, are my *Comtesse*, and I am your loyal man."

The room filled with loud cheering as everyone resumed their places, and the feasting recommenced. Ram rose, took Mabelle's hand and returned her to her place, never taking his eyes from hers.

Her tears had started as soon as he knelt before her. She knew what that gesture cost him. Perhaps there was more to this man? He reached over as he took his own seat and, with a smile, wiped away her tears with his thumb.

Hours later, taking her hand, he whispered, "It will soon be time for the bedding ceremony, Mabelle. I've tried, throughout this interminable evening, not to recall the vision of you lying in the grass, your legs half open—inviting." He pressed his thigh against hers again. She felt her nipples tingle and a warmth flood between her legs. Feverish heat washed over her.

I must be ailing for something?

They listened to the toasts given by Antoine, then by her father, who, to her embarrassment, rambled on about traitors and rights and redemption. Then Ram raised his goblet and toasted his bride. "I drink to the health of my beautiful wife, Mabelle de Montbryce. I'm confidant she'll be a good and willing wife."

He winked at her, and she thought he'd probably drunk too much wine.

Such arrogance! Good and willing? We're back to that.

She rose to her feet to return the toast, hoping her trembling legs would hold her up. She too had imbibed more of the excellent wine, not to mention a sip of the fine apple brandy brought from the cellars. She felt somewhat unsteady. She was also nervous about the journey they would undertake on the morrow to England, having never sailed before.

"I thank you, *mon seigneur*, and I drink to your health also." She sat down but not until she'd winked at him, or at least tried to. Winking didn't seem to be a skill she possessed at that moment.

He looks disappointed. Good!

She'd heard gossip in many castles about bedding ceremonies, but had never attended one, being an unmarried woman. They could be affairs bordering on mass hysteria, where the bride and groom were both stripped naked and forced to copulate in front of the whole assembly. Bloodied sheets were then hoisted from the flagpole.

Or, they might be polite and discreet occasions. The bride's maids dressed her in her nightgown, the groom's men undressed him, and then the bishop blessed the marriage bed, the gathering tucked the happy couple up in bed, and left. She fervently hoped something along the lines of the latter would be the case now.

Ram reassured her, "Don't worry, Mabelle, there'll be no running sheets up flagpoles in this castle."

He'd understood her concern, and tried to make her feel better. Or was it that he'd made sure there would be no public display, because he suspected she was no longer a virgin, and there would be no bloodied sheets?

He still thinks me unchaste.

CHAPTER TWENTY

The assembled gathering was merry but not bawdy, as they lifted a broadly grinning Ram, and a blushing Mabelle, and carried them to the bridal bedchamber. It was the first time Mabelle had been in this room since she'd left her letter of farewell. A carved wooden screen had been placed at one end, and she and Giselle stepped behind it so the maidservant could help remove her gown, chemise, shoes and hose. The veil had long since fallen away.

She gasped at the flimsy nightgown that a gleeful Giselle carefully fastened around her. Ram, and everyone else in the chamber, would see through it. But Giselle wrapped a warm bed gown around her, and pulled the belt tight.

"Only for *milord's* eyes, in my opinion. Not those who want to ogle," whispered the feisty maid.

Thank God for the loyalty and common sense of this serving woman.

Ram's friends and brothers were divesting him of his clothing, tossing it here and there, and he eased into a black silk bed robe held out for him by Vaillon, cinching it lightly around his waist. Smiling and waving to the jeering and cheering crowd, he strode proudly across the room and joined a blushing Mabelle. The robe barely came to his knees, and she inadvertently caught a glimpse of his muscled thighs as he walked. She looked away quickly. Had he noticed? She was propped up on a large pillow, having been tucked into the bed by Giselle, after the maid had combed out her hair. The Bishop intoned a brief prayer of blessing, and sprinkled the bed with holy water. Then, despite ribald urgings from the guests to *"Get on with it"*, Ram ushered them out with an imperious wave of the hand, and gradually they left.

"*Allez, tous!*" he commanded, trying to appear serious. "Be gone, all of you."

Their eventual leaving, urged out by Vaillon and Giselle, created an overwhelming silence in the big chamber. Ram slipped off his bed robe. Mabelle averted her eyes as he raised his hips to free the silk from under his body. He threw it nonchalantly to the floor. Turning onto his back, he stretched out his arm to the table for one of the two goblets of mead. She stole a glance at his well-muscled chest and the trail of black hair leading down to his navel and—he turned back to her and offered a goblet.

"Something sweet for my bride?"

She shook her head. Her face was on fire.

"Too nervous?" he asked.

"*Oui*," she whispered, scarcely able to speak. Her insides were churning.

Propped up on one elbow, he took a sip of the honeyed wine and licked his lips. "You should try some, Mabelle. It's bad luck not to."

He offered his goblet to her and raised it to her lips. His eyes seemed to darken as he watched her, and he frowned slightly. "More?"

"*Non, merci*," she murmured. The mead was still lukewarm and she could feel it trickling down her throat.

He smiled, took another sip, then leaned over to replace the goblet on the table, licking the stickiness off his fingers. Her mouth fell open.

Turning on his side, with his head propped up on his muscular arm, he looked at her and said seductively, "Well, *ma belle,* will you let me see that irresistible body without my begging?"

"You weren't going to beg at the lake." As soon as she uttered the words, she regretted them.

He bristled. "*Non*, you're right. Would I have had to beg? I got the feeling you were ready to give yourself up without much protest."

His words cut into her heart.

But my dream was of you—of your kiss.

"What trick do you have in mind to hide your lost virginity?"

Anger swept over her. "You think I'm not a maid?" she murmured, her eyes filling with tears. She wished he'd choked on his mead.

"Maids don't lie half-naked in meadows, covered with flowers. But I don't care. You've cast a spell on me, and you're the one I must have."

Despite his cruel words, the smoldering need in his ice blue eyes made her heart race. She looked away, afraid her heart might break.

Wiping away a tear with his fingers, he admitted, "My male needs threatened to control me, Mabelle, and I'm not proud of it. That's what passion seems to do. I'm a Montbryce, an honourable Norman noble. I was tired after my journey. I thought you were a vision."

As he spoke, he gently tugged away the bed robe and looked at her body, visible through the diaphanous fabric of the nightgown.

"Two perfect circles on two perfect globes," he murmured, a faint smile tugging at the corners of his mouth. He lowered his head and twirled his tongue lightly over each hard nipple. It sent molten waves to the core of her being.

She could feel her heart pounding and couldn't swallow. He kissed her softly, then, as the kiss lengthened and deepened in intensity, she parted her lips and welcomed his tantalizing tongue, warmed by the mead. His lips were sticky and he tasted of honey. He wrapped his powerful arms around her, accepting the silent invitation, licking the corners of her mouth. He groaned.

Sucking on her lower lip, he trailed one hand down her throat and cupped her breast. It filled his hand and he stroked slowly and rhythmically, his fingers straying closer and closer to the expectant nipple. His scorching touch through the silken fabric aroused feelings unknown to her before, and when he finally pinched the pert point between his thumb and forefinger, a spasm tore through her, and she arched up off the bed, wet heat flooding between her legs.

What is happening to me?

With his other hand, he carefully peeled the nightgown from her trembling body. "I've longed to see your glorious body," he whispered, "And to lose myself in you. You are as lovely as I imagined."

She moaned softly as his big hands cupped both breasts. He lowered his warm lips to them, suckling and licking as he tenderly squeezed the other needy nipple. She arched her mons and felt his arousal throb against her thigh. She dared not look.

His kiss then was slow and deep. She sucked his tongue into her mouth. Surrendering to an instinct that overcame the inner voice urging modesty, she opened her legs. With a deep grunt she felt in her toes, he used his hand on the top of her thigh to open her wider, pulling her leg over his. She felt the silken tickle of the hair on his legs, and the hardness of his manhood pressing against her thigh. His fingers stroked her most intimate place. The sensations were overwhelming, but she didn't want him to stop. She couldn't breathe and had to break away from his kiss. She looked into his eyes, expecting to see censure at her wantonness, but instead saw deep need.

He smiled at her and whispered, "Don't forget to breathe, Mabelle. Don't be afraid. Breathe."

The sound of his seductive voice calmed her. He kissed her again, continuing to stroke her, harder and faster now, the other hand squeezing a nipple. Intense heat coursed through her belly, shooting down her inner thighs. She dug her heels into the bed, wanting the sensations to go on—and on.

"Come for me, my lovely," he whispered. "Come for me."

She didn't understand his words, only half heard them, totally rapt in scaling a mountain of exquisite pleasure, and wanted to scream as her body cascaded from the top of it and fell into bliss.

"Your screams excite me," he said huskily. "I want to thrust into you, but I want to see your face again when you reach ecstasy."

No man had ever spoken such words to her. She'd entered a world she'd never known. She wanted to laugh and cry. She wanted all of him.

Where have these thoughts come from?

He bent his head to suckle her, then ran his fingers lightly across her belly and slid one finger further inside her, then another, curling them against the tender flesh, his palm pressed against her mons. She'd never known such sensations and fulfillment came again quickly. But she was so wet. Ram held her tightly as her body convulsed.

Is that me screaming?

She opened her eyes and plumbed his blue depths again. He smiled and whispered, "It's time. You're ready now."

He rose above her on his knees, and spread her legs wider. She summoned the courage to look at his male part and gasped.

He chuckled and whispered, "I know. I'll go slowly—if I can."

His hand guided the tip of his manhood into her throbbing folds.

"I'm wet," she stammered, in whispered apology.

He groaned. "Put your hand on me."

He took her hand and curled it around his shaft.

"Like silk," she murmured.

The memory flashed into her mind of how magnificent he'd looked at the lake—a beautiful aroused male, his excitement barely concealed by his braies—ever since that moment she'd longed for him to join his body to hers. Surely he must see the lust on her face?

"You're beautiful, Mabelle," he groaned. "I've ached to make you mine."

"Please—Ram—please," she murmured, awash with desire, "Possess me—take me."

He took hold of her hands and held them over her head, his fingers entwined with hers, bracing himself. He breathed in deeply as he pushed in. She cried out when he breached her maiden's gate. He stopped and looked into her eyes.

"*Dieu!* I'm the *first*," he choked. "You're truly mine."

She should have been affronted at the tone of surprise in his voice but was too enthralled with the sensations building inside her. She tore her hands from his and grasped his hips, pulling him towards her, then reached up and brushed his nipples with her thumbs. Her eyes glazed over when he gasped at her touch.

He withdrew almost completely and plunged in again, then thrust deeply, over and over, faster and faster. She'd never experienced such a feeling of possession.

This man is mine.

Deep within, exquisite pleasure blossomed. She raised her arms above her head, and he entwined their fingers again. The overwhelming sensations Ram had brought to her body earlier were nothing to what surged through her now, an inexorably intoxicating bliss. Ram's skin sheened with perspiration. She wanted to tear her hands from his grasp and run them across his gleaming shoulders.

She felt his essence burst from his body and rush into hers. He reared his head back and a strangled gasp emerged from deep in his throat. Euphoria filled her. A shudder went through them both, and she screamed out her amazement with a sound she'd never made before. He collapsed onto her, his breathing laboured.

"Sorry," he gasped after a minute or two. "Too heavy—can't move."

"You're not heavy," she whispered, her fingers lazily caressing the back of his neck. His shoulders twitched. She loved the feel of his weight on her, his warm body covering hers completely, his rapid heartbeat reverberating through her.

Rolling away several minutes later, he saw the tracks of tears on her face. "I'm truly sorry. I thought you were not a maiden. You should have told me," he said softly. "Though you were a virgin, that was the most exhilarating—"

Mabelle blushed, elated she'd pleased him, that he too seemed to have been moved by the experience.

"—you took all of me. You were tight, my lovely, but you were wet and welcoming. I could feel you throbbing around my shaft, and I wanted to stay inside you as long as I could."

How to respond? This man she barely knew, who'd preoccupied her thoughts constantly, was saying intimate things that inflamed her. She wanted to arch her body to his, wrap her legs around him, rake her fingers through his hair—but then he would again judge her a wanton.

He has eyes that can make women do foolish things.

He went to the basin, poured water from the ewer on to a cloth. "Would you like me to cleanse you, Mabelle?"

The deep tenderness in his voice brought tears to her eyes, and despite her discomfort at having a man, a warrior, wash her most intimate parts, she nodded. He smiled at her embarrassment over the bloodstained sheets.

"It wasn't a trick," she murmured, not knowing what else to say.

He kissed her nose. "I could tell."

She wanted to offer to cleanse him but was too shy to ask, and before she knew it, he'd left the bed to take care of his own needs. She couldn't take her eyes off him as he walked around confidently and without embarrassment. He was so male, so muscled, so big, so dark, so naked, and so comfortable in this masculine room.

"Do you like what you see, *Comtesse?*"

She felt her face redden.

"*Oui, milord.* I confess to being the wanton you already know me to be. It's a weakness I didn't know I possessed. You've unleashed something I've never experienced before. Despite my anger at you, I can't say no to your passionate embraces."

He sat beside her on the bed and took hold of her hand. "First of all, never call me *milord*. I'm your husband and my name is Ram. Secondly, I'm conflicted. The irony of our predicament strikes me. You did indeed behave like a wanton, but that aroused me. Your actions were inappropriate, but I wasn't blameless. At least we have passion, if we don't have trust. I'm elated no other man has possessed you. I'm also overjoyed to have been the man to bring you to your first experience of ecstasy."

She blushed. "How did you know that?"

He traced a finger down her nose and laughed as she blushed even more deeply. "A man can sense these things. It was the look of utter surprise on your face. Mabelle, you're not a wanton, just a warm, passionate woman. We'll make beautiful children. I'm happy to have a wife who is passionate and lusty in bed. Passion isn't a weakness."

"But I don't know how to be lusty—Ram."

"Don't worry, I'll teach you. *Je serai ton maître.*"

His being her master thrilled and dismayed her.

"Let's sleep now and perhaps in a while—"

He turned her, encircled her with his arms and cupped her breasts in his big hands, nuzzling the back of her neck. They fell asleep quickly.

***

Ram woke before dawn filled with an intense feeling of well-being, and slowly became aware of the naked woman sleeping beside him. His wife! Her back was to him, her breasts and belly pressed to the bed, one long leg straight beneath her, the other bent. One hand rested on the pillow next to her face. Her tangled hair lay like a coverlet over her back and shoulders. He had an urge to put his hands on her lovely round *derrière* but resisted. He wanted to watch her breathe for a few more minutes. They would have to rise soon to prepare for their journey, and he'd already hardened at the sight of her.

He'd longed to possess Mabelle from the moment he'd first seen her, and yet the intensity of the passion they'd shared had taken him by surprise. He was usually a man of few words when he bedded a woman but recalled sharing intimacies with Mabelle he'd never uttered before. What he'd experienced with her was more than a bedding. She'd claimed him, possessed him, just as much as he'd possessed her. It elated him he was the first man to penetrate her. He'd never made love to a virgin. Why had he been sure she wasn't a maid? Would she ever forgive his cruel words?

And he'd cleansed her, something he'd never done for a woman before. He'd done it without thinking. As he looked at her now in the

126

early light of dawn, sleeping peacefully, he tried to imagine what life must have been like for her before they met. It felt good to have her here, beside him, in the chamber he loved but had never shared with anyone. "I swear to you, Mabelle," he whispered, "You'll never want for a safe place to sleep ever again."

She stirred, and he reached over to fondle her hair. She turned lazily and stretched. His arousal intensified and he gathered her into his arms, feathering kisses along her neck. She blinked, seemingly disoriented for a few moments. Then she smiled. "Do we have time to do it again?" she asked.

"We have time."

CHAPTER TWENTY-ONE

"The Saxons are to endure the unspeakable humiliation of seeing the Conqueror crowned on the anniversary of Christ's birth," Ram remarked, as he and his wife and brothers were breaking their fast before the departure for the coast. "William has a strong feeling for form and law and he's resolved to let no ceremony pass that might strengthen his claim to be regarded as King of the English."

He turned to his brothers. "So we're agreed? You'll take care of things here and at Belisle and Domfort. I imagine you've had enough of England after Hastings."

Both men agreed readily.

Mabelle smiled timidly at Ram. "I can tell you're honoured by the invitation from William, and nothing will keep you away. From the little you've told me, you played a large part in ensuring the victory."

He'd shared something of the details of the battle, though he'd wisely decided not to tell her about his near decapitation. "Are you sure you want to accompany me?" he ventured, not knowing what he would do if she said she would prefer not to. She'd never travelled by ship before.

"Will it be safe?"

"It's a short voyage, and, if we're careful to pick the right tides, you'll be safe with me. But the castle at Ellesmere—it's not like Montbryce—we can't live in it yet."

Why did he feel a compulsion to take her with him? It would be a difficult and dangerous life, perhaps for years, and there would be a lot of travelling back and forth to Normandie.

"I don't want to be left behind, Ram."

They travelled to the coast. Decorum dictated she ride her mare side saddle.

"My back feels as if it's broken," Mabelle lamented to Ram. "It would be more comfortable riding behind you on Fortis. Then at least I could feel your warmth. I'm cold."

He looked at her with a teasing smile and reined in his horse. Perhaps having a wife who had spirit wasn't such a bad thing? "I too would enjoy your riding behind me, pressing your beautiful breasts against my back."

Soon she was mounted behind him, and they made better progress. He reached behind and patted her thigh. "I now see the advantage for me of your riding astride."

The winds were with them and they took ship for the English coast. She weathered the crossing well, but Ram was seasick from the moment they cast off. He'd told her about his ailment. "I'm sorry. I did warn you. When I think of the last time I sailed to England, with William, it seems a lifetime ago. I didn't know if I would ever see you again."

Mabelle huddled closer to him. "You thought of me?"

Another bout of retching prevented his response.

She wiped his brow. "I'm not a good wife. I have no idea how to help your malady."

"Nothing can be done about it, Mabelle. Believe me. Nothing helps. I have to stay outside, but if you're cold, you should seek shelter in the tent they rigged for you."

"*Non*, I love the tang of the salty breeze on my face, and I would rather be with you."

"This wind is filling the sail and should carry us quickly across the Narrow Sea. We're fortunate." He didn't want to mention this stretch of water could be deadly if weather and tides turned against them.

They came ashore safely. "Welcome to England, Mabelle. I'm content you're here with me. This is our new country, the land of opportunity for us and our children."

William had arranged for an escort to take them into London. They were given opulent accommodation at the royal residence next to the Abbey and were to be among the distinguished guests at the coronation in the church of Saint Peter, called Westminster.

They made their way there the next day and Ram thought he would pass on to her something of the Abbey, so she would know the history of the magnificent building. "Edward the Confessor chose Westminster as the site for his palace and church because it lay close to the famous and rich town of London. It was surrounded with fertile lands and green fields near the main channel of the river Thames, an important trade route. Of course, London isn't the seat of government. That's in Winchester."

Mabelle gazed around in wonder. "I know the Confessor grew up in Normandie."

"*Oui*, and he looked to Norman architects to build his abbey, because they were more advanced in their craft than the English. He was aware of the great abbey churches built at Caen and Bernay, and of the development of our architecture. The Abbey was Edward's great gift to the people of England, magnificent and innovative even by our standards. It was consecrated on Holy Innocents Day, in the year of our Lord One Thousand and Sixty-Five."

Once again, Mabelle surprised him. "But Edward was too ill to attend. My father and I were in Arques, and the castle was full of rumours of his imminent death. We were at Montbryce when he died on the vigil of Epiphany. Like Moses and the Promised Land."

He squeezed her hand. He hadn't known she'd been at his father's castle for that long, but said nothing. "*Oui*, but on Christmas Day in the Abbey, William, *Duc de Normandie*, is to become the third man in this eventful year to wear the English crown. He will be King of his Promised Land."

Ram's chest swelled with pride as he escorted Mabelle into the Abbey. She wore a velvet surcoat dress of emerald green, trimmed with ermine, made for her by Bette, at Montbryce, before the terrible day of their intended wedding. Her girdle was of spun gold. The ruffled pleats of the sleeves of her satin chemise reflected the light of the thousands of candles. Over her dress she wore a voluminous semi-circular matching cloak, pinned in the centre with a brooch bearing the Montbryce crest. The cloak too was trimmed with ermine. On her head, where her hair was closely coiled with a few curls at the forehead, she wore a wimple wound about her golden hair and thrown over her shoulder. A snood of embroidered green silk. held the wimple in place.

As they proceeded to their places, he whispered in her ear, "You're stunning. Even in this illustrious gathering you turn heads."

There was a substantial guard of Norman men-at-arms and knights posted round the church to prevent any treachery on the part of resentful townsfolk.

In the presence of the bishops, abbots, and nobles of the whole realm, Archbishop Ealdred of York consecrated William *Duc de Normandie* as King of the English and placed the royal crown on his head. The Archbishop of Canterbury had refused to officiate. William's coronation robe was ornamented with gold and costly gems. Hundreds of amulets of gold and silver hung from it.

"Each amulet contains a saint's relic," Ram whispered to Mabelle.

When Archbishop Ealdred asked the English, and Geoffrey, Bishop of Coutances, asked the Normans if they would accept William as their king, all proclaimed their agreement with one voice, but not in one language. Ram shouted proudly with a resounding, "*Oui!*" thrusting his fist into the air in salute to William, filled with conflicting emotions at the memories of the horrific battles, and what William's victory had cost him. His other hand held Mabelle's tightly.

The Archbishop led William to the royal throne in the presence and with the assent of the bishops and abbots gathered there.

However, the armed Norman cavalry outside, hearing the harsh English accents, believed treachery was afoot. They set fire to some of the buildings surrounding the Abbey, putting people to the sword. The fire spread rapidly and the crowd took fright, rushing out of the church.

"Ram?" Mabelle cried, clutching his arm.

She was plainly terrified. "I won't let any harm come to you. Hold on to me. We must stay together."

He led his trembling wife to safety, his arm firmly around her, sword drawn. He delivered her to his men-at-arms with instructions to take her back to the palace.

Only the bishops and a few clergy remained in the sanctuary to complete the consecration of the king. Ram elbowed his way back to the new King's side. William seemed badly shaken by the course of events. Once he got William's attention, Ram urged, "*Majesté*, you must make an appearance to the people, to reassure our fellow Normans you've been crowned."

William regained his composure, nodded and walked regally to the door of the Abbey. The sight of him in his Coronation robes calmed the largely Norman crowd. He looked distraught over what had happened, but he was King.

"I've sworn to maintain the Church, and all Christian people in true peace, to prohibit injustice and oppression, to observe equity and mercy in judgments, and to rule my people better than the best of kings before me, if they are loyal to me. I am determined in my heart to make England a country where something other than anarchy can reign. I will pursue the King's Peace with warlike fervour. With the help of the Confessor's Norman advisors and courtiers, and allies like you, *Comte Rambaud le Noir*, I will be invincible."

***

Frantic with worry for Ram, Mabelle paced back and forth, biting her nails. She'd shed the cloak and wimple. She rushed to embrace him when he arrived back at the Palace.

"Everything is peaceful now. Our Duke is King William the First of the English, despite the best efforts of our own Norman soldiers to ruin the day for him."

They looked at each other and laughed with relief.

"We shouldn't let your beautiful *ensemble* go to waste, *Comtesse de Montbryce*," he purred, undoing the girdle of spun gold, as he pressed her to his body. "This is a day for celebration."

As soon as he touched her, she felt the clenching low in her belly. It wasn't long after they were naked that her body ached for him. She called his name over and over as he knelt between her legs, draped them over his shoulders, lifted her hips, bent his head and kissed her place of pleasure. He held her firmly as he made love to her with his warm mouth, his tongue as deft as his fingers had been. It seemed natural. She trusted him with her body. Why could she not trust her heart to him?

"I savour every tremor of pleasure vibrating through your body, Mabelle."

He smiled the smile that made her quiver. Keeping her legs draped over his shoulders, he put a bolster under her hips and slid his manhood into her. She smiled back as their rhythmic dance inflamed her. Throbbing with release, her sheath welcomed his surging seed.

"Your hair's getting longer," she whispered later, as she twirled her fingers through it. "It smells of wood smoke."

***

Long days and nights of celebration followed the coronation.

"The King wishes to formally name me Earl of Ellesmere at tonight's banquet," Ram told his wife on the third day. "Beforehand, he wants to meet to discuss the problems in the Welsh Marches, and how he perceives my role in dealing with them. There's no definite border between England and Wales, so we must establish our authority in the region."

When they were ushered into the King's antechamber, William strode to Ram and embraced him warmly *"Non, mon ami,* you will not kneel. I wouldn't be wearing this crown today without your help. I am desolate about your father."

Turning to Mabelle, still in a deep curtsey, he took her hand and kissed it, pulling her to her feet. "My dear *Comtesse* de Montbryce. At last this fool friend of mine has had the good sense to marry you."

"Merci, Majesté."

"My dear friend," the King turned to Ram, wasting no time, "I want to talk about these irritating Welsh rebels."

"Sire?"

"Ram, you have time and again proven your worth, both militarily and in governance. The situation in the Marches requires such skills. You've been there and seen for yourself. I also need someone I can trust implicitly. I envision my Marcher Lords having more power than an ordinary earl. Rebellion is ever in the air. We need to consolidate our victory."

Ram wanted to tell William what he thought of the *castle* at Ellesmere that he had indeed seen for himself, and fervently hoped rumour of the fiasco with Rhodri hadn't reached the King's ear. He bit his tongue.

The King's next words broke into his thoughts. "Ah, here come d'Avranches, Montgomerie and Fitz Osbern, the other men I've chosen for the job."

I am indeed in illustrious company!

He wondered if the castles with which the other men had been rewarded were as dilapidated as his. After the appropriate introductions of the lords and their ladies had been completed, and the social niceties observed, the ladies withdrew to a nearby alcove.

The discussion continued for several hours, with William outlining the powers he planned to give to his four Marcher Lords. Ram's Earldom of Ellesmere occupied an area close to Wales, between Chester and Shrewsbury, sites of two of the proposed earldoms. Hereford in the south was the other.

When time came for the feasting, Ram went in search of Mabelle. The ladies had long since left to prepare for the banquet.

"This is one of the proudest moments of my life," he whispered to her as they were announced, and he entered the massive hall, his beautiful wife on his arm.

"I'm happy to be here to see you honoured."

"It's your presence here that makes me proud."

Why did I think she wouldn't make a good Comtesse?

"I have mixed feelings," he admitted. "The King has indeed honoured me beyond measure, but it's an honour that's not without its dangers. The Marches are not a safe place to bring my wife and start our family. It certainly won't be the comfortable life we enjoyed at our castle in Normandie, at least not for a while."

"I don't care, Ram. I would rather be with you."

"I can't envision leaving you alone in Normandie, Mabelle, I need you by my side."

Before the food was served, King William called his four appointees to the dais and commanded them to kneel. "*Mes seigneurs, Comtes* d'Avranches, de Montgomerie, de Montbryce and Fitz Osbern, I confer upon you the titles of Earl of Chester, Shrewsbury, Ellesmere and Hereford. You are hereby invested with greater powers than any noble has ever enjoyed before."

It was a long and involved ceremony, and later, during the feast, Ram and William Fitz Osbern began discussing the castles they'd been granted. Ram was aware Fitz Osbern was an accomplished castle builder.

"Hereford is in reasonably good shape," Fitz crowed. "If Ellesmere is in need of renovation, I would willingly give you aid with the task. We must work together to strengthen our position throughout the border regions."

"I accept your offer, Fitz Osbern, and I thank you," Ram replied, his heart lifting a little.

CHAPTER TWENTY-TWO

While the Conqueror and his Marcher Lords were celebrating, Lady Ascha Woolgar spent a lonely Yuletide in the manor house at Ruyton, and by the New Year suspected she had conceived. The possibility became a reality a few sennights later, and she was filled with elation one moment and dread the next. Her condition and her fear exhausted her. She was afraid Roussel, the steward appointed by the Earl, would notice.

Ascha recognized her good fortune with Ram's generous arrangements. Many Saxons had been thrown out of their estates by the invading Normans. Her stubborn Saxon pride wouldn't let her grovel to him now she carried his child. He would probably reject her and the child. If he accepted the child, it would grow up a bastard, an outcast.

She determined to survive the ordeal alone. At least the child would be a cherished remembrance of her brief liaison with Ram. It was ironic that in all the times her brutish husband had used her, she'd never gotten with child.

Her maid Enid, who'd served her for many years, was the only person in whom she confided. "No one can ever find out, Enid. We must tell people my child is the issue of my late husband, Sir Caedmon."

"That would be easier to accomplish if your tenants and servants didn't know Sir Caedmon left here well before the Battle of Stamford Bridge, my lady. If he was the father of your child, the babe would be born by May, but you'll not give birth until much later."

Enid was right, but Ascha could see no way out of her dilemma. She fretted so much about her pregnancy becoming evident, she worried she might fall ill.

"Roussel will soon start putting things together and spread word of my condition at Ellesmere. He may tell Lord Rambaud. I'm sure he already wonders why the Earl is generous towards me. Perhaps I'll just have to stay in the manor house and not let anyone see me." How impractical that would be. She couldn't hide the child away, once he was born.

"My lady, if this child makes you unhappy, we should perhaps try to procure an abortifacient for you. I could—"

"Never, Enid!" Ascha cried. "I want this child desperately. But Lord Rambaud must never know. We need a miracle."

***

Roussel was perplexed. The lady of Shelfhoc Hall looked worse every day. Should he mention this to Lord Rambaud? He decided against it. His explicit instructions had been to take care of the house and estate. Nothing had been said about the welfare of the Saxon woman who lived there. The whole arrangement was strange as far as he was concerned. He couldn't understand why the Norman Earl had taken on responsibility for this remote manor, far from his own lands.

"You're to administer the rents and lands, and take care of the house, Roussel," Gervais had told him. "And you're to provision the men-at-arms left there to safeguard the manor. All accounting and revenues are to be given to the Lady of the house. The Earl doesn't want to be bothered with it."

"Am I to take a commission on behalf of *milord?*"

"*Non.* You'll be recompensed directly by me, and then by the Ellesmere steward, Bonhomme, when he arrives."

Oui, the whole arrangement is very strange.

***

In the early spring, three riders were challenged by the Earl of Ellesmere's men as they approached the rampart protecting Shelfhoc. "State your business at the Hall, Saxon," the captain sneered.

"Who are you to demand I tell you my business?" one burly nobleman replied angrily.

"I am captain of the guard assigned to protect this manor, and you will not pass until you tell me who you are, and what your business is with Lady Ascha Woolgar."

The visitor urged his mount forward. "Lady Ascha Woolgar is my sister."

Seemingly satisfied, the soldiers gave way.

The three rode into the courtyard. Sir Gareth Bronson dismounted and rapped with his fist on the door of the manor. "Ascha! It's your brother Gareth. Open the door."

His squire Edward and his son Gawain dismounted, and Edward took the reins of the three horses then handed then over to Roussel who'd emerged hurriedly from the stables.

"Gareth!" Ascha exclaimed as she flung open the door, throwing herself into her brother's arms. She hadn't seen him for two years, not since she'd married Caedmon Woolgar and come to live in Ruyton.

"Ascha! How do you fare?" he asked as he strode into the manor, his arm around his sister, Gawain close behind him. "I'm sorry I couldn't come sooner. It's impossible for Saxons to travel now with these cursed Normans everywhere. The Conqueror boasts about the *Peace of God* and safety for all, but—"

"Never mind, Gareth, you're here now."

"I should have come before, my dear, as soon as I received your message about Caedmon's death at Hastings. I'd suspected he may have fallen there. You look pale. Are you well?" He embraced her. "How are you coping with his death?"

"As well as can be expected. I was never happy with him. He wasn't an easy man to live with."

Gareth took a good look at his sister. "No. But a woman can't survive alone these days here in England, especially a Saxon woman. Who is the Norman who took our horses? And you have Norman soldiers guarding the Hall?"

Has he guessed?

"He's a steward assigned here by the Earl of Ellesmere who has generously provided me with protection, and a steward to help me manage the estate. He provides an accounting of the revenues."

"Why would a Norman earl do that?" young Gawain asked suspiciously.

Ascha fidgeted nervously with her hair. "There's the ever present danger of attack from the Welsh here in the Marches. This is a valuable but vulnerable estate. He's protecting his own interests. Gawain, why don't you go to the kitchen and see what Cook can find for you? You must be hungry after your journey."

She was relieved the notion appealed to him, and he left.

Her brother waited until Gawain was out of earshot, then continued, "Nevertheless, Ascha, you can't stay here alone. I'm getting the feeling you've already suffered at the hands of these Norman invaders."

Ascha's betraying hands went immediately to her rounding belly. "As I thought."

She clenched her fists. "But where would I go, Gareth?"

"You'll come with us to Scotland."

Her hands flew to her face. "Scotland?"

"King Malcolm Canmore hates the Normans as much as we do. He has made it clear he welcomes to his court in Edwinesburh any Saxons who don't wish to remain as subjects to the Normans. We'll make a new life there, free of the Norman tyranny. Many of us have made the decision to follow the hundreds who've already fled."

"But what about Shelfhoc Hall?"

"I'll speak to this steward of yours and inform him you'll be travelling to my home for a while. He needn't know you're never coming back."

It's the answer to my prayers—but Scotland?

"As you have rightly guessed, Gareth, I'm with child but without a husband. Will such a woman be welcomed in the court of King Malcolm?"

"You're my sister, Ascha. Many Saxon women have fallen victim to the rapacious appetites of these murderous Normans. You'll be under my protection. Gawain's mother died years ago. You and I will be good companions for each other. I'll safeguard your secret."

Ascha chewed her lip. "And you'll speak with Steward Roussel?"

Gareth thought for a while. "I'll instruct him to continue taking care of things as usual. I see no reason why he can't send you a yearly accounting and the revenues, if we send back word of where we are once we arrive. Normans are obsessed with form and order. He'll probably be happier to be in charge of a manor where there's no-one to constantly look over what he's doing."

"True, perhaps, though he'll still be ultimately responsible to the Earl, and he's a man it's not wise to cross." Her heart was heavy as she remembered her brief but fulfilling liaison with Rambaud, a man she could never have. Would he be angry if he ever found out she'd borne his child and not told him?

Three sennights later, a wistful Lady Ascha Woolgar left the land of her birth, wondering what the future had in store for her and her unborn child. Gareth had taken care of the arrangements as he promised.

A score of souls made the harrowing journey in ten gruelling days. Upon their arrival, they were greeted warmly by the Scottish king and his queen Ingibjorg, and were provided with help and support by other Saxons who'd fled before them to make a new life.

By the time her son was born a few months later, Gareth had procured a house for himself, his son and his sister, along with their squire Edward, and her maid Enid. She named her son Caedmon. The name of her dead warrior husband would be perpetuated, if not his bloodline, and would make it easier to conceal Caedmon's parentage.

She could not choose a Norman name for him but gave him the second name Brice, which in her language meant *son of a nobleman.* She took satisfaction in knowing she would be the only one who knew the true significance of the name. But she vowed never to tell her son of his true father. It wasn't an ignoble thing to be the son of a martyr of Hastings—whereas the bastard of a Norman.

In thanksgiving for her miracle, she would devote her life to this precious child.

CHAPTER TWENTY-THREE

The castle at Ellesmere gradually took shape, and Ram decided it was at least habitable and Mabelle could move there, after spending six months at the Palace. They saw each other infrequently. Each time he came to visit she threw herself into his arms. Westminster was a lonely place for a Norman woman alone.

"I've missed you, Ram. How long are you staying this time?"

She's ached for me as I've ached for her.

"As long as it takes to pack."

"I'm returning with you?" she asked happily. His nod was the assurance she needed. She rushed off to get Giselle started on their packing.

Ram had rarely seen William during his previous visits to the Palace. Once, however, when he did manage a brief audience, he was amazed to hear the King remark on how useful some of Mabelle's intimate knowledge of Normandie had been. "It's astonishing, Ram, what people will say when they think they're speaking in front of someone unimportant."

More often than not though, the king was away, riding extensively throughout his new kingdom, confiscating lands and building fortified wooden castles. Then he appointed his half-brother Eude and William Fitz-Osbern as co-regents, and went back to Normandie.

Catching up with his wife, Ram told her, "We've been delayed by the rebellion that broke out in Fitz-Osbern's earldom shortly after he was named Regent. It took him away from work on our castle. However, he has suppressed it, with great brutality, I might add." Looking around furtively he whispered, "I'm getting increasingly worried about the capacity for cruelty of some Norman Lords."

***

140

It touched Ram's heart to see how Mabelle struggled to conceal her dismay at her first sight of Ellesmere. However, little by little, she added her personal touches to the castle. *La Cuisinière* sent a young Norman woman from Saint Germain, whom she'd trained in the finer arts of cuisine.

"Trésor is proving to be the treasure her name implies," Mabelle remarked to Ram one evening after they had supped in the half-finished Hall. "She brooks no nonsense from the Saxon and Welsh servers and scullery maids, and her rule in the kitchens is supreme."

"I agree, and visitors speak highly of the fine food we serve here."

"Giselle is relishing her role as head of the household, selecting and training the maids and houseboys to meet her rigorous Norman standards."

"*Oui*, now we have Fernand's son, Mathieu, here as our steward, it seems like home."

They augmented their household staff by bringing to the castle a local Welsh healer, Myfanwy, who was recommended by the village midwife.

"Myfanwy has a special healing touch, your Ladyship," said the stout red faced midwife, who'd inspired Mabelle's confidence as soon as she'd met her, despite being Saxon. Mabelle was reassured that, when she did conceive, she would be in good hands. Haunted by the memories of the deaths at the time of the pestilence, and how powerless she'd felt then, Mabelle suggested to Ram they should always have a healer on hand in their home, and he agreed. The Welsh woman was amenable, and Mathieu Bonhomme allocated her a small chamber within the castle.

Mabelle spent much of her time supervising the menus, preparing herbal remedies and salves under Myfanwy's supervision, and doing embroidery and weaving. She made wimples, chemises, shifts and dresses, and shirts for Ram, though most of her husband's clothes and the fancier items were made by local tailors.

They enjoyed their first Yuletide in Ellesmere, and celebrated in the chapel with the usual religious observances, but also enjoyed the Festival of Fools. A jester was elected to be a mock bishop. He dressed in fake vestments and led people to church, where he delivered a mocking service in gibberish nonsense, and sang rude songs. It gave them a sense of being back at home in their beloved Normandie, and relieved some of their homesickness.

"I miss our beautiful Calvados," Mabelle confided later when they were in bed. They'd laughed hard at the Festival and it had relaxed them.

"As do I, but as long as you're here, I can bear the homesickness. When the weather improves, we'll return home for a visit."

He turned her so her warm back was tucked into his body, and enfolded her in his arms, cupping her breasts.

"When I hold your breasts, I'm in Normandie. I hold my homeland in my hands."

She felt his erection against her back.

"What is this spell you weave around me?" he whispered, nuzzling her ear. "I've only to touch you and I become insatiable."

They made love, pleasuring each other, until they tumbled together into mindless oblivion, calling each other's name, drugged by the overwhelming feelings of sensual rapture.

"You're my lifeline in this sea of foreign hostility," he murmured sleepily.

CHAPTER TWENTY-FOUR

"After everything I did for Edgar the Aetheling when he had the good sense to capitulate at Berkhamsted, the ungrateful wretch rebelled against my authority."

King William clenched the arms of his throne. He was incensed as he addressed his advisors, though the news they brought him of Edgar's defeat was welcome indeed.

"He incited Morcar in Northumbria to rise up again. I should have kept him in Normandie after I took him hostage at Berkhamsted, rather than bringing him back with me."

"Your Highness, worry no longer. He has fled to Hungary with his sisters, Margaret and Cristina, after his defeat at our hands."

William had risen. He glared at them. "They were born in Hungary, when their father was in exile. Their mother is Hungarian. They'll find support there."

"Surely that can't hurt you, Sire? Hungary is far away."

William snarled. "Capturing him would have been a better outcome."

***

Ascha Woolgar wondered what the commotion was about when her nephew Gawain burst into the room where she was playing with her son, Caedmon.

"Have you seen father?" he panted.

She frowned. "I believe he's in his chamber."

"I must find him and tell him the news from Court. Edgar the Aetheling's ship has foundered in a gale off the coast of Fife. He and his sisters have been rescued and brought to King Malcolm's court."

Ascha's mouth fell open. "The Aetheling? Our true King? Sailing off the coast of Scotland?"

Gawain nodded his head so vigorously, Ascha worried it might fall off. "He was part of Earl Morcar's rebellion in Northumbria against the Normans but was defeated. His plan was to flee to Hungary, the land of his birth, when the ship went down."

"The hope for ridding England of the Normans still lives?" Ascha asked excitedly, stooping to pick up Caedmon, who'd struggled to his feet, hanging on to the folds of his mother's dress.

"Yes." He swallowed and took a deep breath. "The other astounding news is the newly widowed King Malcolm is smitten with young Margaret, Edgar's sister. Apparently he rode from his residence in Dunfermline to welcome the royal refugees. Imagine if he marries her. What a political manoeuvre! It would bring Malcolm an alliance with the old royal house of England, and a large dowry given her by the King of Hungary. Edgar would benefit enormously from having a brother-by-marriage who is already a formidable opponent of the Norman usurpers. I'm confident Malcolm would support Edgar if he attempted to regain the throne again."

Ascha planted a kiss on Caedmon's nose, then put her hand on Gawain's shoulder. He quivered with excitement. "Your father will be delighted with this news. I'll help you find him."

***

As Gawain and the whole Saxon community in Scotland hoped, King Malcolm Canmore, the Great Chieftain, became besotted and did marry Princess Margaret. He agreed to support her brother Edgar in his campaign to reclaim the English throne. When a major rebellion broke out in Northumbria early the following year, Edgar returned to England with other rebels who'd fled to Scotland, to lead the revolt. Gawain and Gareth Bronson were among those who went with him.

After early successes the rebels were defeated by King William at York, and Edgar again sought refuge with King Malcolm. Gareth was wounded, but Gawain managed to get him back to Scotland safely. Ascha took care of him and he recovered.

In late summer that year, the arrival of a fleet sent by King Sweyn of Denmark spawned a fresh wave of English uprisings in various parts of the country. Edgar and the other exiles sailed to the Humber, where they joined with Northumbrian rebels and the Danes. Their combined forces overwhelmed the Normans at York and took control of Northumbria.

Edgar then led a seaborne raid into Lindsey which ended in disaster, and he escaped with only a handful of followers to rejoin the main army. Gawain was among them, Gareth wasn't. He died instantly, felled by an arrow through the heart.

Ascha grieved for her dear brother, her protector and champion. Gawain, his heir, assured his aunt she and little Caedmon could remain in the house.

Late in the year, King William fought his way into Northumbria and regained York, buying off the Danes and devastating the surrounding country. After Yuletide he moved against Edgar and other English leaders, who'd taken refuge with their remaining followers in a marshy region, and put them to flight. Edgar returned once more to Scotland. Gawain drowned in the marshes. Since he had no heirs his property devolved to Ascha.

***

Ram was angry as he strode out of the recently furbished Map Room at Ellesmere into the corridor, where he found Mabelle, walking by with a servant.

"What is it, Ram?" she asked.

"The news from Northumbria and York is dire. I hope we can resolve the Welsh problem without having to resort to the tactics William is using in the north," Ram replied, running a hand agitatedly through his hair. He glanced at the servant, whom Mabelle promptly sent away.

"What's he doing? Hasn't the rebellion had been quashed?"

"It has, but he's bought off the Danes and is harrying the whole region. The devastation includes setting fire to the vegetation, houses and tools to work the fields. It's inevitable anyone who escapes slaughter will starve. Walk with me to our chamber. I feel safer talking there."

Once they reached their sanctuary, he continued, "After such cruel treatment, neither the people nor the land will recover for many years. You know I want the firm establishment of Norman rule, but William has let his anger get the better of him. It sickens me. He wants to terrify the English into obedience. These actions won't benefit us in the long run."

He could voice these treacherous notions to his wife. She would never betray him. "What worries me in particular is that in this region some of the other Marcher Lords are capable of similar atrocities."

***

Malcolm Canmore, King of Scotland, was a fierce and passionate man. He'd embraced the cause of his brother-by-marriage Edgar, not only for the sake of his beloved wife Margaret but also because he despised the Normans. He had designs on Cumbria and Northumbria, which he'd tried to bring under his rule for years before the advent of the invaders.

He welcomed Edgar back once more, frustration evident in his voice. "The news from Northumbria and York is dreadful Edgar. The Normans are putting everyone to the sword, and everything to the torch. If they continue with this strategy, there'll be nothing left of the borderlands for us to win. What does the Conqueror have to gain from such cruelty? Margaret is devastated. You know the depth of your sister's piety."

Edgar drew his cloak more tightly around his shoulders, trying to ward off the chilly draughts of the castle. His harrowing experience in the marshes of Holderness had resulted in an ague. He was exhausted and discouraged. "William has let his anger get the better of him. In the long run this harrying will result in greater hatred for the Normans amongst the people—if they survive."

Malcolm slapped him on the back. "Don't be discouraged, Edgar. We Scots will keep trying to oust these barbarians from the lands we want, and I'll continue to support your claim to the throne."

Edgar, a Saxon, privately thought it amusing the king of an uncivilized horde such as the Scots would refer to the Normans as barbarians. He could admit Saxons might be inferior to the Normans in the arts and learning, but they'd brought a much greater degree of civilization to the southern reaches of Scotland than had existed before.

But he needed Malcolm's support, and the old warrior doted on his pious sister.

***

In the year of our Lord One Thousand and Seventy-Two, King William invaded Scotland with a large and well organized army, in retaliation for Malcolm's invading the north of England yet again. William's march took him through Lothian and across the river Forth at Stirling, then on to the River Tay. The whole population of Lothian was in panic, especially the exiled Saxons.

Malcolm knew his forces were no match for the powerful host of Norman knights and men-at-arms, and refused to give battle. William offered to talk terms at Abernethy, on the Tay.

"This is getting tiresome, Malcolm," William said to him condescendingly as they sat together to hammer out a treaty. "You can't win. I'm getting frustrated by your delaying tactics. As part of our agreement, and to guarantee you'll not attack again, I demand your son Duncan as a hostage for peace."

The infuriated Malcolm had no choice. He gave his son by the late Queen Ingibjorg into William's hands, and agreed not to harbour the king's enemies. Edgar fled to the protection of the Flemish *Comte* Robert the Frisian, an enemy of the Normans.

Malcolm told his nervous courtiers, "William views the treaty as a formal act of homage by me, the King of Scotland, as his vassal.

I see it only as recognition of English suzerainty over Cumbria and Northumbria, and don't consider myself bound by it in any way."

CHAPTER TWENTY-FIVE

Despite the ongoing problems with Welsh discontent, Ellesmere prospered. The spacious Great Hall was completed, and Ram proudly showed off the intricately carved tables and large impressive hangings from Normandie.

Mabelle grew to love the region around the town. A few Normans had settled in the region prior to the conquest. There were mountains, moorlands, farms, wooded river valleys, and quaint villages. Ram explained to her it had come to be known as the Marches, because the Anglo-Saxon word for boundary was *mearc*.

True to his promise, William granted Ram virtual independence and what amounted to kingship over his lands. Marcher lords ruled their lands as they saw fit, unlike other English lords who were directly accountable to the king. Ram could build castles, administer laws, wage wars, establish towns, salvage, claim treasure-trove, plunder and was allowed to fish for royal fish. The King's plan was to subdue the Welsh without having to do it himself.

As the Earl, Ram was often away dealing with Welsh incursions, holding courts which could try all cases except high treason, and administering his territory. He encouraged immigration from Normandie, established markets and expanded trade, especially in fine cloth and wine. Sheriffs received their appointments from him. Occasionally, he had to confiscate the estates of felons, and redistribute them to other more trustworthy folk. His experience administering the Montbryce family estate was of great benefit to him, and he became known in the Marches as a firm but fair ruler, and a soldier to be reckoned with. He believed if people had enough food and the basic necessities of life, and were treated fairly, they wouldn't want to rebel.

"I could do none of this, Mabelle, without your presence here at Ellesmere. You've proven to be a formidable Countess. I never worry about the castle when I'm away."

In recognition of Ram's contributions, King William granted him another vast tract of land in Sussex in southern England, which brought four score and three manor houses under his control. It was also an area vital for the defence of England. He decided to deed ten of the estates to Hugh and ten to Antoine.

Ram's power and wealth were growing, as he'd hoped. He'd succeeded more than he ever thought possible in bringing honour, wealth and prestige to the Montbryce name. There was only one fly in the ointment.

"The years are going by, Mabelle, with no sign of your getting with child. Why don't you ask Myfanwy's advice? You're still relatively young at five and twenty, but I'm approaching a score and ten, and the lack of an heir is beginning to worry me."

"Me too," she admitted.

If I'm barren, he'll have to put me aside. I'll die of grief.

Joy surged though her when, after only one month of Myfanwy's herbal ministrations, she missed her flux.

Ram often chafed Ellesmere wasn't as fine as the castle de Montbryce. He worked tirelessly to make improvements to the buildings and grounds, determined to make their home in this foreign land as grand as the ancestral one in Normandie. Knowing she was pregnant, she waited until he once more began his complaints about Ellesmere. They were alone in their chamber when Ram finished his usual lament with, "I only want a castle suitable for my beautiful wife."

"—and child," she added.

It took him a few moments to understand her meaning, and then he leapt from his chair and embraced her. He picked her up and twirled her around until they were both dizzy, then set her back on her feet and kissed her deeply.

"Are you sure?" he rasped. "It's been so long."

"I've only missed one month but I'm sure."

"This is the perfect way to welcome in the new year of our Lord One Thousand and Seventy-Two, and you're the perfect wife," he crowed.

Mabelle laughed. "Yes, I am, but I couldn't have done it without the perfect husband. Apart from you and me, only Giselle and Myfanwy are aware of it. Can we keep it that way for a while?"

"Of course, my beloved. But it will be hard for me not to climb up to the battlements and shout it from the rooftops."

Did he realize he'd called her *beloved*?

***

When she told him of her condition and happiness and relief swept over him, Ram's suspicions were confirmed.

I'm in love with her.

But he had to be wary. He was first and foremost a soldier, the King's man. His steadfast commitment to the King would bring more handsome rewards.

What is this alchemy we have between us?

He had only to touch her for his manhood to harden. Not even touch—the mere sight of her was enough. And now she would bear him a child. He was a happy man. He couldn't imagine life without Mabelle. If he'd been forced to acknowledge his wife was barren and seek another—it was something he didn't want to contemplate.

***

In August of the year of our Lord One Thousand and Seventy-Two, as King William and King Malcolm were confronting each other in Abernethy, Mabelle was giving birth to a son. As the time for the birth of her child drew closer, Mabelle grew ever more nervous. She hoped Ram would return home from the sortie against the Welsh before the event occurred, though she was confident all would go well.

Her every need had been taken care of for several sennights, and she'd grown bored. She felt fat, bloated and unattractive, despite the fact her husband had told her repeatedly she looked lovely and lush. She longed now for his attentions, as she lay in bed, unable to get comfortable, resigned to being awake as the dawn broke. Gradually she became aware of a dull ache permeating her belly.

"What was that?" She lay perfectly still. The ache had passed. Perhaps she should call Giselle to prepare a bath for her, to soothe her troubled spirit.

As sleep claimed her, the ache came again, this time more sharply and for a longer period. She'd never borne a child before, and had assumed the pains of labour would be sharp, intense stabs. Now she wondered if perhaps these aches were signals her child wanted to be born. She rolled out of bed slowly, pausing as the ache caught her again.

Oui, something is happening.

"Giselle, Giselle, *viens vite*, come quickly!"

The maidservant came bustling in from the connecting chamber, her red hair uncharacteristically awry, her face flushed with excitement. "*Milady*, is it the *bébé*?"

"Fetch the midwife, and Myfanwy."

Fifteen hours later, sitting on the birthing stool brought days before in readiness, bathed in sweat and screaming loudly, Mabelle could believe death was at hand. But the experienced midwife told her calmly everything was normal, and saw no reason to be anxious. "It's a good idea to scream. It will make you feel better."

Bertha used simple and natural procedures, relying on pepper to provoke sneezing, which would in turn cause birth. She used various soothing herbal remedies and oils. "I'm confident you'll not need the shroud you made for yourself, at the behest of the bishop. But it's as well you obeyed his insistence on confessing your sins."

Mabelle sought solace during her labours in praying to Sainte Margaret, the patron saint of pregnant women. As her child came into the world and her last cry of relief rent the air, Ram rode into the bailey.

"Mabelle!"

Ram gasped her name as he threw open the door of their chamber. His wild eyes fell upon his wife as she lay back, spent and dishevelled, Giselle supporting her shoulders—and then their child made his presence known with a lusty wail.

"You're beautiful," he called to her as she smiled at him weakly.

"My Lord," cried Bertha, ushering him out, "You shouldn't be here. Don't worry. You have a fine healthy son, but your wife needs to rest now. I'll bring the child to you when we've cleaned him up. He too has had a long journey."

As Ram was shooed out, the midwife said to Giselle, "Trust the father to turn up as soon as it's over."

The four women laughed, though Mabelle barely had enough strength left to do so, as Myfanwy handed her a steaming bowl of chamomile tea.

***

Ram had ridden hard to get home, soon working up a sweat in the warm August weather. He'd experienced a premonition his child would be born that day. Though exhausted, joy overwhelmed him that he'd been present when his son was born.

When Berthe appeared with his babe swaddled in warm wrappings to keep out the unavoidable draughts of the castle, he took his heir into his arms and gazed upon him. He could scarcely believe he and Mabelle had created this wondrous being he held. What a wife she'd turned out to be. They would name the boy Robert, after the King's father and son.

"Robert de Montbryce," he murmured, cradling the child, "I'm your father, Rambaud de Montbryce, son of Bernard de Montbryce. It's to my everlasting sorrow my father didn't get a chance to see you. What does life hold in store for you? You're the long awaited heir to a rich Norman heritage. Wherever your travels take you, I hope you'll always remember that."

Ignoring the strident admonitions of the midwife, he strode off with the babe still in his arms, to the chamber where Mabelle lay. The women had moved Mabelle to her bed, and washed her and combed her hair. She was exhausted, but he saw only her radiance. Smiling, she reached out her arms for her child, and he carefully handed Robert to her. She held the child's face to her breast and he tried to latch on. Ram's shaft hardened.

"I was nervous about holding a baby," he confided with a grin, "But I'm good at it."

Mabelle had noticed it too. "You are, Ram." She smiled at his obvious physical discomfort, brought on by her suckling the child. "In many noble families the father never touches the babes. I know only too well how a child needs a father's love."

***

By February of the year of our Lord One Thousand and Seventy-Three, Mabelle had conceived again over the previous Yuletide. As the time for the birth approached, she liked to sit by the window with her ladies, sewing busily, looking up from her work to see the fields in lambing-time, and watch the shepherds in rough sheepskin clothes drive the sheep into enclosures.

Soon I'll have another little lamb of my own.

She liked being a mother. Robert was a strong, healthy lad. Everyone who saw him admired his dark hair and blue eyes, and commented on his resemblance to his father. She wondered what her next child would be like. She spent a lot of her time in the nursery with her son, and preferred to nurse him, instead of using a wet nurse. She often told him how much she loved him, words she'd never heard from her own father.

How is it I find it easy to tell my child I love him but I can't tell Ram?

When Ram pined for Normandie, Mabelle chided him, "Remember, Ram, our son was born in this foreign land. It's his land."

"Robert is a Norman first and foremost. When I'm gone, it's the Norman lands that will pass to him. They're the important holdings and titles, the ones passed down in our family before. The Montbryce legacy."

Idly patting her belly, he smiled. "Our second son will inherit our English lands and titles. Those lands I've won for myself. They are Ellesmere lands."

In September of the year of our Lord One Thousand and Seventy-Three, Ram and Mabelle welcomed their second son, Baudoin, another almost identical copy of his father. Again, everything went normally, and the midwife and Myfanwy saw her through it.

As time progressed, and the boys grew, Ram didn't get to spend a great deal of time with his young sons, but when he was with them, he treated them much as his own father had treated him—with a firm hand but with love. He often remonstrated with Mabelle she doted on them too much. Robert and Baudoin were excited to see him return from his travels. Whenever he was away fighting the barbaric Welsh, Mabelle was consumed with worry for him.

***

The following year, Edgar the Aetheling returned to Scotland. Shortly after his arrival he received an offer from Philip, the King of France, who was also at odds with King William, of a castle and lands near the borders of Normandie, from which he could launch raids on his enemy's homeland.

Malcolm tried to dissuade him, but he embarked with his followers for France. Once more he became the victim of a shipwreck, this time on the English coast. Many of his men were hunted down by the Normans, but he managed to escape overland with the remainder to Scotland. Following this disaster, he was persuaded by Malcolm to make peace with William and return to England as his subject, abandoning any ambition of regaining his ancestral throne of England.

The despondency among the Saxon refugees in Scotland was palpable. They congregated more and more at Court, drawn by their patroness, Margaret, Queen of Scotland. Many among the Scottish nobility resented what they considered to be the Anglicization of their Celtic court, but they were afraid to voice their criticisms, given Margaret's well known piety, and her husband's besottedness.

Ascha felt more and more isolated after the deaths of her kinsmen. Caedmon was her only solace. She instilled in her son, and encouraged among the Saxons at court, a sense of great pride that he was the son of Sir Caedmon Woolgar, *housecarl* to the dead King Harold, who'd fallen with his king at Hastings. It was the stuff of legend that the king's *housecarls* had fought to the death, rather than surrender.

At seven years of age, Caedmon Brice Woolgar was a strong, affectionate boy, a mirror image of his real father. Ascha was unconcerned about the resemblance, finding comfort in it. She was confident the two would never meet.

CHAPTER TWENTY-SIX

One of the powers granted to the Marcher Lords was the right to raise militias, and Ram often recruited and trained new soldiers. While the ranks might consist of local people, the commanders of these men were always Normans. Giselle frequently dropped hints to the Earl her sons would make fine commanders if they were only given a chance to come from Normandie.

Mabelle didn't pay attention to any of the details regarding these men, busy as she was with her home and children. One winter's day, just after the turn of the year of our Lord One Thousand and Seventy-Five, she was sewing with ladies of the household, chatting about the impressive tapestry they'd heard Bishop Eude had commissioned to commemorate the Conquest. It was being made in England by the Anglo-Saxon seamsters at Eude's *demesne* at Canterbury in Kent but would later be sent to Bayeux in Normandie. Robert and Baudoin were playing with their nursemaids near Mabelle's feet.

"I hear rumours it will be over two hundred feet in length," Giselle commented. "The Anglo-Saxons are famous for their needlework."

"I heard it will show the historic events of the battle, as well as those leading up to the invasion," added Mabelle. "If it's being embroidered, then it's not a tapestry is it? That would mean it would have to be woven."

One of the nursemaids asked, "My lady, why is it being sent to Bayeux?"

"Bishop Eude is building a cathedral there."

While they were talking, her husband entered with some of his commanders. She glanced over to watch him. Even among this group of physically fit elite fighting men he stood out. She fought the urge to rush over and knead his powerful iron-hard thighs. The soft black hair hidden beneath the fine linen of his shirt called to her, and she smiled at how shocked they would be if she tore the shirt off his muscled body, right there, right then—

Heat rose in her as he shifted his stance, and her eyes went unbidden to his sex, just there, hidden under the long doublet, nestled, ready to spring to life if he looked up and saw her hungry gaze. She averted her eyes, aware her face had flushed, that she'd been almost drooling.

Pray no one noticed!

The men's voices drifted into her returning awareness. They were discussing a new Norman noble, who was to arrive soon to take over command of one of the divisions.

"Seems he asked to be assigned to Ellesmere, *milord*," Gervais, Ram's Second in Command remarked.

"Interesting. I wonder why?" Ram replied.

He glanced over to see if Giselle was within hearing. He obviously didn't want to get into that hornet's nest again.

"I expect he knows where the power is, *milord*." The other men chuckled their agreement with this assessment. "He probably knows you have sons. Your heirs will inherit your lands, and they won't revert to the King. That kind of stability leads to opportunity."

"What's his name?"

"Giroux. I've good reports on him. He arrived recently from Normandie. Good family. Capable soldier."

"Sounds familiar—but I can't place it."

Mabelle's heart thudded and she suddenly felt cold. Had she heard correctly? Could this be the son of the man her father had blinded and mutilated years ago? It wasn't a common name, and why had he asked specifically to come to Ellesmere? She'd heard nothing of the Giroux family since coming to England but they were partly responsible for the years of wandering exile she'd endured. She resolved to speak to Ram about it.

Later that night he reassured her. "I'm sure there's nothing to worry about."

He'd remembered where he'd heard the name before but was in the process of seductively undressing his wife. "After your brother's death, I heard no rumour of any ongoing threat from that family."

"But why would he ask to come here?"

"News of our power and reputation has spread throughout Normandie. He's probably an ambitious young man seeking opportunity for advancement with a powerful Marcher Lord. Don't worry," he cajoled, playfully rolling her hardening nipple between his finger and thumb, grinning at her, "I can assign him where you'll never have to meet him."

She lost coherent thought, as the passion that always took hold of her the moment Ram touched her, did just that.

***

The moon had waxed and waned since Giroux's arrival. Ram mounted Fortis, intending to ride out to inspect the Saturday market. He'd always been an accomplished horseman, and was puzzled as to why his favourite mount seemed frenzied. It was a spirited horse, but that was the sort of steed he liked to ride. He'd been relieved the stallion had adapted well to his new life in England, after the rigours of Hastings.

Try as he might, he couldn't seem to calm the snorting animal, which reared so suddenly Ram was thrown heavily to the hard ground. Giroux rushed from nearby to calm the distraught horse. Gervais ran to his earl's side, pulling him away from the flailing hooves. Ram was having difficulty rising, only managing it with the help of his Second. He knew immediately he'd at least cracked a rib or two.

"What the devil is wrong with that horse?" he shouted, as pain snaked through his chest, bending him double.

"I'll look him over, *milord,*" Giroux answered. "He seems calmer now. I'll see to him."

"Gervais, help me to my chamber. I fear my wife will need to assist me. I believe I've broken something."

Mabelle had heard the commotion and hurried to his side. Gervais, almost carrying his Earl, told her what had happened. She began issuing commands to the servants as she helped her husband climb the steps. They assisted Ram to their chamber, where he sat on the edge of the bed. He was shaking.

Giselle and Myfanwy, the Welsh healer, arrived with armfuls of linen cloths. Myfanwy prepared a potion for pain, and Ram downed it in one, knowing firsthand how effective her potions were. The women tore the cloth into strips and bound him, after Myfanwy's gentle examination confirmed the likelihood of broken ribs. "*Yr Arglwydd* Montbryce," Myfanwy said with authority, "You must rest for at least a fortnight. The only time you may get out of bed is when I come to bathe you in knitbone. Only thus will the bones start to heal."

He started to protest, but his argument became less forceful when the draught she'd given him took effect.

"Thank goodness you've at least stopped shaking, Ram," Mabelle murmured with relief, helping Myfanwy tuck warm linens around him.

He wasn't an easy patient, protesting loudly at the indignity of being forced, every second day, to soak in a tub of hot water, darkened by the green of the knitbone. It necessitated the removal of his bindings, and their reapplication afterwards. He was such a big man, the women couldn't manage getting him into the tub, and his squire, Vaillon, had to enlist the aid of another male servant.

"That cursed Welsh woman will kill me."

Mabelle stood with her hands on her hips. "Ram, much as I adore your magnificent body, it's not a pleasant task for me to dry you after you've been soaking in the wretched comfrey. But it will help take down the swelling."

Ram squirmed, aware he'd imposed the duty on her. "I'm sorry. I don't want any of the servants doing it. It's humiliating."

Mabelle seemed to be enjoying baiting him, as she carried on, "And you're ruining every pair of braies you have, with your insistence on keeping them on in the tub. The laundress is less than pleased."

"I don't feel very magnificent," he whined, secretly wishing he had the energy to display his magnificence for her. "And I'll not expose myself to all and sundry."

An active, virile man, he couldn't abide spending time in bed, particularly since he wasn't able to make love to his wife. It was torture. Her nearness in the bed at night, or when she came to sit with him during the day, never failed to arouse him.

"It's difficult for you too. We've never been able to temper our passion for one another."

After close to a fortnight in bed, he was stroking her breasts and bemoaning his plight yet again when she rose and knelt between his legs. "Lay still, Earl of Ellesmere."

She feathered light kisses up the inside of one thigh, and down the other. Bending his legs slightly, she tenderly stroked the backs of his knees. His erection had sprung to life before she'd started the kisses, and now she grasped the base of his manhood, and leaning forward, ran her tongue up the length of him.

"Mabelle," he gasped, trying to keep as still as he could, flattening his palms against the bed to brace himself.

She moved her mouth rhythmically on his rigid manhood, as she cupped his sack with one hand and echoed the movement of her mouth with the other on his shaft. He groaned with every tug. Reaching for her breasts, he rasped, "I can't wait. Straddle me."

Mabelle lowered her slick womanhood onto his throbbing phallus, the sensation of deep penetration sending a wave of well-being coursing through him, from his toes to the top of his head.

"You're already wet, my lovely. But—I can't thrust. You'll have to do the work."

He grasped her hips. "*Oui,* that's it. I can feel you gripping me. Ah!—*Dieu*—Ride me hard, *ma belle.*"

Her nostrils flared, her strong thighs braced tightly against his hips as she rode, back arched, hands threaded into her golden hair, breasts thrust forward proudly. She looked like a wild woman. Glancing to where their bodies were joined seemed to inflame her more—the golden and black curls intertwined. She stared into his eyes and he stared back. She smiled at him, and he smiled back. They crested and peaked together, never turning their gaze as fulfillment clouded their vision.

Mabelle was careful not to collapse on top of him. Rising from the bed, she went to the ewer and poured water on a linen cloth. "Now I'll cleanse you in the loving way you've always cleansed me."

Loving? Of course I love her but could I bear the pain if she doesn't love me in return?

She dried him with her hair, and kissed his sated manhood.

"Cursed horse," he moaned, touching his bound ribs gingerly.

"Didn't you enjoy that, my darling?" she teased.

"*Oui,* of course, but these ribs are not healing fast enough. I can't wait to be riding again."

"And I can't wait to see that broad chest of yours again."

They laughed together. He remained on his back, and she curled into him as sleep claimed them.

***

Ram was a healthy, robust and active man, and it didn't take him long to heal. He was happy to play with his sons when they were brought from the nursery.

"I want to get back on a horse, but if Fortis is still acting wildly, I'll have to find another mount," he told Mabelle sadly. "Much as I appreciate a steed with spirit, I also need a horse I can rely on when I ride against the Welsh. It will be hard to replace Fortis."

He was pleasantly surprised, however, when the horse was demonstrably glad to see him, and he mounted easily, only a twinge pricking his abdomen. He rode out to the town market with his men-at-arms.

"So, you've recovered from whatever upset you that day, *mon vieux*?" he said lovingly, patting the horse's neck, still puzzled by its uncharacteristic behaviour.

On his return, he mentioned it to Gervais, who told Ram that some days after the accident, he'd discovered a deep wound on the horse's flank, under the saddle, as if something sharp had been pressed into its flesh.

"See. There. I didn't think it important at the time, but it was odd."

"Perhaps there was something stuck to the underside of the saddle?"

"Not that I could see, but I wasn't the first to handle Fortis after the accident."

CHAPTER TWENTY-SEVEN

The castle, and its environs grew as buildings and defences were completed. With prosperity and expansion came more people, and with them the need for more healing skills. Myfanwy did what she could, aided by Mabelle and Giselle, but the old woman complained she needed more help. She asked Ram if she could take two girls from nearby villages under her wing, and pass on her skills to them.

"I'm not getting any younger," she cackled. "If something happens to me, you'll need others to tend the wounds of your men, and nurse the illnesses of your people."

Ram looked at her skin, wrinkled like old parchment, and knew she was right. He gave permission for two young women, Morwenna and Rhonwen, to come to the castle to be the healer's apprentices.

They'd been there a fortnight when Ram remarked to Mabelle, "The two apprentices are complete opposites. Where Morwenna is fair of hair and face, Rhonwen is dark, moody, and, I must confess, hard to read." They were dining in the Hall, and could see both girls sitting several benches away, though not together.

"*Oui*, Morwenna braids her long hair, whereas Rhonwen's hangs around her shoulders like a black cape. Morwenna smiles a lot, and Rhonwen doesn't."

Ram took hold of Mabelle's hand. "Don't be angry, but I've noticed Morwenna has beautiful blue eyes with long blonde lashes, and Rhonwen's are huge round pools of grey."

Mabelle made a pretence of rebuking him, wagging her finger and shaking her head, but then she smiled. "Have you noticed how

Rhonwen's high cheek bones accentuate her look of constant surprise?"

Ram chuckled. "*Oui*, and Rhonwen is small and delicate, whereas Morwenna—well, a man notices these things. You know—breasts—and hips that promise fertility."

Now I might be in trouble.

He supposed Mabelle had decided not to rise to the bait when she only smiled again and remarked, "Both girls are quick studies, and Myfanwy is delighted with her pupils. I confess I like Morwenna, but I find Rhonwen uncommunicative and shy. However, I can't fault the way the girl works when faced with a wound to cleanse, or a fever to tend. It sometimes seems people heal faster when Rhonwen takes care of them. She has a special healing touch."

Ram replied, "I'm pleased the castle will have three expert healers."

"*Oui* and the four of us are spending many hours replenishing the stock of herbs, and mixing fresh potions and salves."

"Speaking of salves, I'm leaving for the border on the morrow. Would you like to come and soothe my ache?"

***

One warm spring day, not long after her conversation with Ram, Mabelle and Myfanwy were gathering herbs together in the garden, when the Welshwoman made an observation that they must be sure to replenish certain ones. Mabelle recognised them as herbs used in child birthing. She blushed, wondering if Myfanwy had guessed what she suspected. It would be useless to deny it to this perceptive Welshwoman, whom she'd grown to love and trust.

"I believe you may be right, Myfanwy. I'm with child again, I think. I haven't had my courses for two months, and I'm nauseous every morning."

"Does *Arglwydd* Montbryce know?"

"Not yet, but I know he'll be pleased. I plan to tell him on the morrow, when he returns from Wales."

"I can prepare something for the nausea, my lady, if you wish."

"Thank you, Myfanwy."

That evening, as she sat in her lonely chamber, looking forward to Ram's return the next day, Mabelle heard a soft tap at the door. Morwenna entered, the usual bright smile upon her face, carrying a wooden tray with a goblet. "My lady, Myfanwy has sent this special draught for nausea but says it must be taken the night before, to be truly effective."

Mabelle was upset the Welsh healer had evidently shared news of her condition with the apprentice but decided not to make an issue of it. She thanked the girl, dismissed her and took a sip of the potion. It had a bitter taste, and she could only take a few sips at a time. She might prefer the nausea to this gall. She called to Giselle in the next chamber to assist her to undress.

"You're no doubt looking forward to *milord's* return on the morrow," enthused the little Norman woman, who'd become Mabelle's only real confidante.

"*Oui*, I am, Giselle. I love him dearly, and I miss him when he's away."

Giselle helped her lady lift the dress over her head. "So, you've come to see that what you feel for him is love?"

"*Oui*, for many years I didn't think I could experience love. As you know, I spent my childhood growing up with a father who didn't know the meaning of the word. And Ram and I—well—you're aware of the difficulties we had at first that I thought I would never forgive him for. But he's the person I was meant to marry. He's the other half of me."

Giselle knelt to remove Mabelle's shoes. "Have you told him you love him?"

"*Non*, I'll probably never tell him. You know Ram. He's a man of action, a soldier. Such men don't allow themselves to fall in love. He's a good husband and father, and he cares for me, and our passion is sometimes—overwhelming, but for a man that's natural lust, and I wouldn't want to tell him I love him, and receive no words of love in return."

Giselle smiled and patted Mabelle's belly. "*Milady*, you're mistaken. When he looks at you I see love in his eyes. When you tell him about the *bébé* on the morrow, why not tell him you love him?"

Now Mabelle smiled—even Giselle had guessed she was with child.

Suddenly the room swirled around her. The smile left her face as intense pain sliced through her abdomen, bending her double in agony—no time to reach the chamber pot before vomiting. She gripped her shoulders and started to shake and sweat.

"Giselle, *aide-moi*. Something is wrong."

Giselle ran to the door of the chamber, calling loudly for help. *"Au secours! Au secours!"*

Soon both Morwenna and Rhonwen had been roused from the chamber they shared, and brought to assist. No one could find Myfanwy. They managed to get Mabelle off the floor, where she writhed in agony, into the bed. She lay doubled over, crying out as the debilitating pain wracked her slender body, and the vertigo held her in its thrall.

Giselle noticed the empty goblet on the tray. She seized it and inhaled, desperate to ascertain what her lady had drunk. She smelled myrrh and coriander. Morwenna told Giselle that Myfanwy had sent the potion. Rhonwen said nothing but kept bathing her lady's forehead with cold cloths.

"That Welsh witch has poisoned my lady!" Giselle cried. "Oh, my lady."

"No, it can't be true," Rhonwen burst out.

The three anxious women stayed with Mabelle through the long dark hours of her awful torment, replacing the spent candles as they burned down, and changing the soiled linens and Mabelle's shift each time she vomited.

"There's blood." It was the first time Rhonwen had spoken since her outburst concerning Myfanwy. She'd started to change the linens, and suddenly saw the pool between Mabelle's legs. "My Countess was with child?" she cried.

"God save us!" cried Giselle. "The witch has given her an abortifacient. She's losing the baby. Help her."

Rhonwen and Morwenna worked feverishly to try to stop the bleeding.

"I'll need to give her a draught, to help the pain and stop the bleeding. The child is lost," Rhonwen acknowledged sadly to Giselle.

The fearful maid's face was streaked with tears. "You may give it to her, but you'll drink of the potion yourself first."

Rhonwen prepared the potion and drank of it, without hesitation.

As the dawn broke, Mabelle settled into a deep sleep. Reassured by Rhonwen that the bleeding had stopped, Giselle went in search of Gervais. She told him to root out the Welsh healer from her hiding place, and throw her in the dungeon.

***

When Ram arrived home several hours later, Bonhomme awaited him, and he could tell by the expression on the man's face something was wrong. "My children?" he asked, as fear gripped him.

"*Non, monseigneur. Ta femme, la Comtesse—*"

Ram felt his legs buckle beneath him, and his heart raced. How could he face life without Mabelle? "Where is she? Is she—?"

"She's in your chamber, and the healers are with her. We're seeking the witch Myfanwy. She poisoned your wife."

He didn't later recall how he got to the chamber but was gasping for breath when he arrived. What he saw made his heart clench with anger. He would kill whoever had done this. The bile rose in his throat as he looked at the ravages the poison had wrought on the fair face of his beautiful wife. She looked like she'd been dragged to hell.

He didn't think he'd uttered that thought aloud, and yet a moment later, as if sensing his presence in the room, Mabelle opened her eyes and murmured in a barely audible voice, "Ram, I was at the gates of hell. I wanted to spit in the Devil's face, but my throat was too dry."

He rushed to the ewer, then helped her sip the life sustaining liquid Rhonwen had brought from the nearby holy well at Halliwell. The poison and the vomiting had left her throat raw. She could hardly speak. "Ram. Our baby. I've lost our baby."

"Baby?" he murmured, his fury intensifying. He clutched his wife's cold hands and brought them to his lips. The only sounds were Mabelle's sobs and his own heavy breathing as he struggled to control his emotions. He became dimly aware the two Welsh girls, looking exhausted, were standing in the far corner of the room. What struck him as odd, in that fleeting moment, was that tears were streaming down Rhonwen's face, but Morwenna stood stonily expressionless.

Giselle entered the room, and Ram ushered them out into the hallway. "I thank you for taking care of her, for saving her life. What happened here? Where is Myfanwy, and why are my men hunting her?"

Giselle recounted the story, and Morwenna confirmed it was Myfanwy who'd given her the draught and instructed her to take it to Mabelle. Wiping away tears with her sleeve, Rhonwen told Ram that Mabelle had miscarried a child, and she cautioned her mistress was still very ill.

"She might yet die?" His heart and his head were pounding.

Rhonwen averted her eyes. "The abortifacient she ingested was powerful, and it will take a long time for the poison to leave her body. We'll need to watch her carefully. Also, *Arglwydd* Montbryce— I hope you'll forgive me if I speak of these things, but sometimes when a woman loses a child—she loses the will to live, and my lady is already very weak."

Ram grimaced.

This could kill her.

"Get some sleep now. I'll watch her."

He returned to stand by his sleeping wife's bedside, dropped to his knees, rested his elbows on the bed and prayed, weeping for her terrible pain and his own.

***

The bloated body of Myfanwy Dda floated to the surface of a nearby lake two days later, her throat cut. Ram had left his wife's side only to visit with their children in the nursery, and to bring them to see their mother as she slowly grew stronger. When Gervais brought him the news of the discovery, he left Mabelle with Morwenna and went to discuss this latest development.

"Her confederate evidently didn't trust her to keep quiet," Gervais suggested.

"But why would she try to poison my wife, and kill our child? Though she was Welsh, she's lived in England peaceably for years. She had a position of honour and respect here as our healer. She's saved the lives of hundreds of our people. I had complete trust in her."

He returned to his wife's bedside and told her the sad news about Myfanwy. She shook her head. "I can't believe Myfanwy would do this. What would she gain? Who would she conspire with, and why would they kill her?"

"Did she know you were with child?"

"*Oui*, she'd guessed as much and we talked of it in the herb garden. She told me she would prepare something for me to take, so I didn't question when Morwenna brought me the potion."

"I do recall now that Morwenna brought it to you."

He turned to ask Morwenna where Myfanwy had been when she gave her the potion, but the girl had slipped out of the room, without his noticing.

Strange.

It was stranger still that Morwenna's hair was unbraided. Perhaps after a long and difficult two days, she'd not had time to braid it this morning. With his Norman sense of order, he had a vague feeling something wasn't right, and it didn't sit well with him.

"Morwenna doesn't seem herself," he remarked.

"You're right. I hardly recognised her with her hair down. And the poor child has not smiled much today. I'm getting the feeling that of the two of them, it's Rhonwen who'll prove in time to be the better healer, and I wouldn't have thought that before. While I lay in pain, I could feel Rhonwen's compassion as she tended to my needs. It was mystical. I didn't feel that from Morwenna. In fact, I felt malevolence emanating from her."

"I'll tell Gervais to have someone keep an eye on her."

It soon became apparent Morwenna had fled the castle. The alarm was raised and the town thoroughly searched, but she couldn't be found.

"Perhaps she was murdered too, for her part in the plot," Ram suggested.

"*Non*, my husband. I think Myfanwy was a victim of this crime. I sense it was Morwenna who poisoned me. What do we know of her? Until recently she still lived in Wales. Myfanwy knew only of her family. Perhaps we were blinded by the beautiful smile and braided golden hair."

"Ah," her husband replied with a wink, squeezing her leg. "It wouldn't be the first time that has happened to me."

As a familiar ache assailed her loins, Mabelle silently thanked God the poison hadn't destroyed her ability to feel passion for this handsome man she loved so dearly.

***

Myfanwy's death was declared to be murder by persons unknown, and she was buried with dignity and solemnity in hallowed ground. Mabelle grieved for the Welsh healer, and knew in her heart the woman hadn't been involved in the plot to kill her. Whoever was responsible remained at large, probably with Morwenna. Rhonwen seemed inconsolable over the death of the crotchety old woman. She was probably the closest thing to a mother the girl had ever had.

Attending the funeral exhausted Mabelle, and Rhonwen helped her back to bed. "I learned much from her, my lady," Rhonwen's voice was unsteady. "Who'll teach me now? Who'll protect me?"

It was an odd choice of words, but Mabelle replied, "You have great inner abilities to heal people Rhonwen, a natural touch, which will stand you in good stead, and never fear, we'll seek others to help us learn more. I'll protect you."

***

Ram suspected the Welsh barbarian, Rhodri, was involved in the plots against his family. He and his well trained trackers tried many times to follow his trail into the mountains but always returned empty handed. He couldn't understand these stubborn Welsh folk, with their strange Celtic beliefs, and their incomprehensible language. He grudgingly admitted they had difficult geography to deal with, and admired the way they used the impossible terrain to their advantage.

However, he had a personal desire to see Rhodri captured after the humiliating incident at Ruyton, and was determined to put a stop to his interference in the future prosperity of England, and William's plans to expand his control into Wales.

He assumed Rhodri had spies in his own castle. Perhaps Morwenna had been one? He didn't like to believe any of the educated Normans under his command would ally themselves with a barbaric Welshman.

CHAPTER TWENTY-EIGHT

In the late spring, Ram and Mabelle visited Normandie. He'd made the journey many times in the nine years since the invasion. The defence of the castle merited constant attention given the volatile political climate in Normandie. Ram's brothers were not far away in their own castles, but Ram had trained an elite garrison under the command of *Capitaine* Laurent Deschamps, a man with whom he had fought, a man he trusted. He was never disappointed in Laurent's preparations and felt Montbryce was secure.

This time Ram and Mabelle took their sons with them. Ram felt it was important they visit the castle at Saint Germain. They were the sons of a Norman *Comte,* and it was imperative they know their ancestral home. Despite the unseasonably fine weather, it took them a sennight to reach the coast, but the crossing was calm, and even Ram managed not to become seasick. Robert and Baudoin enjoyed the voyage and were excited to be going to Normandie.

As their cavalcade rode into the bailey of the home where he'd been born, Ram was hard pressed to hold back his emotion. This edifice held many memories and so much history. "How can I impart that to our children?" he shared with Mabelle. "I hope this will be the first of many visits for them. One day Robert will be the *Comte* here. Perhaps in time the Welsh problem will be solved, our King will no longer need my services in England, and we'll return to Normandie for good."

"*Oui*, Ram, I would like that too. While you're now wealthy and powerful, it has been costly."

Ram looked at her wistfully. "The way we Normans constantly insist on alienating people with our brutality, the less likely it seems there will ever be peace."

He took his children to show them the fields and orchards around the castle. Fernand Bonhomme, looking old and stooped, found a malleable horse so he could ride with Baudoin on his lap, Robert sitting behind him, holding on to his Papa, squealing with delight. Everyone was happy to see their liege lord returned, and commented on the handsomeness of his children. It was the first time they'd ever spent time as a family, with no external pressures on them.

"This is a place of intense memories for me," Mabelle confided to her husband. "I recall the dark handsome knight, conjured from the lake, who became my husband, a man who has brought me the most exquisite pleasures." The smile left her face. "But there are more difficult memories of my father and yours. I grieved alone for him here. And you can tell Bonhomme has never recovered fully from Vangeline's death."

He noticed she made no mention of the wedding day incident, so he decided not to either.

"*Oui*, his son, Honoré, does most of the work now."

They took the boys to the crypt, explaining the tombs and their grandparents. It was evident the shivering lads were uncomfortable, as they stared up at the long shadows cast by the flickering candles on the vaulted ceiling.

Mabelle picked bluebells with the children while Ram watched, and they exchanged smiles at the memory. The blue flowers held no interest for the boys, who preferred to run through the fields, laughing and shouting. They took them swimming in their special lake, and Ram knew his eyes betrayed his need as they looked at each other close by the place he'd first found her. The bittersweet memory washed over him like a rushing river. Trying to break the tension, Ram remarked casually to his sons, "*Maman* once threw Papa's sword into this lake."

"Why *Maman*?" Robert asked curiously. "You must have been very angry with him."

"Oh, *oui, mon fils*, I was angry." she replied, grinning at her smiling husband.

"It's a good thing you didn't stay angry at him, *Maman*," Robert said innocently.

Their contentment at being back in the land of their birth carried over into their bed chamber, and they made sweet love every night, as their bodies joined with flow and grace. Ram loved fondling and caressing Mabelle's breasts, and now, after the birth of two children, they were fuller and more sensitive and he suckled them, knowing she would be enthralled in her need for him. He loved the way her responsive bud swelled under the tender touch of his fingers, and never tired of feeling the inner texture of her. He loved to hear her call out his name in the throes of passion and wondered if she did indeed love him. She'd never told him she did.

"Would you like to go for a picnic in the meadow?" he asked innocently one day. "You could pick bluebells. Fernand can look to the children for a while."

Mabelle eyed him curiously, and he struggled to keep his feigned composure.

"It *is* a beautiful day," she agreed. "And I do love bluebells. I'll get *La Cuisinière* to prepare a hamper."

She scurried off to the kitchens, leaving him to wonder if she'd guessed his plan, to get her to the enchanted pool. He wanted to try to erase any bitter memories they both may be harbouring. Why did he care? Did he need her to love him? Were the physical pleasures not enough?

When she came into the Great Hall, carrying the picnic basket and a blanket, he was pleased she'd changed into a simple chemise and belted sage green overdress. She was barefoot.

"Will you be taking your sword to the meadow, *milord Comte?*"

He laughed. "I think not, saucy wench." He took the hamper and blanket, and they strolled out of the castle together, their bodyguards following at a discreet distance. He ordered the men-at-arms to stop outside the walls. They would keep watch from where he stationed them, and felt it was safe enough.

When they reached the meadow, he spread the blanket on the ground, and lay on his side, his head resting on one hand. He felt comfortable in his linen shirt and loose fitting knee breeches, especially once he took off his boots.

His gaze followed Mabelle while she picked the blue flowers, humming as she gathered them to her breast.

She was doing this the morning I found her.

He watched her, and recognized he cared too much for this woman. He suspected Mabelle would never forgive him completely for his accusations and suspicions, though he intended to try to erase that memory today. But could he let go of his pride, his need to control? He came lazily to his feet, wandered over and took hold of her hand as she bent to pick another flower. The grass felt good beneath his bare feet.

"Would you like to take a swim, *milady*?" he drawled seductively.

Her grasp on the bluebells tightened, but as he kissed her, the flowers fell to the ground. "Gather them up and bring them to the lake."

He led her to the water's edge, out of sight of their bodyguards, took the flowers, then undressed her, brushing his hands against her breasts as he lifted the clothing from her body. He smiled at her naked beauty, disrobing quickly. As he led her into the shallow water, she reached out tentatively and grasped his erection in her long fingers. Even the cold water couldn't dampen his arousal as she slowly moved her hand on his phallus.

"I'm not a good swimmer, Ram," she teased. "I need to hold on to something."

He took her hand from his throbbing manhood and lifted her. "You have other talents and skills which are far more important. I fear I may release too soon if you continue that," he teased.

She entwined her legs around his waist, locking her ankles behind him. He walked over to the shallows, where a smooth moss covered rock met the water's edge. The friction of her wet female cleft against his shaft sent ripples of sensation up his spine. Leaning her back against the rock, he feathered kisses on her throat, neck and nipples.

She groaned with pleasure and swirled her tongue around the rim of his ear. "The moss feels like velvet against my back," she crooned.

"Mabelle," he rasped. "I have to come now."

He thrust inside and her sheath clenched him tightly in response. Her legs gripped his torso, trying to draw him deeper as he pressed her body against the rock. She clung to him, keening her pleasure and her breasts rubbed against his chest.

In his passionate haze, he caught a glimpse of speckled trout flashing by in the knee-deep water. He curled his toes into the mud. She raked his scalp with her long fingers, and cried out *'Ram!'* as his seed erupted into her and a powerful spasm tore through her body.

She lowered her head to his shoulder and her hair enfolded them like a golden cloak. Staying inside her as long as he could, he carefully made his way to the deeper water, eased on to his back and floated for a while, with her on top of him, moving them effortlessly through the water with one arm, both of them completely relaxed.

"You're as light as a feather," he murmured into her ear.

She's purring.

He guided them back to the shallows and carried her to the grass, where he laid her down and spread out her hair. With great care, he took the bluebells and laid them reverently on her body. He posed her legs as he remembered them from that bittersweet day, as awestruck by the sight as he'd been then.

"On the day of our intended wedding," he managed to say hoarsely, "I thought you were a vision. Your beauty struck me senseless, and you're more breathtaking today. What happened that day embittered us both, but if you'll allow me to continue to pleasure you today, *milady*, we can perhaps atone for our mistakes? I hope whatever you were dreaming of that day will come true for you."

"It has already come true, Ram. I was dreaming of being kissed by you, my handsome husband."

Antoine was right. I'm an idiot.

***

The day they were to leave, she awoke shortly after dawn, dressed and went down to break her fast. Ram had risen before her, and she couldn't find him anywhere. She decided to make a last private visit to the crypt, and a strangled cry escaped her as she entered the shadowy chamber. Ram knelt before the tombs of his parents, and a tiny posy of bluebells lay atop each. She sank to her knees beside him and took his hand, and they clung together.

"Swear to me, Mabelle, that if I die in England, you'll return here with my body, so that I may be laid to rest with my parents. It's in Normandie I belong."

"I so swear," she whispered, stricken by the notion of life without him.

CHAPTER TWENTY-NINE

I t was because of Ram's well tried and proven methods of governance that the towns and villages around Ellesmere grew and prospered. September brought with it the affirmation of another child firmly planted in Mabelle's belly. Both she and Ram were thankful the abortifacient seemed to have done no permanent damage. It had been a year since she'd been poisoned. The resilience of her body surprised her, considering the difficult life she'd led before she met Ram.

The long summer had been particularly hot, relieved only by gentle rainfall in the early evenings. She often felt uncomfortable and was nauseous every morning. But the weather produced a bumper harvest and there was much celebrating at the Autumn Fayres held in the towns and villages. No one would starve this winter.

Rhonwen continued to show great promise as a healer, but they heard tell of another renowned healer in the village of Whittington, which hadn't yet held its Fayre. Mabelle received Ram's permission to take Rhonwen with her to the Whittington Fayre so they could seek out the healer. The young woman was gleeful at the prospect.

"Perhaps we'll convince her to return with us to Ellesmere, my lady?" she enthused.

"Perhaps we will. But if not, we'll try, over the course of the few days we remain there, to learn as much from her as we can about the things we don't yet understand."

As planning for the excursion progressed, it occurred to Mabelle how wonderful it would be for her sons to accompany them to Whittington. "They enjoyed the fayre at Ellesmere," she argued, when Ram was less than enthusiastic. "They have few chances to be little boys. Please let me take them. Giselle can accompany us and keep them busy while we're with the healer."

Ram relented, insisting they be protected by a company of ten men-at-arms as their escort, but he was uneasy he couldn't go with his family. He wasn't interested in what they would be discussing with the healer but might enjoy the fayre with his wife and children. "We have too few opportunities to be together and enjoy life, as we did during our visit to Normandie."

"Don't be concerned, Ram," she laughed. "Your men will take good care of us. We'll be surrounded by people at the fayre and it will be perfectly safe. The Welsh won't encroach as close as Whittington. In any case, the beginning of October is too late in the season for them to leave their mountains."

Ram put his hands on her waist and leaned his forehead against hers. "You're right, but I still don't like the idea of my pregnant wife and my children leaving without me."

***

As soon as Mabelle met Caryl Penarth she thought the woman embodied the meaning of her name, which Rhonwen explained was the Welsh for *love*. Caryl would share her knowledge of the healing arts with the two women and agreed to consider coming to Ellesmere, at least for a few months, to instruct the local women, as well as Rhonwen.

When they weren't with Caryl, they enjoyed the minstrels, theatre, jugglers, magicians, and human chess games. They laughed at the bright costumes of folk dressed as such varied characters as King Arthur, mermaids, and the fayre's king and queen. Mabelle hadn't seen her sons laugh as much since Normandie. They tended to be serious little boys.

Everyone enjoyed the fruits of the bountiful harvest, and the ale and wine flowed freely. The women and children were never without their armed escort, and Mabelle enjoyed herself immensely. After three days they mounted their horses for the slow ride back to Ellesmere. Caryl promised to come to the castle in a sennight.

They'd travelled only a short distance and were entering a copse. Rhonwen commented on the beauty of the autumn leaves. Without warning, masked men, clad in sheepskins and leather breeches, dropped like stones from the trees. The Norman soldiers were rendered harmless before they knew what had happened. Mabelle could do nothing. The furtive attackers seized the reins of their horses and led them deeper into the copse.

Mabelle lost sight of Robert. "*Maman, Maman,*" her son shouted

"I'm safe, *mon fils*, don't worry. I'm here. Look to your brother," she shouted in reply, trying to sound braver than she felt.

None of the men made any move to harm them, and she considered that a good sign. It didn't seem they would be murdered immediately at least.

Other brigands were concealed deep in the copse, with horses at the ready. The attackers mounted. One took Robert on his lap and another took Baudoin. Stealthily, the caravan made its way deeper into the woods. The men spoke to each other in a language foreign to her, but the terrified Rhonwen could understand them and she surmised it was Welsh.

Neither of her sons had cried since they were taken, but she constantly called words of reassurance to them, hoping her voice didn't betray her fear. "Don't be afraid, *mes enfants*, I'm here, as are Giselle and Rhonwen. We'll be safe. Don't worry."

It broke her heart to remember her children's joy at riding on their father's lap.

They rode at a steady pace for about an hour. Mabelle was relieved they hadn't travelled at a gallop. Perhaps the child she carried might survive this ordeal—if she did. She had a sense they were travelling west, probably into Wales. When she saw the village of Oswestry in the distance to her left, her suspicions were confirmed. Trying to occupy her mind and divert it from the sheer terror threatening to engulf her, she wondered how the bandits had known the Montbryce family would be at Whittington. This hadn't been a random act. She and her family had been targeted. The traitor within was still at work.

Other than comforting words spoken to the children, the three women said nothing, exchanging only glances whenever the roadway caused their horses to be close to each other. A bandit led each of their horses and they had no chance to control their own mounts. There was no possibility of escape.

Though there was no marker, Mabelle could tell an hour later that they'd crossed into Wales when they reached the village of Rhydycroesau. Their captors became more relaxed and the tension eased. The scowling faces of the villagers told Mabelle all hope was lost. No one had pursued them. There would be no rescue. Ram would never see his family again. She prayed her husband would discover the identity of the traitor and cut out his heart.

After another hour in the saddle, Mabelle's body ached. She asked their captors several times if they might be allowed to dismount for a few moments for the sake of the children, but was ignored. Did the men speak her language? They came to a village and on the western edge reined in the horses at a cottage.

"You'll sleep here tonight," one of the bearded men said gruffly in Norman French, holding out his burly arms to help her dismount.

She didn't want to accept his aid, but would have fallen flat on her face if she didn't. When her numbed feet hit the ground her legs wouldn't sustain her, and she had to lean on the horse. The man didn't take his hand from her elbow as she waited for the feeling to return to her legs.

When he grew impatient, Rhonwen spoke to him in Welsh. She assumed the girl had told him Mabelle was pregnant. He seemed surprised and allowed her more time to regain her equilibrium.

Once they were inside, the man bolted the door of the cottage, imprisoning his captives, and her sons ran quickly to their mother. Neither boy had cried throughout the ordeal and she told them how proud she was of their courage.

Baudoin struggled to control his fear. "Will Papa come to rescue us, *Maman?*"

"I'm sure Papa will do everything he can to rescue us, *mon petit.*" From the looks in the eyes of Giselle and Rhonwen, they didn't share her optimism.

Bread and cheese and ale had been provided for them. The cottage was cramped but clean. It afforded them a chance to sleep indoors and take care of their personal needs. Giselle did her best, with the limited means at her disposal, to tend her lady. Rhonwen massaged Mabelle's back and applied to her feet a salve Caryl had given her, which she'd packed in her saddle bags. Mabelle hadn't started to bleed and prayed the child within her still lived.

Mabelle slept fitfully on a pallet, which, to her surprise, was furnished with clean linens, and her sons cuddled into her. Giselle and Rhonwen clung to each other on the second pallet.

At dawn the following day, a loud banging on the door of the cottage signalled departure. Andras, the leader of the captors, opened the door and brought in bread and honey for them to break their fast. Fear made her choke on the food, but she was determined to eat, to keep up her strength. She encouraged the children to eat.

"Rhonwen, do you know where we are?"

"My lady, I think this village is Llansilin. I believe they're taking us to the mountains."

Fear crept up Mabelle's spine. Their suspicions were confirmed when they left the cottage. Their horses had been replaced by sure-footed Welsh mountain ponies. She smiled when Robert seemed to forget the terrible trouble they were in and exclaimed with excitement, "Look, *Maman*. Ponies."

***

"Trussed up?" Ram shouted. "Ten of my finest men-at-arms? Knocked out and trussed up like piglets for the spit? How can this be?"

He raked his fingers through his hair, scratching his head, completely distraught over the desperate news from Whittington.

"My lord Earl, it appears they were ambushed," Gervais replied.

Ram snorted. "Of course they were ambushed. They're Norman soldiers, supposedly prepared for ambush."

Gervais hesitated. "Perhaps they'd enjoyed the delights of the fayre a little too much, *milord*—the ale—"

Ram stared coldly at his Second. His voice dripped ice as he replied, "Then I'll execute them myself. I entrusted my family to them and they failed me."

Gervais remained silent.

"You believe they're already dead, don't you?"

Again Gervais kept silent. The minutes dragged as Ram paced.

"Summon my commanders to the map room. We'll pursue them."

Gervais threw up his hands. "But, *milord*, we don't know where they've gone."

"They've gone into Wales!" Ram continued to shout, knowing only too well who'd taken his family.

"But, *milord*, winter comes early to the mountains of Wales. We could easily lose our way and become trapped. The local people won't help us—"

"I told you to summon my commanders. We'll follow them into Wales."

Gervais' shoulders sagged. "*Oui*, milord."

***

At least with the ponies the women were able to ride astride and hold the reins themselves. However, the track had become a narrow twisting path. They rode single file, with some of the men in the lead and the others behind them. Flight was impossible.

Robert and Baudoin were now on a first name basis with the ponies they shared with their captors, and Mabelle was grateful they were distracted from their fear.

The path rose steadily for the next three hours. The scenery became wilder, the terrain more rugged. When they entered a remote village and the men began calling out to each other, confirming the direction to take, Mabelle looked to Rhonwen who told her they were in Llanrhaeadr-ym-Mochnant. She didn't know why she asked. She would never remember these tortuous names, and what did it matter anyway? Who could she tell?

***

"In your best estimate, Gervais, where do you think they've been taken?" Ram asked impatiently as he and his commanders pored over the latest charts they had of the area, not knowing if they were accurate or not.

"They may have taken the route through Oswestry, and crossed the border at Rhydycroesau. After that, it's more difficult to say. If Rhodri is behind this, we don't know where his camp is. They may have gone north west to Llanarmon, or south west to Llansilin. Or he may have taken them to Powwydd Castle."

Ram followed his Second's finger as he traced the routes on the charts. "Rhodri is behind this. Of that I have no doubt. But what does he plan next?"

Phillippe de Giroux stepped forward. "*Milord*, if he planned to murder them, why have we found no bodies? Why take them into Wales? Perhaps he has ransom in mind?".

Gervais spoke again, looking directly at Ram. "*Milord*, I'm as anxious as you are to rescue my Countess and your family, but you must see it's futile to ride into Wales. We could search for sennights and not find them. You know yourself how difficult the terrain is, not to mention the weather that will soon turn against us, if it hasn't already."

Ram understood Gervais was right, but his heart was broken. He dismissed the other men with a curt, "Leave us."

He slumped into a chair. "You're correct, Gervais, but I can't sit and do nothing."

"You have no choice, *milord*. But it may not be long before they send a message. I think Giroux is right and they'll demand ransom.

179

However, they too know winter is setting in and won't want to wait until spring."

***

It was getting colder. They'd left Llanrhaeadr far behind at least an hour before, and were still climbing. The Normans had dressed for the warm autumn weather in Whittington and the children were shivering. The brigands had provided blankets at the cottage, but Mabelle's fingers and toes were freezing, and she could tell Giselle and Rhonwen were suffering the same problem as they blew on their hands and rubbed them together, trying all the while to keep the ponies on the narrow track.

She became aware of the sound of rushing water. Judging by the roar, it must be a high waterfall. Suddenly they came upon a cascade which fell two hundred and fifty feet through a stunning arched rock formation. The raging torrent was thunderous. Some of the water had already started to form into ice crystals at the edges. The men called a halt as everyone gazed at this natural wonder. One of them took the opportunity to give each captive another hand woven *brychan*.

"Pistyll-Rhaeadr," Rhonwen yelled to her fellow captives. "I've heard of it many times. It's the most beautiful waterfall in all Wales."

They headed into the woods. This path led into a wide valley. After a few hundred feet they were down in the valley floor, and then they turned onto a track going in the opposite direction up the hill on the other side.

They made their way up the opposite side, then onto a trail which wound up from the valley floor. Once the tortuous path reached the head of the valley, the men turned in their saddles to view the incredible scenery behind them. Mabelle followed their gaze and it took her breath away.

Even barbarians appreciate a beautiful view. I'm beginning to understand why the Welsh are passionate for their wild land.

The path then crossed and followed a stream, and soon they came across a sight which made the first stunning vista they'd seen pale in comparison. There was a lake far below them in a deep crater, backed by craggy mountains and ridges. Mabelle hoped the faraway vista wasn't where they were going. She'd never seen a lake of the same colour as the one below them, as blue as the *bleu de France* favoured by the heralds of the French king.

The leader signalled another halt, and the captives were allowed to dismount. They sat together on rocks in a clearing. One of the men gave them bread and cheese to eat and ale to drink.

"Ask them where they're taking us, Rhonwen," Mabelle urged, though she was hesitant to put the girl in danger.

Rhonwen got only a grunt and a disdainful look in reply.

The climb for the next two hours was strenuous. They came to the top of a crag and had to hug the side of the mountain. It was the strong hind legs of the ponies that saw them through. The path was wet and slippery. If they fell, they would fall to their deaths.

Once they'd crested the crag, they headed along a wide ridge path. They reached a rocky knoll and Mabelle was astounded to see a wooden fortress loom out of the mist, built into the side of the mountain. Some of the roofs of the buildings seemed to be covered with turf, others with what looked like slate. Though she couldn't see the rear of the fortification, she was sure it was perched on the edge of a deep ravine. Any army wanting to attack would have to send its soldiers in one at a time. It was impregnable. This was probably the reason for the evident lack of armed men on the high balustrades. They'd reached their destination and her heart plummeted. She surveyed the magnificent scenery of high mountains on every side.

It's a beautiful place to die.

CHAPTER THIRTY

Darkness fell as the captives were led through the gates of the forbidding fortress. The towering palisades, made of stout trees lashed together, were as tall as two men. Once inside, they were led to a chamber. Andras quickly lit several candles, and Mabelle could gradually see the room was clean but spartan.

"We're expected," she whispered sarcastically to Giselle.

Five palettes piled high with sheepskins and furs had been installed at one side of the room, and a chamber pot placed discreetly behind a screen, along with a basin and ewer full of water and drying cloths. An empty wooden bathtub stood propped against the wall. A roughly hewn table and six stools completed the furnishings. The comparative warmth of the room led her to believe none of the walls was an outer one. They were completely within the fortress.

"My children are hungry, Andras," she began, but he didn't reply. She heard the heavy door being bolted after he left. She glanced at her children and then at Giselle and Rhonwen. The women understood—they would have to be careful what they said in front of the boys. It was a relief none of them had been raped. They had been treated relatively well by their captors. With the natural curiosity of children, her sons began exploring their new surroundings, and the women sat down to wait.

They didn't have to wait long. Andras reappeared and ushered them to follow. He led them along a dimly lit corridor, outside across a rocky pathway, then into a great hall, full of light from scores of torches. Mabelle blinked rapidly. It was difficult to believe such a place could exist so high in these bleak mountains. It must have taken considerable skill and perseverance to build.

The high vaulted ceiling was supported by huge wooden crossbeams from which hung banners she didn't recognize, wafting gently on the currents of air. The walls were decorated with a motley collection of shields, weapons, furs and antlers. The air was hazy with smoke and heavy with the aroma of roasted game. At least a hundred dark-haired, swarthy men, bristling with daggers, lined the walls, standing erect, dressed in sheepskin jerkins, leather breeches and boots. It was the devil's army.

At the front, on a dais, sat the only furniture—two massive wooden chairs—one slightly smaller than the other. Andras urged the Normans forward, until they were standing directly in front of the chairs.

A large, muscular man lounged in the bigger chair, his long fingers caressing the intricately carved dragons on the arms of his chair. He wore breeches and boots but no shirt, and a sleeveless sheepskin jerkin open in the front. His face bore the trace of a smile. A blonde woman sat on the edge of the other chair, looking malevolently pleased.

A gasp escaped Giselle. "Morwenna," she whispered to her mistress.

Mabelle couldn't at first recognize the girl. Her once tightly braided hair now flowed in a wild tangle down to her waist, softened only by two braids on either side of her face. The end of each braid was adorned with brightly coloured beads, and she wore a narrow leather thong around her forehead. She too was clad in leather breeches and boots, and a sheepskin jerkin. The smile Mabelle had been used to seeing was now replaced by a look of malice and triumph. She made a move to rise and speak, but the big man stopped her with a barely perceptible movement of his hand.

Mabelle knew without being told this man was Rhodri ap Owain. He'd been a constant thorn in the side of the Marcher lords for a long time. Even before the Conquest, his frequent sorties into the border counties of England from his stronghold in the Welsh mountains, left a trail of fear and destruction in their wake. It was said he hated Saxon and Norman equally and burned with Celtic fervour for a Wales free of their domination.

She contemplated him nervously now—at more than six feet he was a towering figure, with curly black hair which hung down his back, flowing freely, except for two tight braids at either side of his face, each bound at the end with amber beads. He looked in need of a shave, but she suspected that was always the case.

He embodied primitive masculinity and vitality, with eyes like green jade and the tanned, weathered skin of a man who lived his life in the open air. Around each of his muscular biceps, a narrow band of Celtic knots had been etched into his skin.

He was intimidating to behold, and Ram had told her the mere mention of his name struck fear into the hearts of those living on the English side of the Welsh border. To them he was a feral force. To his own people he was a folk hero of mythical proportions. Though few had ever met him, all knew of his deeds, and the Marcher lords could get no information from the Welsh villagers to help them find him.

Rhodri stood. "Lady Countess of Ellesmere, I bid you welcome, and I apologise for your difficult journey. I wasn't aware you're with child. Permit me to introduce myself. I am Rhodri ap Owain ap Dafydd ap Gwilym, Prince of Powwydd."

He bowed slightly.

Whatever Mabelle had expected from a Welsh rebel chieftain, this man, this wasn't it. He spoke courteously, despite his primitive garb. A memory of her father rattling off his long list of lands and properties flitted into her head, but she'd learned enough about Welsh naming traditions to recognize this man's pride was in his ancestry, not his lands. She was also well aware this was the man her husband thirsted to kill after their encounter at Ruyton.

"Lord Rhodri—" she stammered, trying not to let her fear enter her voice. She returned the bow, but not too deeply. Courtliness aside, this man held their lives in his hands.

"My lord, my children and my serving women are in need of food and clean clothing. And—I am in need—of an explanation—as to why we have been—?"

He silenced her with the same slight movement he'd used with Morwenna. "Forgive me, Countess, I haven't yet finished my introductions. I believe you're acquainted with my betrothed, Morwenna verch Morgan ap Talfryn?"

Mabelle looked straight at the girl and felt Rhonwen tense beside her. "Yes. Morwenna, murderess of my unborn child and of Myfanwy Dda."

Morwenna protested. "It wasn't I who murdered that foolish old woman—"

Again Rhodri silenced her with a look, and she sank back into her chair, scowling.

Mabelle now knew for certain there was a traitor in Ellesmere Castle.

"As to why you're here, Countess, it must be obvious by now we intend to ransom you to your husband. He and I have met before, you know."

Mabelle's knees went weak with relief. But was he referring only to her when he spoke of ransom? Seeking protection for her children and her companions she asked, "Do I have your assurances then, Lord Rhodri, that my children and my serving women won't be harmed while we're here? Your men have already killed my escort at Whittington."

Rhodri strode quickly from the dais and reached the captives in a trice, his hand on the hilt of the large dagger tucked in his belt. Before the exhausted Mabelle could react, Rhonwen moved to protect the boys, and stood defiantly between them and the aggressor. Rhodri seemed to be taken aback for a moment as he glared at the girl, apparently noticing her for the first time. It was a few moments before he turned back to Mabelle.

"Not a single one of the soldiers in your escort was killed when you were taken. I give you my word, as Commander of Cadair Berwyn and Prince of Powwydd, that no harm shall come to any of you as long as you're in my care. Unless, of course, you try to escape."

He laughed and winked at Mabelle.

Suddenly he turned back to Rhonwen, and speaking to her in Welsh, asked her name. She replied in Welsh, "I am Rhonwen, a healer, daughter of Myfanwy Dda."

Had Rhonwen uttered Myfanwy's name? Mabelle wasn't sure, since Welsh was an unintelligible language to her. She assumed Rhonwen had told of being a protégé of Myfanwy's. Rhodri looked at Rhonwen with surprise for a few seconds, but the healer didn't turn away from his insistent gaze.

***

Fear chilled Rhonwen's spine but strangely, it wasn't him she feared. This man's aura of primitive power drew her and brought on conflicting feelings. As a healer, she recognised and admired a strong, healthy body when she saw one. The mystical side of her, passed down through generations of Dda's, drew her to him. She sensed an affinity that transcended the physical and it alarmed her.

She wanted to reach up and touch his dark face, fondle his braids, run her hands over his tattooed biceps, feel the controlled strength that radiated from him. His deep, sonorous voice evoked the memory of the rich, melodious Welsh folksongs they'd enjoyed at the fayre in Whittington.

Her thoughts made her blush. How childish to expect a Celtic prince to welcome the attentions of a lowly woman such as her. She determined to quell her feelings, knowing with dire certainty she would avenge her mother's death by killing Morwenna, his betrothed. It was a harsh knowledge for a woman who'd dedicated her life to healing, to saving others.

***

Rhodri returned to his chair. Morwenna glared at Rhonwen. She hadn't failed to notice the brief exchange that had taken place between Rhodri and the healer. She smiled at him, but her thoughts were black.

You look at her while you're betrothed to me. A curse on you! I have another who'll give me much more than this windblown fortress.

"I want to kill the healer," she told Rhodri after the captives had been escorted back to their chamber, and food ordered for them.

He looked directly into her eyes, his voice cold. "You'll not kill any of them, Morwenna. I've sworn an oath they'll be protected here. They're worth nothing to us dead. We need the coin their ransom will bring. It will allow us to buy the things we desperately need to continue our struggle. Our people have to be fed, clothed and armed. Many in the villages will starve without this ransom money."

He turned to Andras. "We don't have much time. I'll write the ransom. Prepare four men to ride to Ellesmere. We must act before the weather turns against us. The Countess is expecting a child, which I wasn't aware of. We don't want the babe born here, then he'd be a Welshman! When is our loyal friend from Ellesmere expected to arrive?" he asked with a hint of sarcasm.

"On the morrow, Lord Rhodri."

Morwenna's blue eyes lit up.

CHAPTER THIRTY-ONE

Phillippe de Giroux arrived at the isolated fortress of Cadair Berwyn exhausted and frustrated. He'd lost his way twice. Despite his peasant garb, he'd been unable to ask for help because he didn't speak Welsh, and was afraid his manner of speech would jeopardise him. Once he found the right trail, his pony almost lost its footing on the high path.

"Curse this wild country, and curse these ignorant Welshmen with their fanatical obsession of defeating the Normans," he muttered as he stabled the pony and went in search of Rhodri. "They'll find out to their regret we can't be defeated, but till then, I'll use them to my purposes."

He found Rhodri in the great hall, now filled with tables and benches. People were gathered for a meal. The air was redolent with the aroma of venison. He helped himself to a chunk of it from the large trestle table at the side of the room, hacked off a large piece of coarse black bread and poured a goblet of ale.

Rhodri came down from the dais where he and Morwenna were sitting, and joined the treacherous Norman who'd helped him secure the prize. Rhodri detested spies who betrayed their own countrymen but tried not to show his contempt.

Giroux glanced in Morwenna's direction and asked, "All went well?"

"*Ydi*, yes. Very well. I thank you for your help."

"Has the ransom been sent?"

"*Ddoe*," Rhodri automatically replied in Welsh. He saw how irritated Giroux was he'd spoken to him in Welsh. "Yesterday, *hier*," he added. Giroux had betrayed Montbryce for his own reasons, not for the freedom of Wales, and he wondered what had caused the anger that drove a man to seek revenge at such a high risk.

"I didn't see your men on the trail," Giroux began, and then quickly changed the subject. Rhodri would know he'd become lost if he continued. "The weather is already bad in the passes. I hope they get through."

"They're Welsh, they'll get through."

***

Rhodri was mistaken. The blinding snowstorm howled out of the frigid peaks and caught the messengers unawares. Though autumn blizzards weren't unheard of in these mountains, the sudden ferocity of this one forced them to seek shelter in a shepherd's hut.

The snow stopped after two days, but they had to wait another sennight before the weak autumn sun melted it sufficiently to make the track safe enough for travel. They'd used up their supplies. If they got to Ellesmere, it was unlikely there would be time to return to Cadair Berwyn with the reply to the ransom demand they carried. If they were able to leave Ellesmere alive, they would have to winter in the foothills, and return to the mountains in the spring.

***

"*Capitaine* Gervais?"

The Earl's Second in Command looked up from his task in the Map Room to see one of their most trusted commanders. The man was obviously exhausted, and Gervais knew why. He braced himself. "What is it, Brémonde?"

The commander shifted his weight, evidently unsure how to begin. "*Mon Capitaine*, I'm a loyal servant of the Earl. I came with him from Normandie. I grew up at Montbryce. I would never question anything he does."

Gervais waited.

"But—the men—well—we're exhausted. We're warriors, used to working hard, to rigorous training. But *milord* Earl is pushing us beyond our limits."

Gervais had expected this conversation. "But he pushes himself equally hard."

"It's true. He does, and we know he's grieving. We all want the safe return of our beloved *Comtesse*."

"It's difficult for him. He blames himself. He cannot seem to break free of a deeper and deeper melancholia. He's lost interest in the affairs of the manors in Sussex. I have to admit, I'm at a loss."

They stood in uncomfortable silence. Gervais was on the point of dismissing the man when they were disturbed by another soldier, who knocked on the open door and entered.

"Forgive the interruption, *mon capitaine*, but you need to know. There are four Welshman at the gates. They say they have a message about our *Comtesse*."

Gervais ran to the hall, where Ram sat slouched in a chair by the hearth, gazing into the charcoal embers.

"*Milord*, there are messengers from the barbarian Rhodri."

Roused from his constant berating of himself for not adequately protecting his family and household, Ram leapt to his feet and instructed his commander to lead him to the Welshmen.

"They're in the cells. Preparations are being made for their torture."

"Take me to them."

Ram could see the four prisoners had undergone a difficult journey. They were dirty, and battered, their beards unkempt. Yet there was dignity in their bearing. He could sense when a man was afraid, and these men showed no sign of fear as he strode into their dank cell. He wondered how long they'd been on the road to his castle with the message.

Their leader didn't wait to be spoken to. "Earl of Ellesmere, *Comte* de Montbryce?"

His enemy was an educated man, a warrior. "I am he. Who are you and what is your message?"

"I'm Aneurin ap Norweg," he replied, withdrawing a small metal tube from inside his sheepskin jerkin. He handed it to Ram. "I have a message for you from Lord Rhodri ap Owain, Prince of Powwydd."

Ram snatched the tube, willing his hands not to shake in front of these enemies. He pulled out the parchment coiled tightly inside. It was damp, but the message still legible.

To Rambaud de Montbryce, Earl of Ellesmere
Herein my requirements for the release of your wife, children and household servants.
Two thousand pounds in Fleury pennies to be brought back to Wales by the messengers.
If they are killed, and no ransom paid, you will not see your family again. I guarantee the safe return of the captives upon payment.
Rhodri ap Owain, Prince of Powwydd.

Ram's gut tightened. It was impossible. He shook his head. "I can't comply with these demands. This sum is the equivalent of a year's income from all my properties. For all I know they're already dead."

He could barely speak the words, and yet, in the depths of his despair, he'd never sensed his beloved wife and children were dead. He thrust the document back at the Welshman.

Aneurin refused to take it. "My Lord Rhodri is a man of honour. He has sworn an oath that none in your family or household will be harmed, if the ransom is paid."

Ram smirked. "Your Lord must have a different code of honour from ours if he thinks kidnapping women and children is honourable."

He spat out the words, though he knew some Norman knights thought such misdeeds acceptable in time of war. Aneurin remained silent. This *was* war and they were both warriors.

Ram stood looking at the Welshmen for long minutes. "We're both aware of the atrocities men are capable of. However, I will not send you off with a chest full of coin. You wouldn't make it back before winter. I assume you've taken them deep into the mountains. My family wouldn't be able to travel out in the winter. Why have you come so late?"

Aneurin reluctantly agreed, explaining the delay of the blizzard. "We'll take whatever message you send back to the foothills, and wait until the spring to return to the mountains."

Ram wanted to shout that his cherished wife was pregnant, that he feared for her life if she gave birth in the wilds of the Welsh mountains, but his fear made him swallow the words.

"But Rhodri will believe you've been killed," Gervais interjected.

"He may think that, but won't act upon his suspicions until our deaths are confirmed."

These men held their leader in high regard. "I could order you be tortured until you reveal where Rhodri is holding my family." It was an empty threat. Such toughened men wouldn't succumb to torture.

"I'll save you the trouble and tell you they are in the fortress of Cadair Berwyn. If you could find it and arrive there alive, it would profit you nothing."

A flicker of hope blossomed in Ram's heart. Aneurin spoke as though he truly believed they were alive and safe in Cadair Berwyn. He paced in the dark cell, trying to ignore the bile rising at the back of his throat, brought on by the stench in this squalid place and his own fear.

He gave a curt order. "Gervais, escort these men to a chamber in the North Tower. Provide them with pallets and a bath, and food. Bolt the door."

He left the cells before Gervais could protest.

CHAPTER THIRTY-TWO

"Aneurin has not returned, Rhodri. It's been a month since they left. The Earl has murdered him and his men. We must kill the hostages."

Morwenna and Rhodri were eating the evening meal in the great hall. The Earl of Ellesmere's family and servants had been given leave to eat their meals in the hall, and Mabelle had been grateful. "Thank you, Lord Rhodri. It will give the boys a chance to mix with the other children in the fortress, and ease their boredom. It's amazing that children can ignore the circumstances that have brought them together, and treat each other with friendliness."

She and the other two women ate at a separate table from the others, however, and as her pregnancy became more evident, she seemed to appreciate this bit of decorum and privacy.

Morwenna had badgered Rhodri with her demand for their deaths every day for a sennight. He too worried about the messengers, but why did the woman have such a blood lust? It wasn't clear to him how he'd become involved with her. How had their betrothal come about? He supposed when her father had proposed the union, he'd been smitten with her beauty, but now he saw how hatred distorted her lovely face. Even her ample breasts did nothing to rouse his lust. She sickened him. He also suspected, if they married, she wouldn't come virgin to his bed.

And now I'm smitten with another.

He understood passion. He was as passionate as anyone for his beloved country but had no personal hatred for the Earl of Ellesmere, whom he recognized as an able administrator, a fair man who strove to better the lives of the people who lived in his lands. He could have killed the Earl years ago, at Ruyton, if he'd wished, if he was the sort of man who killed adversaries who'd been knocked

192

into oblivion by a blow to the head. He wanted none of the Norman usurper's earls ruling his own country, and would fight to keep them out, but saw no reason to slaughter the Earl's wife and children. He'd given his oath they would remain safe, and he reminded Morwenna of that again.

She rose to her feet abruptly and angrily stormed out of the hall. Though the hostages were too far away from the dais to know what had been said, he suspected they sensed the woman thirsted for their deaths.

My constant staring probably makes them nervous too. They likely think I'm musing on how best to kill them. They would be surprised to learn who it is that draws my gaze. They must know the messengers haven't returned and that it will be spring before they're able to. The Countess will have to soon accept her child will be born in these mountains.

***

That same night, the Prince of Powwydd had a powerful dream. He sat amid his children. There were five of them, and two had flaming red hair. A hazy vision of his grandfather, Gwilym, drifted across the dream, his titian hair ablaze in the sun. It was a happy dream, different from the ones he usually had when he returned from raids. He didn't enjoy killing, and death often stalked his nightmares.

Like his Celtic ancestors, his belief in the power of dreams ran deep in his blood, and in this dream, Arianrhod, the virgin white goddess of birth, was revealed to him. It was a dream of hope and promise for the future. The goddess conjured an image of the mother of his children. She was a diminutive woman with long black hair, high cheekbones and eyes like grey pools, the woman he'd been unable to stop thinking about since setting eyes on her.

When he woke, he spoke her name, "Rhonwen." He gave thanks for the honour the gods had bestowed on him. She wasn't high born. Her mother was Welsh, but her father? She'd never lived in Wales, only in the Marches, and he sensed she burned with a desire to kill his betrothed, to avenge her mother's murder.

He only hoped he would be worthy of her and could win her heart. Then the dream could be fulfilled.

***

The Normans had been escorted back to their chamber after the meal, and Giselle soon had the yawning boys tucked up in their pallets. In consideration of her condition, Rhodri had provided a bed for Mabelle, but the lads liked their pallets.

"What brave little soldiers you are," Mabelle whispered, gazing at their tousled heads.

A tapping at the door made them instantly wary. They were usually left alone at night. Rhonwen opened the door a crack, and Mabelle heard a voice speaking Welsh.

Rhonwen's shoulders tensed and she turned to her mistress. "Rhodri has sent for me, my lady," she whispered, her big grey eyes wide with apprehension.

"For you?"

Before Mabelle could reach her and refuse to let her go, the healer was gone and the door barred once more. Mabelle and her maid exchanged desperate glances. Being called to Rhodri at this time of night could mean only one thing for the girl. They wept for the loss of her innocence, and for the failure of the barbarian Rhodri to keep his word none of them would be harmed.

**

Phillippe didn't knock, knowing Morwenna would be alone in her chamber, waiting impatiently. They exchanged no greeting. By the time he reached her, she'd torn off her shift and was naked. He devoured the site of her thrusting breasts and the heated promise in her eyes. Their kisses became ravenous. Their mouths remained locked together as they both worked frenziedly to remove his clothing. She sucked his tongue into her mouth. He bit her lip, then her earlobe. His hands squeezed her breasts roughly and she arched her mons to meet his erection. His tongue darted in and out of her mouth and she groaned huskily. "Phillippe, Phillippe. Fill me now. I need my Norman stallion."

Throwing her onto the bed, Giroux leapt on top of her and rammed his phallus into her throbbing sheath, already weeping for him. She sank her teeth into his neck. She liked him to be rough and that suited him too.

"We're a perfect match," he rasped.

After their passion had taken them both to the edge and over it, they lay physically spent but still full of anger and plotting.

Morwenna pouted. "The weak willed Rhodri refuses to kill them."

"He'll come to his senses. I'll make sure of that," Phillippe replied casually. "Mabelle de Valtesse will pay dearly for her father's crimes against my family."

"And, my lusty Norman knight, you'll repay me for my help by taking me as your bride to Normandie, and I'll be the *Comtesse* de Giroux."

He reached for his clothing. "I must return to my own chamber. We don't want anyone becoming suspicious."

He kissed her carelessly, opened the door carefully to make sure no one was in the hallway, and stepped silently from the room.

A perfect match. I wouldn't trust the Welsh bitch as far as I could throw her.

Phillippe snickered. He would have to be careful not to let his disdain show. He mustn't give away that he had no intention of taking this barbaric woman as his wife.

To Normandie? My family and friends would think I'm as mad as my father. When she's served her purpose, I'll be rid of her, or perhaps leave her to make Rhodri's life wretched.

CHAPTER THIRTY-THREE

When Rhonwen stepped into Rhodri's chamber she was trembling. The escort remained outside. She was afraid of what this Welsh warrior might do to her but had been drawn by his magnetism each time she'd set eyes on his Celtic beauty. She was afraid he *wouldn't* do the wild things she'd imagined him doing to her. She too had Celtic blood in her veins.

He sat in a massive wooden chair by the hearth in the centre of the room. He wore a long sleeve linen shirt dyed pale red, the sleeves rolled up to his elbows. A string of beads, reflecting the firelight, drew her gaze to his neck, and she licked her lips, suddenly aware she was perspiring. His long curly hair was tied back at his nape with a brown leather thong. The tight braids were gone, making him less intimidating. Leather breeches clung to his muscular thighs. His feet were bare, and she noticed fleetingly how long his toes were.

His usual weapons were nowhere in evidence. The only light in the room came from the flickering embers. A bluish pall of smoke, wending its way up to the smoke-hole canopy in the roof, hung around him. The chair beside him was empty.

"Don't be afraid, Rhonwen." His voice was soft and held no threat. "Come, sit by me," he said in Welsh, holding out his big hand to her. "Let the fire warm you."

She shivered and walked towards him slowly. Her breasts tingled and a strange ache throbbed in her nether regions. "I'm not afraid, my lord," she lied as she sat in the other chair, her hands holding on to the arms tightly, in case she might have to flee suddenly.

Slowly, he leaned forward to rest his bare forearms on his muscular thighs, and stared at her. She blushed as the fire of his gaze warmed her body. She tried not to look at him but was held by the green depths of his eyes.

"It's as I thought," he pronounced huskily after several minutes. "You're as drawn to me as I am to you."

Rhonwen stared at her knees. "You're betrothed to my enemy, my lord."

He sat back in the chair, his frustration evident. "Ah yes, the lovely Morwenna."

He remained silent for several minutes. She couldn't take her eyes off his face as he wrestled with his demons.

"I'll not marry her."

Icy chills raced up and down her spine. It was what she wanted to hear but made the situation more confused. "My lord?"

He stood and said softly, "Please, call me Rhodri."

She suspected this powerful man didn't use the word *please* often. She trembled as he stood behind her chair and placed his big hands on her shoulders. As soon as he touched her, she felt the overwhelming heat of his body flow into hers. She stifled a groan.

"My lord—Rhodri," she stuttered, "I cannot—we cannot—I'm your captive—I'm a maid."

He bent his head to whisper in her ear, "My Rhonwen, it's you who have captured me. I can't stop myself from wanting you, from making you mine. But I'll not force you against your will. I'll resolve the problem of Morwenna and send her back to her father. He won't be pleased I've broken the betrothal, but I have no wish to live my life with her blood lust. It's you I want."

Her mouth fell open. The room had tilted. "But you've known me only a short while."

Rhodri chuckled. "The same could be said of you, and yet you've no doubt in your mind about your feelings for me. Do you?"

She longed to tell him her feelings for him threatened to overwhelm her, but remained silent.

He took his hands from her shoulders and a moment later she felt him fasten something around her neck. It made her shiver. Reaching up instinctively, her hands felt the smoothness of his string of amber beads. She looked down and saw how beautifully formed they were—an object an artisan had worked on lovingly, an object of great worth. The heat of his body lingered in the cold beads. She wanted to turn, to look up into those piercing eyes, but was afraid of what she might see there.

"Return to your chamber, Rhonwen. The fates have destined we meet. I know in my heart our future paths lie together. Accept this as a token of my pledge to you. You'll come to my bed when it's the right time, and you will be my wife."

He took her by the arm and helped her rise from the chair. She was so stunned by his words, and his gift, she could barely make her legs work as he walked her across the room to the door.

"Take the healer back to her chamber."

***

Rhodri sank back into his chair. His body had betrayed him as soon as she'd entered the room. He had moved to stand behind her so she couldn't see the physical effect she had. He'd already been aroused, but his erection became rock hard when he touched her. He'd had to remove his hands from her. Good thing she hadn't turned to look at him when he fastened the amber beads around her neck. Looking into those round grey pools would have undone his resolve.

He'd been afraid to kiss her when she left—afraid of the emotions such a kiss might unleash. It had taken a great deal of effort to keep his voice steady when he ordered the guard to take her back to her chamber.

***

Agitated and conflicted, Rhonwen stumbled along in an effort to keep up with the escort holding the torch lighting their way. Her mind was a jumble of emotions. A furtive figure emerged unexpectedly from the dark shadows of the corridor where Morwenna's chamber was located.

He paused for a moment when he saw them but then continued to walk, and she gasped as they came face to face. She recognized him as a Norman by his shaved head and was sure she'd seen him before, in Ellesmere. Who was he and what was he doing here? He gave her a look of pure hatred and she immediately looked away. His eyes terrified her.

When she stepped hastily into Mabelle's chamber, the other women mistook the cause of her trembling.

"What has that brute done to you, Rhonwen?" Mabelle demanded.

"No, my lady. Rhodri did nothing to harm me. He was kind to me." She felt her face flush. "But I've just had an encounter in the hallway which has scared my wits out of me. There's a Norman soldier here, one of your husband's men."

"It's Giroux," Mabelle hissed, clenching her fists. "I now see clearly the malevolent hand behind the Earl's riding accident, Myfanwy's murder, the loss of my child, and my own near death after the abortifacient, and now this last betrayal, our kidnapping and probable death at the hands of a Welsh rebel."

"Who is he? Why has he betrayed you?" Rhonwen asked.

Giselle told Rhonwen the story of how Guillaume de Valtesse had blinded and mutilated Charles de Giroux and endured years of wandering exile with his daughter.

Mabelle slumped onto the edge of her bed. "I didn't know you knew the whole story, Giselle, but I'm relieved I didn't have to tell it."

Rhonwen had listened open-mouthed. "But if you and your father were cast out of your home, was that not revenge enough for the Giroux family?"

Mabelle sighed. "Apparently not. My father died several years ago, and I inherited Alensonne, Belisle and Domfort. I can't believe his reckless actions long ago have resulted in this threat to my own life, and those of my children and servants. From the grave he reaches out to hurt me and mine."

Rhonwen grasped Mabelle's hand. "Forgive me, my Lady," she cried tearfully, "It's not just that I saw the soldier. He knows I saw him. He came from the direction of Morwenna's chamber."

"We must think," Mabelle murmured. The three women sat huddled together on Mabelle's bed, careful not to wake the sleeping children. "What did Rhodri want of you anyway?" she whispered.

The healer blushed. "He's drawn to me."

Giselle sneered. "You mean he lusts after you."

"No. He was kind and gentle. He spoke of—love—of my becoming his wife." It sounded ludicrous. "He gave me this necklace of amber beads." It was incomprehensible.

Mabelle looked at Rhonwen and whispered, "And you feel the same for him, don't you?"

Fearing the censure of her lady for her foolish feelings, Rhonwen could barely murmur, "Yes."

The countess squeezed the healer's hand. "Rhonwen, a woman never knows when love might come along and knock her off her feet."

Rhonwen couldn't believe she'd heard these words from the Countess of Ellesmere. She looked wide-eyed at Giselle, who for some reason was silently nodding her agreement. "We must hope Rhodri's love for you will protect us from Giroux," the maid whispered.

***

Phillippe, burst into Morwenna's chamber. "They know it was I who betrayed them."

She looked up at him with a bored expression. "It's not a good idea to come here during the day, Phillippe."

He strode towards her. "That's not important now. The healer saw me."

Morwenna rose immediately from her chair. "Does she know who you are?"

He ran his hand back and forth over his shaved head. "Perhaps not by name, but I'm sure she recognized me as a Norman. It's only a matter of time before she and her accursed mistress deduce who I am. The Earl believes I'm in Normandie, and must never find out who betrayed him. My life would be worth nothing."

"We'll wait and watch for a good time to kill them, my lover," she purred as she pressed her body to his and kissed him. "I suddenly like the idea of bedding you in the afternoon."

***

After that, Phillippe made no effort to avoid being seen by the hostages. He appeared for meals in the hall and scowled at them, his hatred and lust for vengeance plain to see.

Rhodri thought it curious but didn't reprimand him. He did notice, however, the occasional exchange of heated looks between Giroux and Morwenna. They'd conspired together in England to trap the Countess, and he had serious questions about their relationship now.

CHAPTER THIRTY-FOUR

Rhodri sent for Rhonwen every evening. At first they sat in the chairs talking as before. Sometimes he ran his fingers through her hair, inhaling its fragrance, feeling the texture of it, telling her how beautiful it was. He gazed at her for several minutes at a time. He sensed she had resolved to keep a tight rein on her emotions.

She's drawn to me but can see no future for us.

As she became more at ease with him, he encouraged her to sit on his lap. The soft pressure of her small body against him was pleasant torture. He loved the feel of her slender form in his arms, and as long as they stayed in the chair, he would be able to control his male urges. His steadfast belief that this woman was his soul mate strengthened him, and he didn't want to hurt her or drive her away. They talked of many things. Rhonwen told him of her love for healing and the things her mother had taught her. Rhodri shared tales of growing up in the castle at Powwydd.

One night, after she'd sat upon his lap for a sennight, they were laughing over a story he'd told her of a prank he and his brothers had played. Her smile gladdened his heart. He put his fingers on her chin, drew her face to his and kissed her on the lips. The kiss deepened and she responded to him, parting her lips as he coaxed with his tongue. She slid her arms around his neck.

She's not afraid.

They kissed for a long time, exploring each other's mouths, necks, throats and ears. Rhodri was intoxicated by the innocence of her responses and her eagerness to please and explore him. He loved the feel of her small hands on his face.

"Rhodri," she whispered as he nuzzled her ear and bent his head to kiss her again, "What of Morwenna? She's your betrothed. Surely what we're doing is wrong?"

He tensed. "I'll send her back to her father in the spring."

"But she risked a great deal for you. She murdered my mother, and helped to deliver my mistress to you."

"Morwenna didn't do what she did for me, or for Wales. Murdering your mother wasn't part of my plans."

Rhonwen relaxed back into his arms. After a few moments, she took a deep breath and asked, "Do you believe she's still a maid? I didn't believe her to be one when we shared a chamber at Ellesmere, and I have stronger suspicions now."

He smirked. "The Norman, you mean?"

She sat up and he could feel her fear. "I saw him coming from her chamber. He knows I saw him. He wishes me dead, and my mistress and her family."

"Why would he want you dead? There's no gain for anyone in that."

"He doesn't care about gain. It's revenge he seeks."

"Revenge for what?"

Rhonwen told him who Mabelle suspected he was, and why he was driven with a thirst for her blood as the daughter of the man who'd blinded and mutilated his father. Rhodri didn't confirm her suspicions about the man's name, but resolved to double the watch on the Norman and on his betrothed.

They sat in silence for several minutes, listening to the beating of each other's heart. He wanted to reassure her. He squeezed her knee and turned her face to his. "I've given my sworn oath nothing will happen to any of you. I'll defend you with my life if necessary."

Rhonwen ached with the pain of knowing there was no future for her with Rhodri. She still could scarcely believe his interest in her. But when he touched her hair, all she wanted to do was curl her body into him, rest her head on his chest and bask in the warmth and comfort she experienced in his arms. She loved the soft tickle of his silky black chest hair against her nose. He never wore his braids when they were together, and she longed for the courage to untie the leather thong that kept his hair bound at his nape.

His first kiss had rocked her to the core. For the first time in her life, she felt like a desirable woman. There was desire in Rhodri's kisses, and in his eyes, and in the delicate touch of his big calloused hands.

Was it a mistake to trust him? He could have taken her against her will, but he hadn't. His patient wooing warmed her heart. The bond she'd sensed through forces beyond her understanding was becoming stronger and stronger. She wished each day away, longing for the sun to go down, anticipating his summons.

The parting would be unbearable.

***

Rhodri stood unmoved as Morwenna's fists beat against his chest.

"I defy you to send me back to my father. I defy you to break our betrothal."

"I'll not marry you, Morwenna."

She sprang away from him and spat in his face. "My father will kill you. You have no right."

He wiped the spittle from his cheek. "I have every right. A bridegroom expects his bride to come to his bed chaste. What will your father have to say about your rutting with a Norman soldier, a spy at that?"

She seemed taken aback for a moment, and then sneered, "And what of your precious Rhonwen, will she come to your bed chaste? I think not."

Rhodri grasped her wrists and forced her to her knees. His voice was quietly menacing. "Nothing about Rhonwen should concern you. She is light where you are darkness, joy where you are hatred, innocence where you are corruption. Beware what you say and do while you remain here."

He released her hands. "Go to your chamber."

Morwenna went as she was ordered, but she glared at him defiantly, intense hatred in her eyes.

She'll seek revenge for my turning to Rhonwen.

"She must be watched at all times," he told Andras. "And the Norman."

"It will be done, my lord."

That evening, Rhodri told Rhonwen, as she sat on his broad lap, that he'd banished Morwenna from his life and that the evil woman would be leaving as soon as the weather broke.

"It's still many sennights away," she murmured, returning his gentle kisses.

"I'm having both her and the Norman watched."

Rhonwen imparted this news to the other hostages when she returned to their chamber but didn't tell them how Rhodri had lovingly caressed her breasts, or how he'd made her nipples harden with the strokes of his calloused hands. She mentioned nothing of the wanton feelings these actions had produced in her, but she did share that Rhodri had again proclaimed his love for her.

Mabelle sensed the healer was deeply in love with the rebel chieftain. She felt sorrow for the hopelessness of the situation, and thought longingly of her husband, whom she'd not seen for months. She was consumed with mixed feelings about Rhodri's declaration of love for Rhonwen. Her husband Ram had never told her he loved her, though she believed in her heart that he did. But she'd been slow to recognize she loved him. Now was probably too late. If they ever saw each other again, he would never believe she hadn't been raped while a captive. He would no longer want her, even if she declared her love for him.

CHAPTER THIRTY-FIVE

"The Norman sleeps in Morwenna's chamber every night, Lord Rhodri," Andras reported.

"I don't care, my friend. So long as the two of them stay away from the hostages, they can rut to their heart's content."

He wished he could go to Rhonwen's chamber, but the other hostages were there. Rhonwen would never accept a chamber of her own, when her noble mistress had to sleep with her maid.

"Bring the healer to my chamber."

Andras nodded and left.

Rhonwen entered a while later. Would his body always react as strongly to her presence? This time he didn't wait for her to come to him at the chair but strode to her side, lifted her into his arms and returned to the chair. She giggled and put her arms around his neck.

His lovemaking began with gentle kisses and progressed slowly to stroking and then suckling her breasts. He knew she could feel his erection against her bottom, and that she wanted to touch him, but he held her firmly, and slowly caressed the inside of her thigh beneath the woollen tunic. He'd never cared much in the past about a woman's pleasure, but now he derived great satisfaction out of Rhonwen's delight in the new found awareness of her body.

"I want to bring you pleasure, Rhonwen. Let me touch you."

"Your touch brings me more pleasure than I've ever known," she whispered, but he could tell she didn't know what he intended to do.

Throaty murmurs escaped her as he stroked further and further up her thighs, until his fingers found the tight black curls of her mons. Still suckling her breast, he opened her legs and stroked the swelling bud with his thumb. Her eyes flew open and she almost fell off his lap, but he held her firmly and continued to stroke.

"Hush, my sweet Rhonwen. I won't hurt you."

She soon gasped his name, lost in the ecstasy of her first release. For long moments he cradled her, rocking gently, his heart full.

She recovered from her euphoria and became embarrassed when she saw she was sprawled on his lap with her tunic up around her hips, her legs open.

"Nothing we do here is wrong my love. You're my woman, and I want only to give you pleasure. When you're mine completely, I'll show you ways to paradise that will make tonight pale in comparison."

He felt her body heat at his words. He brought her to release after release that night, slowly sliding his fingers inside her. She cried out with intoxication and surrendered completely to the passion he was patiently teaching her to enjoy.

***

At the Winter Solstice, Rhodri's people held a ceremony to honour the sun and he explained to Robert and Baudoin this was to encourage the sun to come back someday. Despite the remoteness of the fortress, it was well supplied. It had its own large communal kitchens made of stone which were separate from the wooden structure. There were two huge fireplaces for cooking. Most of the meals were surprisingly good and food was plentiful, but at Yuletide they enjoyed a special banquet, which began with mulled cider, followed by venison and fenberry pie. When Giselle asked where they'd found fenberries, she was told they grew readily in the bogs of Wales.

Both Mabelle and Giselle almost fell off their bench when a roasted boar's head was carried in. "At least this one isn't green and yellow," they exclaimed together.

Giselle reddened. "Everyone is looking at us strangely, wondering what we're laughing at."

An oak log was burned for twelve hours using the remnants of the previous year's log to light it. Rhonwen explained that once it had been burnt the people would keep the remnants for next year, but the ashes would be saved to spread on the fields in the valleys below at the time of planting. This would encourage a good harvest.

The doors had been decorated with holly. The Welsh believed the evergreen with its blood red berries was a sign of fertility, and its spikes would capture evil spirits before they entered.

As the New Year neared, Rhodri was the one to go outside before midnight and be the first to enter the Hall after midnight, because it was good luck for a tall, dark and handsome man, bearing food and fuel, to be the first inside the door.

That first night of the year, after watching Rhodri stride in confidently when the massive door opened to his insistent pounding, Rhonwen also had a dream. She and Rhodri were making love. It was so vivid, she was afraid she'd cried out her passion. She awoke to find she'd touched herself, just as Rhodri had touched her. But she felt no shame. He'd taught her things about her own body she'd never known and unleashed passions she'd been unaware of.

If only it could be.

Only Mabelle heard Rhonwen cry out and recognised the sounds of anguish and longing. She'd lain awake many nights, aching with need for her husband, remembering the touch of his hands on her breasts and the fulfillment of his hard manhood deep within her. Had she cried out in her sleep, as Rhonwen did now?

CHAPTER THIRTY-SIX

Robert and Baudoin were growing boys who often became restless with their captivity. With Mabelle's permission, Rhonwen was teaching them Welsh, and they were proving to be good at it. Mabelle and Giselle learned a few words as they listened to the lessons. They passed the time sewing and weaving with the Welsh women in the camp, or spinning wool with a drop spindle.

Mabelle blamed herself more and more for the kidnapping. She'd been the one who'd insisted on all of them going to Whittington. Ram had been right to be wary. Her carelessness might yet cost them their lives. Her husband would likely never forgive her.

Another worry nagged at her. Perhaps Ram had pursued her captors and been killed or injured in Wales. Perhaps he lay at the bottom of some deep crevice.

The weather was foul most of the time and they were unable to spend much time outdoors. Rhodri and his men seemed impervious to the bitter cold, and spent hours honing their fighting skills in the frigid mountain meadow, keeping in good physical condition. The Norman women were amazed by the cleanliness and grooming of the Welshmen when they came to the hall, despite the fact they spent many hours in physical activity. The hostages were provided with hot water whenever they asked for it.

The young Welsh boys were included in the training and were equipped with small wooden swords, daggers and shields with which to learn the rudiments of self defence and attack. One day, Rhodri asked Mabelle's permission to include Robert and Baudoin in the boys' training sessions. He brought with him a sword, dagger and shield for each of them. She noted he had waited until the boys were with her. Their eyes lit up when they caught sight of the miniature wooden weapons.

"*Maman*," Robert pleaded, "Please say we can go."

They often grew bored, and would benefit from the outdoor exercise, not to mention the awesome skills they would learn, but thought it incongruous Rhodri should want to train the sons of his enemy, and she told him as much.

"There's no glory and no honour in defeating an unworthy enemy. The Earl is a worthy opponent, as his sons will be."

She consented, and her sons became Rhodri's pupils in the arts of raiding warfare. They loved it and were full of tales of their prowess when they returned.

Mabelle worried about her unborn child. She was constantly nagged by the worry of Giroux's presence in the fortress, and yet the child seemed to thrive and grow. Morwenna and the Norman spent most of their time in her chamber and were seen rarely.

Mabelle had entered her ninth month when she experienced sudden hard labour in the hall. She collapsed to the floor with a strident shriek as the pain hit her. This hadn't happened with her other deliveries and she panicked. Giselle and Rhonwen rushed to help her, but it was Rhodri who reached her first, lifting her effortlessly despite her bulk and carrying her to his own chamber.

"Fetch the midwife," he yelled to no one in particular.

"You'll have privacy here, lady Countess." He laid her on his own bed. She expressed her thanks that her children wouldn't have to witness her labours, then the pain hit again. It was so severe, she vomited.

"I'll send clean linens. Warrior I may be, but I've no intention of involving myself in this battle for life."

The hours crawled by as Mabelle's screams echoed around the fortress. She called her husband's name over and over, not in recrimination, as Rhodri had heard people say women did in the midst of childbirth, but with longing and regret. He shut out the image of his beloved Rhonwen undergoing the same agony for him, but knew in his heart she would call his name with love when the time came.

Suddenly silence reigned. His heart plummeted. He would be truly sorry if the courageous Norman noblewoman had died in childbirth. The Earl of Ellesmere must love this remarkable woman very much and would seek revenge. Then a thin wail pierced the still night air, and Rhodri smiled at the immense relief he felt that at least the child lived.

An hour later, he was enjoying a tankard of ale with Andras in the Hall when Rhonwen appeared, carrying a bundle. It was a tiny baby girl, wrapped in swaddling cloths and a *brychan*. She moved the coverings away from the babe's face.

"She can only stay a few minutes. She's come into the world early, and needs to be with her mother, but I knew you'd want to see her."

Rhodri stood and took the child, looking up at Rhonwen. He was awed at the love on her face for this child that wasn't hers. "The babe is fair, like her mother. The lady lives then? She has survived her ordeal?"

"Yes, she's strong. She's lost a lot of blood and will need to rest, but I'm confident she and the child will flourish."

"She had a good healer to assist her," he said lovingly.

"No, the skill of the midwife saved them both," Rhonwen replied modestly. "And her own stubborn determination."

***

A sennight later, Mabelle had recovered sufficiently to join the others in the hall for a meal. She brought the newborn for everyone to see. Rhonwen carried the babe around proudly as people commented on the fairness of the blonde child, who was already thriving. After a while, people drifted away, off to their beds. Only Rhodri and the captives remained. Morwenna suddenly burst into the hall, brandishing a dagger, her distorted face reddened with rage.

"You're mad," she screamed at Rhodri. "This is the spawn of a Norman invader, a man you hate." She lunged at Rhonwen and the child, but the healer bolted out of her way. Rhodri jumped to his feet and ran to disarm the madwoman, twisting her wrist. The dagger clattered to the floor. She sprawled at his feet sobbing and screeching, pounding the planking with her fists.

In the noise and confusion, no one noticed Phillippe de Giroux enter the room. He crept stealthily in the shadows towards Mabelle and her sons, sword drawn. Mabelle screamed when she saw him. "*Mes fils!* Robert, Baudoin!"

Phillippe grabbed her by the hair and forced her to her knees. "*Tais-toi*, Valtesse bitch. You'll watch in silence while I despatch your wretched spawn to hell, and then I'll kill you. Your cursed father turned my father into a raving lunatic who made life a living hell for his children." He raised his sword. Rhonwen gasped in horror when she saw the sharp blade poised to behead Robert. The boy stood rooted to the spot.

"*Non!*" Mabelle screeched.

Suddenly, Phillippe's rabid eyes lost their focus. His death grip on Mabelle's hair slackened. His disbelieving gaze fell to the dagger embedded deep in his chest. He dropped his sword and slumped lifeless to the floor, a spurt of blood from his gaping mouth spraying across the front of Mabelle's dress. She lunged for Robert, clutching her son tightly, sobbing.

"Phillippe!" Morwenna shrieked. She'd seen Rhodri throw the dagger that had ended her lover's life. She sprang to her feet and picked up the weapon forced from her hand. She ran towards Rhodri, who had crouched to retrieve his dagger from Philippe's body. He cursed as she thrust the blade, deflecting the blow intend for his heart. The steel sliced into his bicep.

Giselle gathered up the wide-eyed Baudoin. Rhonwen rushed to place the new born infant into the safety of her sobbing mother's arms, and ran to aid Rhodri, struggling with the frenzied Morwenna. Rhonwen grabbed the hair of the woman who'd murdered her mother, determined not to let her slay Rhodri. She could see he'd been wounded and it infuriated her.

Morwenna turned her attention and her wrath onto Rhonwen, who bolted and ran out of the door, down the passageway and through the gate to the outside, where she stopped dead at the sight of a blanket of thick fog. Morwenna was pursuing her. She had to keep going, though she had no idea where she was running, having been outside rarely during her captivity.

She felt her way along the wooden palisades, glad she could draw Morwenna away from the man she loved. She could hear the demonic woman screaming and cursing not far behind. The mist cleared for a moment. She was on a narrow precipice with only the palisades behind her. Before her yawned the chasm of the ravine.

I'm standing on the edge of the world.

She spread-eagled her body against the palisades, clutching at the rough bark, and raised her face, trusting her fate to the spirits of the mountains. A feeling of power surged through her.

A manic Morwenna appeared out of the smothering fog and attacked Rhonwen. The healer looked into Morwenna's eyes. Death lurked there. They struggled briefly, but Rhonwen felt no fear.

Suddenly Morwenna slipped, fell and was gone, swallowed silently by the stoic mountains.

"I didn't hear her scream," Rhonwen thought numbly. "Surely, she must have screamed?"

Rhonwen braced her back against the palisades, digging her nails into the bark of the wooden pilings, panting hard and now afraid to move. Fearing she might freeze or faint if she didn't get inside, she wasn't sure which way to go when she heard Rhodri calling to her. Reciting incantations whose meaning she didn't understand, she edged her way along the precipice towards the sound of his voice, until she stumbled into him. He grabbed her away from danger and held her to his body.

"You're safe now, my Rhonwen, you're safe. I have you."

"Morwenna is dead." A sob racked her body. She reached out her frozen hand to touch the blood oozing from his arm. "You're bleeding, Rhodri. She's cut you. I must see to your wound."

But the dizziness overwhelmed her and she fainted.

Rhodri took his beloved to his chamber, removed her clothes and massaged her body with rosemary oil to warm her. Gradually her teeth stopped chattering and she regained her wits. He covered her with furs and blankets and sat by her bedside until she stopped shaking.

Later, Rhonwen stitched his wound and applied a healing salve of lady's mantle.

"Your stitches are so delicate, I'll bear but the faintest scar."

The small gap it would cause in the Celtic knot designs etched into his biceps would be hardly visible and unnoticed by most. She couldn't believe he barely flinched as she plied the needle through his flesh.

CHAPTER THIRTY-SEVEN

Three sennights later, a sudden thaw made it possible for Aneurin ap Norweg and his men to make their way from the village of Llansilin, where they'd spent the intervening months, to Cadair Berwyn. He delivered the reply from the Earl of Ellesmere to the ransom note sent by Rhodri.

> *To the Prince of Powwydd*
> *Be informed the Earl of Ellesmere agrees to pay in full the ransom demanded for his family and servants but proposes an exchange at the border village of Rhydycroesau.*
> *Safe passage is to be guaranteed by both parties.*
> *The chests of coins will be carried to the middle of the bridge and left there.*
> *The hostages will walk to the chests with an unarmed escort who will verify the contents and carry the ransom into Wales.*
> *The Earl gives his word for his part of the bargain and trusts Rhodri ap Owain to do the same.*

As he read again the ransom reply, signed by the Earl and bearing his seal, Rhodri sent for Rhonwen. He'd already dispatched a message back to Ellesmere, agreeing to the exchange, and detailing the date and time.

He put his hands on Rhonwen's shoulders, trying to keep his voice steady. "I want you to stay in Wales, with me. I'll free the others on payment of the ransom, but you are mine."

"I've dreaded this moment," she whispered, avoiding his gaze. "I cannot stay, Rhodri. My duty is to my lady who has trusted me and given me a place of honour in her household. She's been like a mother to me, since my own mother was murdered."

He lifted her chin. "Look me in the eye and tell me you don't love me."

Rhonwen shook her head, her eyes brimming with tears. "You're a powerful warrior, a man who must fight for Wales, for what you believe is right. I'm a healer. I fight to heal men, not to wound them. Our lives and our priorities are different. I'll always love you, and treasure what we've shared, but I don't want to be involved in war and bloodshed. I want peace."

Rhodri let go of her shoulders, afraid he might be tempted to force her to stay. "I too want to live in peace, Rhonwen. I seek only peace and justice for my people. Sometimes it's necessary to fight to achieve it."

***

Ram had endured many agonized months of not knowing how his family fared, but had a deep inner sense they were still alive. Mabelle had become such an essential part of his life, part of him, that he would sense if she was no longer alive. His body would have felt the loss. There remained no doubt in his mind that, despite his protestations, he loved her deeply.

Why had he never been able to utter those simple words to her? Why had his stubborn pride and ambition deprived her of the assurance he truly loved her? He prayed fervently he would have the chance to tell her. He sensed she loved him too, though she'd never confessed that to him. But he didn't care. He resolved to tell her anyway.

And what of his children? He loved them and had been a loving father. Unlike his wife, he'd never spoken the words to them either. Why was it so difficult? He swore an oath to tell his sons how much he loved them every day of their lives, if they were returned to him safely. And the child his wife was carrying when she was abducted? Did the child live? Did he have another son, or perhaps a daughter? Could Mabelle have survived bearing a child in the remote mountains of Wales?

He worried the Welsh rebels wouldn't agree to his proposals for an exchange. "I hope my caution hasn't cost my family their lives," he confided to Gervais. "Can we trust Rhodri?"

A messenger arrived with word from Rhodri agreeing to the exchange, and outlining the day and time. Relief flooded Ram.

It's only a sennight from now.

"Send out scouting parties to reconnoitre the area around the border village where the exchange is to take place. We've agreed to the idea of safe passage, but we must position bowmen in strategic locations, as I'm sure Rhodri will do the same. The Welsh archers are famous for their skill and deadly accuracy."

He'd already gathered the sizable ransom from his estates in Sussex, and it lay in his chamber in two iron chests. "Post a two man guard outside my door, and double the guard on the walls and gates of the castle. We don't need a surprise attack on the castle to rob us of the ransom money."

Gervais smiled. "*Oui, milord.* It's good to be doing something productive."

Ram was aware some questioned paying the ransom. The other Marcher Lords had been vehemently against the idea, suggesting pursuit and revenge instead. One Earl had intimated their King felt the same way. "His Majesty is not happy with the idea of financing rebels."

But Ram feared pursuit and vengeance would result in Mabelle's death. He knew with dread certainty that if his King commanded him directly not to ransom his family, he would defy the order. He'd also learned something from an unlikely source. True to her word, the healer, Caryl Penarth, had come to Ellesmere a sennight after the Fayre. She'd agreed to stay when told of Rhonwen's disappearance with Mabelle. Ram had questioned her about the Fayre and her possible knowledge of rebels in the area of Whittington. He'd sensed there was something she wanted to say, but didn't. After receiving the ransom demand, he'd gone to her again.

"There are many who say I shouldn't pay the ransom, Caryl," he told her.

Caryl hesitated a moment before she replied. "Then many will starve, my lord."

Ram arched his brows. "Starve? The harvests have been good."

"Not in Wales. It's a blighted land," she whispered sadly.

Ram knew much of the *blight* had been caused by Norman brutality.

"How do you know what Rhodri intends to do with the coin?" he asked.

"I've heard the whispers of hope on the lips of desperate villagers."

***

215

On the eve of departure from Cadair Berwyn, Rhodri summoned Mabelle and her family to the Great Hall. He'd developed a great admiration for this proud Norman woman, who seemed to have taken her ordeal in stride and maintained her bearing and fortitude throughout.

"My lady Countess," he began, bowing slightly. Had she noticed it was the first time he'd used the word '*my*' in front of her title? "On the morrow we begin our journey back down the mountain to the border, where you'll be reunited with your husband. I trust you have all in readiness? My men and I will accompany you as your escort, and see you safely delivered."

Mabelle returned the bow with a curtsey. She looked surprised that he would accompany them, but she said nothing. She was aware of his love for her healer. Did she suspect he wanted to go with them to be with Rhonwen as long as possible? Did she know he'd asked Rhonwen to stay?

Rhodri continued, trying to keep his eyes off Rhonwen, and his mind on the matter at hand. "It was never my intention to have you killed. I wasn't aware of the reasons for Giroux's involvement in our plans, and Morwenna has paid with her life for her treachery against you, and me. It has been my honour to have you and your sons and servants as guests in my fortress home. You'll never forget your daughter was born in Wales, and I hope one day she'll come to love the country of her birth."

Mabelle bowed slightly and smiled. "I too have come to have respect for you, and your people, Lord Rhodri ap Owain, ap Dafydd, ap Gwilym, Prince of Powwydd. I assure you my daughter will be told of the land of her birth, and I'm sure my sons will carry with them stories of how a Welsh chieftain slew the monster who wished them dead. I thank you for the respect with which you've treated us—all of us."

He knew she was referring in particular to Rhonwen. He nodded his understanding of her words and intent. Did she know how he burned for Rhonwen, how hard it had been to not claim her body and soul, to make her stay.

Mabelle cleared her throat. "I would like to return to our chambers now to make final preparations for the morrow. I'm worried about how the little one will cope with the journey."

Rhodri wanted to reassure her. "The weather is good, and we should have an easy journey. I myself will see to your infant daughter as we descend."

Mabelle seemed about to take her leave but turned back. "One last favour, Lord Rhodri, could I trouble you for writing materials? Parchment—ink. I wish to compose a letter."

Rhodri was curious but replied, "Of course. Do you need a scrivener? We've a monk here."

"*Non, merci.* I can write it myself."

Now it was Rhodri who coughed nervously. "Perhaps you could spare Rhonwen for a few moments? I would like to speak with her alone."

Mabelle turned to her healer. "Of course, if you're in agreement, Rhonwen. We'll go finish our packing."

Rhonwen blushed and nodded.

CHAPTER THIRTY-EIGHT

"Come."

Rhodri led Rhonwen to his chamber and motioned for her to sit by the hearth in her chair. They faced each other, as they'd done at their first meeting alone. After long minutes of silence, he saw her eyes were full of tears. He longed to hold her, to wipe away the tears, to tell her he was sorry he'd hurt her, that he loved her, that she was his destiny. His thoughts were confused and she was conflicted too. He wanted to beg her to stay with him. His dream had convinced him they were meant to be together.

"Rhonwen, don't go."

"I must," she cried, putting her hands to her face to hide her tears. "I can't endure the thought of living with you as a warrior, spending my days amid blood and violence, worrying if you're coming back from the latest skirmish, tending ghastly wounds. But I want some memory to warm the cold, lonely nights without you. I don't know if I'm brave enough to ask, or if you'll consent—Rhodri, I—want to take part of you with me."

"You're taking my heart."

"Rhodri, I'm leaving my heart here with you, but I want—I need to leave you with something else. You've given me love and pleasure, without concern for your own needs. I want to satisfy those needs for you tonight, my love, and I want to leave this place as a woman. I want to leave you with the knowledge you're the only man who'll ever possess my body and my soul."

She was gifting him with her maidenhood. It was folly, but he picked her up in his arms and strode over to his bed.

At least I'll have this memory.

His physical need for her was so great he couldn't stop if he wanted to, but he vowed to make it a night they would both remember for the rest of their lives apart.

Perhaps if I make her mine, she'll stay.

Slowly he peeled the garments from her body, kissing her face and neck, feeling her quiver as she stood by his bed. When she was naked, he gazed at her.

"You're lovely, so pure and innocent," he whispered. He quickly removed his own clothing and stood at her side. Her eyes grew wider and she gasped when she saw his arousal for the first time.

"I'm a healer, Rhodri," she murmured, "And I've seen naked men before. But I've never seen a man as big and as proudly erect. Looking at you heats my body."

She smiled at him and his heart raced. He'd never felt so admired as a man. She was nervous but not afraid. He didn't want fear to dampen the great passion he sensed she was capable of. It had taken all his considerable control to not let her touch him when she'd wanted to. He stroked her hair. "Rhonwen, you have the pure honest soul of an angel."

He picked her up and laid her down on the bed, then lay beside her and took her into his arms, kissing and licking her face, her throat, her shoulders. He kissed her lips, coaxing her with his tongue. She opened for him and he drew her tongue into his mouth, feeling her groan reverberate through his body. She reached up and pulled off the leather thong that bound his hair, then raked her fingers through it as it fell to his shoulders, sending ripples of pleasure from his scalp, down his spine to his toes.

He kissed her dark nipples, flicking his tongue over the sensitive flesh, marvelling at how hard they were already. She arched her body when he suckled. He knelt between her legs and trailed his fingers slowly between her maiden's breasts and down across her stomach. She opened her legs wider. "I ache for you, Rhodri," she whimpered shyly.

Where his hand had led, his lips now followed and he traced kisses down her stomach until he reached the black curls at the top of her thighs, curls as black as his own. He could see the diamond of her desire and he edged his broad shoulders between her legs, grasped her hips, lifted her slightly and licked the jewel in that most private place. She cried out and her eyes flew open as his tongue brought her intense pleasure, but also a blush of embarrassment.

"Rhodri—"

"Nothing we do here is wrong or shameful, Rhonwen. It's a precious gift you're giving me this night and I want to taste you," he rasped.

She closed her eyes and keened as he covered her with his mouth, the taste of her sending new blood rushing to his groin. He slowly inserted his fingers, felt her wet heat. He could wait no longer. He guided the tip of his manhood into her folds. She opened her eyes and placed her hands over his, urging him to enter her.

"I'll try not to hurt you," he whispered. "I'm big, and you're—"

She smiled. "I'm not afraid."

He knew it was the truth.

He entered slowly, sensed the barrier and pushed through. She sucked in a breath and cried out, clutching his shoulders. He clenched his jaw at the effort of holding still.

"Don't stop, Rhodri, please don't stop."

His wild Celtic blood took over on hearing her words. He groaned, withdrew almost completely then plunged in again and again. She screamed his name with wild delight when his seed burst forth into her quivering body.

Still inside her, he lifted her with ease and rolled over so she was atop him. The black hair entwined where their bodies were joined, making them look like one body. He felt her sheathe pulse against him as he softened. It wouldn't be long before he could bring her to ecstasy again.

He'd never known such fulfillment. His soul had left his body and met hers in some ethereal place. He rose from the bed and went to fetch a cloth and water. He cleansed the blood from her thighs.

"Don't be embarrassed, Rhonwen," he whispered with a smile.

"I'm not," she said truthfully. "I'm humbled my mighty warrior is tending to my needs this way. You brought me to rapture with your tender lovemaking before, but this—this was—different. This was fulfillment. The sensations coursing through me as we joined brought me to a mystical release. I've entered a wonderful new world."

She fell asleep hours later, after they'd made love again. He carried her carefully to the chamber where the other hostages slept, and laid her on her pallet. He spread her long hair on the pillow and covered her lovingly with the furs. He gazed down at her and whispered, "You're my destiny, Rhonwen."

She didn't wake, and he left silently.

The only person awake in the room was Mabelle, who saw him place Rhonwen on the pallet, and heard his words. She wept for their heartbreak, and for the unbearable longing for her own husband.

CHAPTER THIRTY-NINE

Rhonwen awoke early, disoriented to find she was back on her own pallet. Glancing around, she saw Giselle and her mistress preparing for the journey. She rose and helped herself to bread and honey. The others greeted her normally, and she sensed no embarrassment from them. Rhodri must have carried her into the chamber, but no one gave any indication they'd seen or heard anything.

Robert and Baudoin were excited to be going home and looking forward to riding the ponies down into the valley. Rhodri told Robert he could ride his own pony because he'd learned quickly in the practice fields. The child was ecstatic.

"I wonder if Papa will come to meet us," Baudoin asked.

"Of course he will," Robert answered, "And he'll bring a huge army and slay the Welsh barbarians."

Mabelle groaned. "Old habits and beliefs die hard I suppose," she sighed to Giselle. "Let's pray there won't be violence at the exchange."

The previous night Mabelle had written a letter to Ram. If anything went wrong, she wanted him to know she loved him. Now she tucked the missive into the folds between her dress and chemise.

The healer wrapped the infant in as many swaddling cloths as she could find. She suggested to her mistress that she carry the child in a sling she'd fashioned, and Mabelle agreed, confident Rhonwen would be better able to manage the burden on the slippery trails than she.

Outside, Rhodri was already mounted on his pony. "Give the child to me, Rhonwen."

She carefully lifted the sling. Rhodri leaned down and she placed the precious bundle around his neck. Mabelle saw their eyes lock for a fleeting moment, then Rhonwen averted her eyes, wiping away tears. Rhodri cradled the baby to his huge body. Mabelle was reassured his body heat would keep her child warm.

"*I Lloegr!* " he shouted to his men, and the warriors and their hostages began their long journey down the mountain to England, as he'd commanded.

Few words were spoken, despite the captivating beauty of the valleys and glades they traversed, painted gold by carpets of daffodils. Mabelle sensed Rhodri and Rhonwen were wrestling with their own emotions, and she was full of fear something would go wrong. Would Ram accept her in his bed when she returned? Would the children remember him? Would they make it safely down these treacherous mountain trails? Her hand went to the letter concealed at her breast.

They stayed overnight in the same cottage where they'd found shelter on the outward journey and were surprised to see their own horses tethered to a post. Lying on the palette, Mabelle thought about the things that had changed in their lives since she was last in this isolated foreign place. She was the mother of a daughter she'd named after her mother. The monk had baptised the child. However, Mabelle felt there was something lacking and had decided to wait for the reunion with Ram to decide what other names the child should bear.

Her sons had grown. For boys they'd demonstrated courage and forbearance during the long ordeal, and she hoped as they grew to adulthood, they would remember some of the good things about the Welsh people they'd spent time with. Giselle had changed too, and Mabelle sensed she had a different perspective about her captors. As for herself, she recognised she loved Ram unconditionally. She hoped desperately he would still want her once they returned.

Rhonwen had undergone the biggest change. Mabelle suspected the healer and the chieftain had been intimate on their last night, yet Rhonwen seemed intent on returning with them to England. She knew the girl loved this wild Celt who now carried her own child down the mountain. Rhodri obviously cared for the child he carried cuddled tightly to his broad chest. Was he thinking of his own children, of what he might have had with Rhonwen?

***

"I don't like this mist," Gervais muttered. "We can barely see the bridge itself, let alone the other end of it. The archers will be hard pressed to find their target, if we need them."

Ram shifted nervously in his saddle as he and his men waited. "We've already been waiting over an hour," he replied. "If the wait goes on, the mist may clear."

He struggled to stay positive. He'd been in many tense situations in his life, but they paled in comparison to the stress he felt now with the lives of his wife and family in the balance. He felt as though the mist had seeped into his head. He dismounted to walk around and stretch his legs, trying to overcome the fear and nervousness he felt. As he strolled into the trees near the glade where they waited, his heart raced when he saw a swath of bluebells.

He could feel Mabelle's presence near him again, and his mind went back to the day they'd met. What if he discovered she'd been raped during her captivity? They'd often jested together about the *Fairies of the Blue Thimbles* and he prayed to them now that nothing would go wrong. The Welsh bowmen were legendary and it was said they could hit a target with their eyes closed. He suspected Rhodri had men hidden ready to strike if necessary, as he did.

"I wonder if there will ever be trust between our two peoples?" he mused aloud. "Peace can only come with trust."

He was weary of the constant conflict that plagued the Welsh Marches. He was a warrior first and foremost, but he was a diplomat too, a good one, and he resolved to try to use those skills to a greater degree than he had before. He'd been picking bluebells while lost in thought. He carried them to his horse and fastened them to the pommel of his saddle.

A faint whinny off in the distance, beyond the narrow humpback bridge, brought him out of his reverie abruptly. His gut tightened.

They are here.

"Earl of Ellesmere," a loud assertive voice came from the mist. "Rambaud, *Comte* de Montbryce."

"I am here," he shouted back, trying to peer through the impenetrable mist, to see any sign of his family. "To whom am I speaking?"

"I am Rhodri ap Owain, Prince of Powwydd. We've met before, you and I. Did you bring the ransom we agreed upon?"

Straight down to business then.

"Yes. I've brought it. How do I know my family is safe?"

There was a pause, then he heard Mabelle's strong, calm voice. "Rambaud? Ram?"

He wanted to charge recklessly onto the bridge. Tears threatened as he tightened his hold on the reins, gritting his teeth and squaring his jaw.

"Ram?" she called again. "We're all safe. Robert and Baudoin are with me, as are Giselle and Rhonwen. And your daughter. Lord Rhodri has taken good care of us. We're looking forward to coming home."

A daughter! Ram's throat constricted. "Robert, Baudoin, you and your mother are well?"

"*Oui*, Papa," yelled Robert. "I've taken good care of Baudoin—and my baby sister."

Ram coughed, hoping to conceal his momentary inability to find words. He could feel the expectant eyes of his men on him. Much depended on what happened next.

"My men will place the chests in the middle of the bridge as agreed. They'll leave them open," he shouted to Rhodri. "If you have the hostages mounted, I want their horses sent across the bridge first."

He didn't want to run the risk the Welsh would turn and flee with the hostages, once they had the ransom. It would make it more difficult if the hostages were on foot.

"Agreed," came the gruff reply a few minutes later. "Then we'll send your family across on foot with four of my men, who will retrieve the chests."

Ram didn't like it, but could think of nothing else he could do to lessen the dangers. The Welshman held the upper hand, and could disappear into Wales without honouring the bargain, if he wished. Ram had to trust him. Mabelle had confirmed they'd been well treated, and Rhodri had left him alive at Ruyton, when he could easily have killed him.

Ruyton brought thoughts of Ascha Woolgar to his mind. Had Mabelle ever suspected what had happened there? He sensed she knew, yet didn't judge him. Did it mean she didn't care, or did she love him so much she could forgive him?

He heard the slow rhythm of hooves approaching. A Welshman appeared out of the mist, leading the horses Ram recognized as belonging to his family and servants. As the man reached the centre of the bridge, he slapped them on the rump and they trotted over to the English side, where his men retrieved them.

Ram took a deep breath. "Gervais, send the men with the chests."

Four of his men-at-arms lifted the heavy iron chests and tramped to the centre of the stone bridge, where they put them down heavily, and lifted the lids. The metallic sounds echoed off the walls and rough cobblestones of the narrow bridge, amplified by the mist and the rushing water of the river below.

Since Ram could see the coins from where he stood, he assumed the Welsh could also see them. His men turned and strode back towards him. He felt a surge of pride in these Norman soldiers who must be aware of Welsh arrows aimed at their backs, and yet they walked slowly, never looking over their shoulders.

Out of the mist came Giselle, leading Robert and Baudoin by the hand. Baudoin waved goodbye to someone. Giselle walked nervously but resolutely to the humpback centre of the bridge, passed the chests, and continued on to the English side. Ram dismounted quickly and ran to take his sons up in his arms. Two Norman soldiers hurried to aid Giselle as her knees buckled and she swooned. She looked at them gratefully, then gasped when she saw these were her two warrior sons, whom she'd not seen for years. She wept as they embraced her. She smiled her tearful thanks to the Earl.

"Papa, papa, did you miss us?" Robert asked.

Ram choked. He was amazed to see how much his sons had grown, but was angry he'd missed that. At least they hadn't been starved. "Of course I missed you. I love you. I love you both."

That wasn't hard after all.

He hugged them, noticing each carried a wooden sword and dagger tucked into the belts of their sheepskin jerkins and leather breeches. They looked like miniature Welsh rebels. He found it amusing, but resolved in that moment never to follow the growing trend of fostering sons out to some other noble lord for their training.

"We rode ponies, Papa. Can we can have ponies when we return home?" Robert asked.

Ram didn't want his children to feel he didn't care about the ponies, but he was desperate now to see Mabelle. As calmly as he could, he replied, "I suppose we could see to that. Now, I want you to wait with Gervais here, while I greet your mother. She's coming next is she?"

"*Oui,* Papa, she and Rhonwen are saying goodbye to Rhodri, and then they'll bring *ma soeur*. Rhodri carried her down the mountain in a sling across his chest."

Ram felt a pang of jealousy at the familiar way his family spoke of this Welsh barbarian. "What's your sister's name?" He felt like he had something lodged in his throat.

"*Maman* named her for our *Grandmaman*," Baudoin answered.

***

After watching her sons walk across the bridge and disappear into the mist with Giselle, Mabelle turned to face Rhodri and thanked him as he carefully placed the sling around her neck. "It's unfortunate, Rhodri, Prince of Powwydd, that our people can't find some common ground, and instead seem to be constantly at each other's throats. I've learned a great deal about you and your country during our stay in your beautiful mountains, and I'll share much of what I've learned with my husband. He's a lover of peace and prosperity, and would wish that for both our peoples."

Rhodri bowed, took her outstretched hand and kissed it lightly. "Peace can only come with trust and respect my lady. I pray one day we shall find that. *Siwrne dda.* Good journey."

She stepped away to look towards the bridge. Rhodri turned to Rhonwen and took her in his arms. He could smell the dampness in her hair, taste the salt of the tears on her face as he kissed her. He couldn't speak. If he did his voice would betray his anguish. The experience of their union had enthralled him, but she intended to leave. He understood why, but couldn't accept it. If she left, he would never again experience the mystical passion their joining had brought him.

"Rhonwen," he faltered. "I can't change what I am. I'll not beg you to stay. Only you know your heart. But you're my destiny, and I am yours."

She was breathing heavily and wouldn't return his embrace. She turned from him, and began the walk towards the centre of the bridge with Mabelle and the infant. Her tears blinded her and she had to grasp her lady's hand.

***

New footsteps on the old bridge caught Ram's attention. He peered into the mist, thicker now, and saw his wife emerge, with Rhonwen at her side, clutching Mabelle's hand tightly. They were accompanied by four Welshmen, longbows over their shoulders, daggers at their belts.

Mabelle walked slowly and proudly, head held high, and Ram had never loved her more. Her steadfast Norman courage had seen her through an ordeal that would have broken many women. She walked across the bridge as if she was out for a stroll, a woven sling across her body that he knew held his daughter. He had a momentary vision of her throwing his sword into the lake. He'd known that day he loved her. Why had he never told her?

He noticed Rhonwen was having difficulty and wondered what ailed the healer. She walked with her head bowed. Was she crying? Her shoulders shook. Perhaps she was ill? The two women paused in the centre of the bridge. The armed men stooped to pick up the heavy chests and walked back into Wales in the same slow and dignified manner his own soldiers had walked. They could nock an arrow to their bow and let it fly before his men had time to blink.

But why were Mabelle and Rhonwen not continuing to walk towards him? Something had gone wrong. His gut wrenched.

CHAPTER FORTY

Mabelle turned to face Rhonwen and took hold of her shoulders. "Rhonwen, you must return to him. He's right. You're his destiny and he's yours."

"But my lady—my duty to you. I'm a healer—how can I live with a warrior, a man of blood and war?"

Mabelle increased her grip and shook Rhonwen. "Because you love him, Rhonwen, and he loves you. You can't turn your back on a great love. It will destroy you both. It won't be easy living with a Welsh rebel, but to live without love is unbearable and creates only bitterness. I've wasted too much of my life trying to deny the existence of love. You must embrace it. You and Rhodri will bear many fine children, and perhaps one day our sons and daughters will live together in peace in these mountains and valleys."

Rhonwen looked back to Wales. "I can't see him, but he's still there. May I embrace you my lady? You've been like a mother to me since my own was murdered."

As the two women embraced, Mabelle asked, "Why did Myfanwy not tell me you were her daughter?"

"She was afraid you'd think she had chosen me because I was her daughter and not because of my skills as a healer. And—she was ashamed I was a base born child, the daughter of a Saxon knight. I said nothing when it was believed my mother had poisoned you, because I was afraid you'd suspect I was involved."

They both looked down at the sleeping child tucked between them, and Mabelle suddenly knew her daughter's name. "My daughter will bear your name, Rhonwen, in honour of your love and courage and as a token of hope for the future."

She kissed Rhonwen on each cheek, made her turn around, and gave her a gentle push. "Now go. And don't look back."

She watched the girl walk slowly towards Wales, then turned and walked towards her husband. As she reached the end of the bridge Ram emerged from the mist and strode towards her. She noticed flecks of silver in his beautiful black hair. "Ram," she breathed, tears rolling down her cheeks.

She felt the warmth of his arms as he encircled her waist and his eyes fell to the baby, sleeping peacefully in her sling. "I want to hold you to myself tightly, but I'm afraid I'll crush the child," he rasped.

Mabelle lifted the baby from the sling and gave her to Ram. "My lord husband, I present your daughter, Hylda Rhonwen de Montbryce."

He looked at the infant who opened her eyes and smiled. "She has your golden hair," he murmured. Then his eyes widened. "Rhonwen? Why have you named her Rhonwen?"

"I'll explain," she rasped. "You'll understand. I cannot speak of it now."

Swallowing hard, he took his wife's hand and, holding the baby firmly in the other arm, walked to where Giselle stood, supported by her sons, having recovered from her momentary dizziness of relief. He kissed the babe's forehead, handed the child to the maidservant, and turned back to look at his wife.

How amazing that the simple touch of his hand can reignite my passion so quickly.

He'd brought Mabelle's warmest cloak with him. He retrieved it and draped it lovingly around her, never taking his eyes from hers. She held her breath. He pressed her tightly to his body, enfolded her in his own cloak and whispered into her ear, "Mabelle, I'm consumed with love for you. Thank you for this beautiful gift. I'm whole again now you're back safe with me. My life has had no meaning with you gone. Can you forgive me and return my love?"

Her legs trembled with the happiness and relief flooding over her. He'd not asked her if she'd been raped, had uttered no words of blame. He'd declared his love for her without any conditions. She returned his embrace and felt the familiar longings she'd striven to suppress during her captivity. Suddenly she caught sight over his shoulder of the posy of bluebells attached to the pommel of his saddle. The memories engulfed her. She could hardly wait to get her handsome husband into bed. She felt his arousal as she pressed against him.

"Oh Ram, I've loved you from the first moment we met, but I was too full of fear and resentment about the past to admit it."

He swept her up into his arms and mounted his horse with her in front of him. "Giselle, please bring my daughter to me."

He nestled the infant into the sling her mother still wore.

"It's good to hold another babe," he rasped.

Mabelle leaned back against her husband's chest and the warmth of his body banished the chill.

"What of Rhonwen?" he asked. "Are we to wait for her?"

"She's gone back to Rhodri. She loves him. They are destined to be together."

"Rhodri ap Owain and Rhonwen?"

"*Oui*. They too share a conquering passion."

Ram shook his head. "To Ellesmere then," he commanded.

***

Rhonwen heard the horses leaving on the English side of the bridge. With them went her family, her security, who though not blood kin, had come to mean much to her. Ahead of her waited the man she loved with a force that threatened to consume her. Something made her stop before the end of the bridge and she took a deep breath to clear her head. Her hand went to her neck where she still wore the fine amber necklace Rhodri had given her on their first night together, when he'd avowed his love. Was she making the right decision? Would he care she was the bastard daughter of a Saxon lord? He was of proud noble descent.

Suddenly Rhodri emerged from the mist. He'd heard the Normans leave. She stood alone in the swirling mist. "Rhonwen? Is it you or a trick of my eyes?

She smiled nervously. "It's me."

Rhodri grinned and put his hands on his hips. "I knew you wouldn't leave me. I had to see for myself you were gone. I trust in the power of my dreams."

Rhonwen held out her hands, shivering with cold. He took off his sheepskin and wrapped it around her, enfolding her like a tiny doll in his arms.

"Rhodri," she began nervously, "I must tell you something. You need to know that my father—well—he was a Saxon. He wasn't married to my mother. You're a prince—"

He looked into her eyes. "The real reason for your reluctance to stay suddenly becomes clear to me. You thought I'd be ashamed of your origins, your bloodlines."

Rhonwen nodded, biting her lip.

"Look at me and hear me well. I'll never mention her name again, but Morwenna's parents were both Welsh, both of noble blood, and yet she was as corrupt and rotten as a worm-eaten apple. You are purity, gentleness and goodness, and I need you to bring light to the darkness of my life. Being a champion for my people isn't an easy burden."

She saw the sincerity and need in his eyes and hers filled with tears.

"Hush, hush, Rhonwen, my Rhonwen," he whispered. *"Mi wnaf dy garu di am byth."*

"As I will love you, forever, Rhodri," she replied, elated he loved her so much her parentage didn't matter.

He lifted her and carried her into the land of her ancestors.

***

As the Montbryce family rode back towards Ellesmere with their escort, they suddenly heard an ominous ear-splitting battle cry behind them.

"Dros Cymru!"

It was a deep guttural yell that echoed to the bone, and they reined in their mounts, sensing danger. They looked behind them. The spring sunshine had burned off the mist. On the opposite side of the valley, a tall man, mounted on a black stallion, held a black haired girl on his lap. He thrust his fist up in salute to the Normans as he yelled his war cry again. "For Wales!"

Rhonwen waved then too, and Mabelle, Giselle, Robert and Baudoin waved back. For some reason he couldn't fathom, Ram raised his fist in a return salute. Rhodri ap Owain turned his horse and rode away, his wild shouts of joy echoing across the valley.

CHAPTER FORTY-ONE

"We'll need to stop for the babe," Mabelle told Ram as Hylda Rhonwen screamed her hunger. "The boys would benefit from a chance to stretch their legs too."

They were half way home. Ram reined in his horse and halted the men close by a stream. Robert and Baudoin darted off to play by the water. "Take care, my sons," their father shouted. He nodded to Gervais to keep an eye on them.

He lifted Mabelle and her precious burden from the horse and helped settle her on a fallen tree trunk, so she could feed the child. As she lowered her dress and chemise to bare her breast, the letter she'd written to him on her last night in Cadair Berwyn fell from the folds. When she'd written it she was unsure of his love. In the excitement and relief of their rescue she'd forgotten it. He'd seen the parchment, intent as he was on watching her suckle their daughter.

"It's a letter," she murmured, blushing. "A letter to you."

"From whom?"

"From me."

He held out his hand. "I would read it."

She handed it to him. He unfurled it with trembling hands.

To my husband Ram,
Mindful of the dangers we face on the morrow, which may yet prevent us from ever seeing each other again, I wish to share with you the feelings of my heart. I've known for many years I'm deeply in love with you. I've always hesitated to tell you of my love. This cruel separation we've endured has made me see the sheer folly of that. What was my

fear? That you wouldn't love me in return? If you have longed for me as I've longed for you over these many months—

Be assured the children and I have not been harmed during our captivity. You will have already deduced it was Giroux and Morwenna who plotted against us. Both are dead, Giroux at the hands of Rhodri himself. It was Rhonwen who avenged her mother Myfanwy's death.

If the Fates decide we not be reunited, I cannot go to my grave thinking you didn't know of my love. I thank you for the deep passion we've shared. You have made my life complete. You're the other half of me. I long to see you again.

Mabelle

Ram rolled up the parchment and tucked it carefully into his gambeson, next to his heart. He looked over to his sons, who were throwing rocks into the stream. "You'd think they were returning from a picnic," he remarked with a smile.

He gazed at his wife and daughter. After a few minutes, he walked over to his horse and took from his saddle bag a loaf of bread and a wineskin. Bending his long legs to crouch down beside Mabelle, he broke off a chunk of bread and held it to her lips. She bit into it. "Mmmm—the bread in Wales was good, but there's nothing like Trésor's."

"Open your mouth, Mabelle." She tilted her head back. He held the wineskin and poured the dark red liquid. Some spilled down her chin and onto her breasts. She gulped, and laughed. "I'm out of practice."

He kissed the baby's head and then licked the trickle of wine from Mabelle's breast to the corner of her mouth, his tongue barely touching her skin. His eyes were full of longing, his body tense with need.

He patted his chest. "I'll carry this letter with me till the day of my death. It will be a constant reminder to me of what a fortunate fool I am. Nothing matters to me as much as my beloved family. I'll spend the rest of my life erasing the memory of the fear you suffered during your captivity."

He tore off a piece of bread, helped himself to the wine, and they continued to share a silent communion, until Hylda Rhonwen was satisfied and sleepy. He took the babe, pressed her to his chest, with her tiny head resting on his shoulder, and sauntered over to the edge of the stream, where Robert and Baudoin were practicing with their miniature wooden swords.

Ram chuckled. "They're good at it," he shouted back to Mabelle. "They had a good teacher."

***

That night Rhodri and Ram made love to the passionate women they adored, Rhodri by the hearth in the cozy cottage in the Welsh hills, and Ram in the opulent bed at Ellesmere, the heavy draperies cocooning him and his cherished wife.

Both noble warriors slowly pleasured their women, kissing and arousing them in the sensitive female places where they knew they loved to be touched. They rejoiced in seeing their women moan and cry out in fulfillment.

For Rhodri and Rhonwen, it was the beginning of their journey to know one another intimately. For Ram and Mabelle, it was a passionate reunion—learning about each other's bodies all over again.

Both warriors called out huskily in ecstatic euphoria as their essence filled the women they loved.

Love is like salt. It gives a higher taste to pleasure, and then makes it last.

About the Author

Anna Markland is a Canadian "Indie" author with a keen interest in genealogy. She writes medieval romance about family honour, ancestry and roots. Her novels are intimate love stories full of passion and adventure. Following a successful career in teaching, Anna transformed her love of writing and history into engaging works of fiction. Prior to becoming a fiction author, she published numerous family histories. One of the things she enjoys most about writing historical romance is the in-depth research required to provide the reader with an authentic medieval experience.

Facebook~Anna Markland Novels
Twitter @annamarkland
www.annamarkland.com
email:anna@annamarkland.com

A Man of Value
The Montbryce Legacy ~ Book Two
Copyright Anna Markland 2011

Set in the 11th century, Book Two of the Montbryce Legacy is the story of **Caedmon Woolgar**, the illegitimate son of a Norman Earl, Ram de Montbryce.

A warrior who has always believed he is the son of a dead Saxon hero of the Battle of Hastings, Caedmon's discovery of his illegitimacy threatens to destroy him and his marriage to **Agneta Kirkthwaite**. He seeks redemption by going off on the First Crusade.

Agneta harbours hatreds of her own after the massacre of her family and the destruction of her home—a crime Caedmon unwittingly participated in.

Can love help them overcome hatred and forge a powerful dynasty of their own?

A MAN OF VALUE is a medieval romance set against the backdrop of the rule of King William Rufus and the attempts of the Scottish King Malcolm to take control of Northumbria from the Normans.

Caedmon's heroism during the First Crusade takes the reader on an emotional journey to find his true identity as he travels across Europe to Asia Minor.

Enjoy this excerpt from A Man of Value

PROLOGUE

Edwinesburh, Scotland, 1087

Caedmon Brice Woolgar liked the sound of laughter, and savoured the guffaws of his friends, already well into their cups. He parted his long hair down the centre, gathered the thick black locks into two bunches, and pulled back tightly. Sticking out his tongue, and rolling his eyes, he continued his mockery. "They say William Rufus, the new King of the English, wears his long blond hair parted in the centre, and off his face, which is always red, as if he's angry. That's why they call him Rufus."

Edgar choked on his ale. "Don't let the fair Aediva see you making that face, Caedmon," he teased. "She'll no longer love you."

Caedmon felt his face redden. "Aediva doesn't love me, though she thinks she does."

"And what of the beautiful Audrey, and the voluptuous Coventina—and the well-endowed—"

"Cease! Can I help it if these women lust after my handsome face?" Caedmon interjected good-naturedly, wiping his mouth with the back of his hand after taking a long swig of his dark ale.

"It's not your bonny face they lust after, my brawny friend," Leofric Deacon commented sardonically, bending his long arm to his head and looking cross-eyed at his own bulging bicep. "It's those impressive muscles."

"Aye!" was the jovial agreement, as tankards clinked together and laughter rang out.

"I hear Rufus is a dandy who dresses in the height of fashion, however outrageous," Edgar Siward cooed, prancing foppishly around the crowded alehouse.

Relieved the jesting had turned back to Rufus, Caedmon carried on, "Rumour has it the new king's eyes are threatening, his voice strident, as if he's trying to intimidate. They say he's a bully who easily takes offense."

Leofric imitated the features Caedmon was describing, giving rise to further fits of laughter.

Despite their levity, Caedmon knew everyone feared the son of the hated Conqueror would be as ruthlessly cruel as his recently departed father.

"The Normans have their problems with all William's ambitious sons. Robert Curthose won't be content to be the Duke of the Normans. He thirsts for Rufus's throne," Edgar opined. "Did you know that when they were boys, Rufus and his brother Henry once stood on a high balcony and dumped a full chamber pot on their brother Curthose's head? Playing dice must have become too boring."

General comments of disgust ensued.

"Perhaps, while they are busy trying to steal from each other, we can help our King Malcolm regain Northumbria?" Caedmon slapped his friend on the back. "Pray you're right, Leofric. I too would like a piece of Northumbria to claim as my own."

"As would any one of us," Siward agreed. "It's ironic all of us were born in this barbaric country, yet we're outcasts, the sons of Saxons who fled the Conqueror after Hastings."

"Aye, and most of us fatherless, our heroic sires dead at Hastings, or Dover, or any one of the innumerable merciless skirmishes with the brutal Normans," Leofric lamented.

"And listen to us. '*Aye,*' Leofric says, as if he's a Scot," Caedmon said. "We sound like Scots, though we're Saxons. We've had to learn the tongue of the Gaels to survive at King Malcolm's court. *Aye,* we sound like Scots, though any Scot knows we're not."

"At least we haven't been forced to learn the hated Norman French," Edgar offered.

Eivind Brede came over from another table and joined the conversation. "Here we are, landless and powerless, but looked upon by our exiled forebears as the hope of the future, the pride of our race. We burn to liberate a country many of us have never set foot in."

Caedmon's Saxon mother, Lady Ascha Woolgar, took such pride in him, and he'd always admired her bravery at risking the flight to Scotland after the death of his father at Hastings—a pregnant woman, with no one but her brother, Gareth, for sustenance. Even after Gareth's death, she'd prospered in Scotland, and become a respected pillar of the exiled Saxon community. His mother made sure everyone recognized him as the son of a martyr of Hastings.

"I wish with all my heart I could restore my mother to her own country, the land of her birth," he declared solemnly.

His friends nodded their heads in silent agreement, and not a word was spoken for several minutes.

They seethe with the same longing, an England ruled again by Anglo-Saxons.

"Now we're getting too serious," he said finally. "We've sworn to help King Malcolm oust the Normans, at least from Northumbria. Let's drink to that."

He leapt up onto his seat. "King Malcolm *Cenn Mór!* Malcolm, the Great Chieftain," he shouted, raising his tankard.

"Northumbria!" came the echo.

"Aye!"

CHAPTER ONE

Bolton, Northumbria, March 1093,
Sixth Year of the Reign of William Rufus

Agneta Kirkthwaite crouched in terror in the abandoned hayloft, shivering, despite the warmth of her mother's arms clasped tightly around her. Her father, Sir Eidwyn, had hurried them into hiding as soon as the outriders had raised the alarm.

"Make sure you have your dagger, Ragna," Eidwyn told his wife, his voice strained.

The barbaric Scots had been increasing their murderous raids on Norman holdings in Northumbria, and though the Kirkthwaites weren't Normans, their manor in the tiny village of Bolton, more prosperous than most, might tempt raiders. Over the years since the Conquest, their isolation, and alliances with the Normans, had spared them many of the ravages experienced by other Northumbrians. Now, in defense of their home, Eidwyn and his sons, Aidan and Branton, had armed themselves and the villagers and were ready for an attack.

Unholy battle cries heralded the arrival of the marauders, raising the hairs on the back of Agneta's neck. Ragna Kirkthwaite pressed her eye to a crack between the old planking of their hiding place.

"God save us," she breathed, making the Sign of the Cross. "They're naked!" She looked away, and dragged Agneta across the rough floorboards, further from the wall.

"Who are they, Mamma?" Agneta whimpered. "Why are they attacking us?"

"Barbarian Scots," her mother spat. "Will they never give up their claim to Northumbria? Stay here."

Ragna crawled back to the chink, and peered out again. She gasped, and scurried back to Agneta, who grasped her mother's sleeve. "What is it?"

"There are Saxons with them."

"But father is a Saxon. Why would Saxons attack us?"

Ragna took a deep breath. "I don't know, but your father and brothers will fight them off, with the help of the villagers."

The mayhem below continued for a long while. Agneta winced at the harsh sounds of metal on metal, screams of pain, and shouts of triumph. Then suddenly—nothing. She clung to her mother for long anxious minutes, until the faint smell of smoke wafted up to them.

Ragna inched closer to the crack. Her mother choked back a whimper and slumped her forehead against the wood.

"What's wrong? What is it?" Agneta whispered frantically.

When her mother didn't reply, Agneta crawled over to the crack and looked.

The house is on fire.

She was about to look away when new shouts came to her ears, and she caught sight of her father. Sword drawn, he was fending off two naked raiders whose bodies shone eerily. Were they covered in grease?

"Papa looks tired," she whispered. She turned to look at her mother, and saw a tear roll down her cheek. She looked back through the crack. No one!

Suddenly, Aidan, her beloved seventeen year old brother, one year older than she, staggered into view and fell to the ground, clutching his chest. A shrieking marauder appeared, leapt onto Aidan, and plunged a dagger into his back.

"*Aidan*," she rasped, her throat dry as dust. She furrowed her brow in anguished disbelief, and rocked to and fro, hugging her knees. "They've stabbed Aidan."

Her mother crawled away from the wall, and curled up, whimpering.

Where are Papa, and Branton, and the villagers?

Agneta couldn't help it. She was drawn to look back at the slaughter. Before long, she'd witnessed the murders of Branton, and her father. Bloodied, broken bodies lay all over the courtyard. The only sounds were the crackling of the burning timbers, and the victorious laughter of the barbarians who'd perpetrated this horror.

Fear gripped her and she couldn't stop the tears streaming down her face. Her mother had gone strangely quiet. Agneta sniffled, wiped her runny nose with her sleeve, and looked through the crack again. Her stomach clenched and she blinked rapidly. A man in chain mail crouched beside Aidan. He turned the boy over, and dragged him into a sitting position, cradling Aidan's shoulders with his arm. Agneta fisted her hands against the wall, her fingernails biting into her palms.

Please don't hurt him.

The warrior smoothed the hair off the boy's face then lay Aidan down again. Agneta flattened her palms against the wall and clawed at the splintering wood. Everything seemed to have tilted and she was afraid she would swoon.

Aidan, Aidan—

Unexpectedly, the man rocked back on his heels and slowly stood, brushing the dirt from his leggings with his gauntlets. With the back of her fist she strangled a cry that threatened to burst from her throat. Even seen from her high perch, he was a giant.

Oh God! He's looking up.

Her insides pitched and rolled, but she willed her body to be still. The man removed his helmet and wiped the sweat from his brow with the back of his hand. Black hair fell to his shoulders. She couldn't look away. Soon another man came to stand beside him, similarly clad.

These are the treacherous Saxons.

The two men conversed together quietly, still looking up. She couldn't move, transfixed with fear and fascination. The man with black hair shook his head when the other put his hand on his comrade's shoulder. Both seemed troubled. They put their helmets back on, turned and walked away.

She swooned against the wooden wall.

11595835R10140

Made in the USA
Charleston, SC
08 March 2012